"I like looking at you."

"Shorts suit you, and tank tops, sweat bands, leotards, swimsuits . . . Everything."

Lauren laughed softly, tilting her head.

Her mouth, when Jack brought his lips to hers, was damp. "You . . . smell . . . wonderful." Between each kiss, he heard her sigh.

She stretched up, wrapped her arms around his shoulders and kissed him. A trembling surge burst through him.

"I don't understand," she said against his jaw.

"What don't you understand?"

"Why me? Why now?"

The touch of her bathing suit was an erotic massage. Everywhere it rubbed him, he felt the silken texture of her skin and then the rough stimulus of fabric. And only that scrap of black kept him from seeing all of her.

"The only answer I can give you is that it's right . . . and it's what I want. Can't that be enough?"

ABOUT THE AUTHOR

Before turning to writing full-time several years ago, Stella Cameron edited medical texts. Her dream then, and even as a child, was to become a writer. Stella, her husband and three children live in Washington state.

Books by Stella Cameron

HARLEQUIN AMERICAN ROMANCE

153–SHADOWS
195–NO STRANGER
226–SECOND TO NONE
243–A PARTY OF TWO
268–THE MESSAGE
306–FRIENDS
360–RISKS

HARLEQUIN SUPERROMANCE

185–MOONTIDE
340–ONCE AND FOR ALWAYS

HARLEQUIN INTRIGUE

50–ALL THAT SPARKLES
83–SOME DIE TELLING
107–A DEATH IN THE HOUSE
123–THE LATE GENTLEMAN

Harlequin Books

TORONTO • NEW YORK • LONDON
AMSTERDAM • PARIS • SYDNEY • HAMBURG
STOCKHOLM • ATHENS • TOKYO • MILAN

For Corinne Meyer, with my thanks

Published May 1991

ISBN 0-373-16391-6

MIRROR, MIRROR

Printed in U.S.A.

Chapter One

Lauren Taylor was a good reason not to leave an otherwise deadly party. Looking at her had a strange effect on a man, oddly disturbing. The rapidly changing expressions on her arresting face held Jack captive; one instant he was quietly fascinated, the next aware of mounting excitement.

"Jack, you listening?"

He nodded, but he wasn't really hearing much of what Barney Middleton said. How long had it been since he'd seen Lauren, except from at a distance? A year, two... more? She was great to watch, even if he didn't particularly enjoy also having her ex-husband, to whom she was talking, in the frame.

Now he remembered their last face-to-face conversation. It was at an earlier version of this same party, Carlsbad's famed May Fling, when he'd awkwardly told her how sorry he was about her failed marriage. And that had been three years ago because he'd managed to avoid the two annual bashes previous to tonight's extravaganza. But he hadn't forgotten the disturbingly vivid impression the quietly controlled Lauren Taylor had made on him.

"You gotta get out more," Barney shouted over the din and elbowed him.

Jack steadied his Scotch and grimaced. He and Barney sat side by side on a white couch so low slung and soft that Jack's knees were at eye level.

"Time you had another woman in your life—the permanent variety. Someone to help look after young Andy."

This was the tape Jack listened to from Barney whenever they met, usually once or twice a week at Barney's restaurant.

"You hearin' me, Jacko?"

"I'm hearing you."

"Four years divorced is long enough and a nine-year-old boy needs a mother figure around. And there's lots of good women out there just dyin' for a chance at you." Barney's bald scalp glistened amid its luxuriant skirt of black hair. Sincerity shone in dark eyes set deep in a round and pudgy face.

Jack undid another button on his tuxedo shirt; the tie already hung loose. "Why doesn't that idea thrill me, I wonder? Damn, Barn, it's like an oven in here."

"Jack, I'm trying to make a point—"

"Yeah, Barney, okay. I get the message." How could Lauren still be civil to that creep Dan Taylor? There wasn't a soul in Carlsbad who didn't know the sordid little details of how Dan Taylor had ditched her. If Jack had the facts straight, the Taylors had been married sixteen years when Danny-boy decided to find grease for his libido with a twenty-three-year-old sales trainee in his real estate firm. Talk at the time was that Lauren was thirty-six, which meant she was now thirty-nine. A very good year on this lady.

The town's "in" people drifted in clumps through the Ocean Club. Elevator-style music rose and fell in insipid waves. The event was a fund-raiser for children's charities and Jack wondered why the organizers didn't save a lot of time and money by scratching the party and making a few arm-twisting personal calls instead. He stretched out his long legs. "How's business, Barn?"

"Stinks. That's why I can lounge around at parties on a Sunday night."

The standard response brought a smile to Jack's lips. Barney Middleton ran one of Carlsbad's most successful restaurants. Money was his middle name, but business always stank.

"How's the flower business?" Barney asked.

"Stinks," Jack said and laughed at Barney's malevolent stare. "No. Seriously, it's a great year so far. I guess the cut flowers interest me most." He considered. "Ah, well, maybe the poinsettia rush beats even that. Who knows? I like it all." He owned one of the leading poinsettia farm, bulb and cut-flower operations in the country and he'd never hankered to do anything else.

He sank into silence. Dan Taylor appeared to be irritated with Lauren and, to Jack's annoyance, she seemed to be meekly accepting whatever he had to say.

She was pale-skinned with sleek, shoulder-length dark hair. Her eyes were almost black, her brows clearly arched, her nose uptilted and her mouth full. Stunning? Maybe compelling would be a better description. And lush was the word that came to mind for her tall, tastefully black-clad body. One classy woman. Jack drank deeply of his Scotch and swiveled his attention to Christie, Taylor's wife number two, who hovered near the soaring ice sculpture of a castle. Her eyes were narrowed in minute scrutiny of the other two. Not a happy camper tonight, this flouncy blond nymph whom Dan Taylor had needed to ease his ego through midlife. The pouting, cutesy type did nothing for Jack, particularly if the woman was . . . eleven years his junior? Christie had to be around twenty-six now, a stereotypical California girl. Evidently she didn't realise she was using a toothpick to systematically spear shrimp with what resembled murderous intent.

"Great pair, huh?"

Jack started. "What?"

"You've been staring at Lauren Taylor all night. And I said she's got a great pair."

"Yeah. Good legs." Jack didn't waste energy on the dirty look he was tempted to give Barney, who was famous for tasteless sexual innuendos and jokes.

"I wasn't looking at her—"

"How's Joannie?"

Barney snickered. "You've got a puritan heart, Jack Irving. My lovely wife is in her usual state of PMS. I can't remember whether that's pre or post at the moment. Doesn't make much difference."

The Middletons fought furiously. They also loved furiously, and Jack accepted the harmless comment for what it was—harmless. "Joannie is lovely," he said of the diminutive golden-haired woman who was Barney's wife. Tonight she was baby-sitting the first and still-new grandchild, or she would have been glued to her husband's side. "I never could figure out what she saw in an ugly, cantankerous guy like you."

Barney wiggled his bushy brows. "It's my body. She can't keep her hands off it. Do you know Lauren?"

The guy never gave up. "Sort of. I haven't seen her to talk to in years. When she and Dan were married they lived out by La Costa, not far from my place."

"Dan still lives there," Barney remarked tonelessly. "With the delectable new Mrs. Taylor."

"Right," Jack said, watching the blonde again. "And baby makes three, I hear."

"You hear right. Only the kid's gotta be two or three by now."

Jack grunted and studied his fingernails. "I think Christie hates her predecessor's guts. Take a look at her. Every time she stabs a shrimp she looks at it as if it's a voodoo doll with Lauren's name on it."

"She got what she thought she wanted. Only I don't think Dan's cut all of his ties to Lauren. Not that I blame him."

"No," Jack agreed slowly. Dan, handsome, as dark-haired as his ex-wife and evidently very fit, rested a hand on the wall behind Lauren while he talked intently. He looked like a possessive...husband? "I use her answering service," Jack added.

"So do we. Very efficient—growing, too, I should imagine."

"Mmm." He ought to change the subject.

"Lauren's some woman," Barney said and the serious note in his voice made Jack glance at him sharply. "One of these days some smart son of a gun's gonna realize what a prize she is and take her off the market."

Jack listened and brooded. He was here under protest and hadn't intended to stay. But two hours had passed since he'd walked through the doors and obviously Barney hadn't taken long to notice where his companion's attention was centered. He hadn't given Lauren Taylor a thought since the last time he'd seen her, so why change the pattern now? He wasn't sure why, but he was certainly thinking about her. The question was: Did he intend to do anything more than think about the lady?

"SO YOU WILL TAKE my advice?"

Lauren sighed. Some things never changed. Dan's overbearing manner was one of them. So was his determination to get his own way. "No. Please drop the subject, Dan." Someone opened the French doors behind her and a blessedly cool breeze blew into the crowded room. She'd have liked to have escaped to the lanai.

"I don't understand you," Dan said. He bent over her so that she had to raise her chin to look into his serious blue eyes. "Have I ever steered you wrong? Have I ever insisted on anything I didn't think was for your own good?"

Lauren glanced away. She didn't love Dan anymore, thank God, but she still cared enough to stop herself from reminding him that he hadn't been considering her "own good" when he'd asked for a divorce because she "couldn't excite him the way Christie could."

"It's the little girl, isn't it?" he persisted. "You're pretending she's yours. Fantasizing about being a parent the same as you did with that boy you had in foster care. That was damn dangerous, too, and—"

"Leave it, Dan." To this day he hadn't figured out how much it hurt that she'd never been able to have a child of her own. Dan had a baby he adored now but he still couldn't relate to Lauren's disappointment. "Betty and Cara rent rooms from me, nothing more."

"You don't *need* to rent out rooms. You've got plenty of money—I saw to that."

He saw to that, in good part with money she'd helped amass. "I'm grateful to you," she said. "But the Floods stay. My town house is more than big enough for three and I enjoy them."

"You enjoy the girl," Dan continued stubbornly. "Why else would you live your life around her while her mother's free to come and go as she pleases?"

Lauren caught sight of Christie beyond Dan's shoulder and smiled. In return she received the frosted stare she'd come to expect. She sighed. "As I've explained many times during the past year, Betty's a night dispatcher for Coastal Ambulance. All I do is be there for Cara—she's only nine, Dan—and run her to school in the morning."

"She could catch the bus."

"The school's on my way to the office."

"Not exactly. They're taking advantage of you."

"How?" Her voice was too loud and she cleared her throat. "How are they taking advantage of me? They pay rent and what I choose to do, I choose to do." *And it's my business.*

"If that boy you took in hadn't gone back to his family you'd probably have had a break-in by now. You don't think things through."

Lauren brushed back her hair. "Joe needed a safe home for a while. For six months I was his anchor and I'm glad." And she'd missed the ten-year-old for months after he'd left. "Contrary to what you thought, his father was down-and-out, that's all, and not a criminal. As soon as he could bring his children together again, he did. Now drop the subject, please."

"Not till you agree to get rid of the Floods."

He was unbelievable. She turned her head and met the dark eyes of Jack Irving—again. He smiled. Funny, she'd never noticed the slow, crooked way his mouth curved up, or how his steady gaze remained serious. Lauren smiled back and he grinned broadly, showing very white teeth. She liked him. Once they'd been almost neighbors and he'd been the type of man who always had a pleasant word. Also, he'd been rejected by a spouse, just as she had, and that made her feel a bond with him.

"Lauren?"

"I told you, no," she said, furious. She avoided parties and wished she hadn't let a good customer browbeat her into attending this one. "I don't understand your preoccupation with this."

"You will when they take off in the middle of the night with your silver."

She didn't have any silver. That had been one of the many things Dan had felt he and Christie would have more use for than Lauren. And she'd agreed. "I'm not discussing the subject anymore. If Betty knew the kind of things you say she'd have cause to file suit against you. She's a very honest woman who had the misfortune to be left alone with a daughter to bring up. And she's doing a good job of that."

"With a lot of help from you. Lauren, I care about you. Whatever's happened between us, we've still got a lot of shared history and I can't forget that—I don't want to."

"I know." She wouldn't try, yet again, to explain that there was a difference between caring and smothering.

Jack Irving had rested his head against the back of the sofa where he sat with Barney Middleton. His curly, dark blond hair was unruly but he gave the impression of casual elegance, despite the dangling ends of his black tie and the open neck of his tuck-fronted shirt. She couldn't recall seeing him up close for ages, but he'd only become more handsome. The lines of his face were lean. That smile had produced deep dimples beside his mouth and the light picked out high cheekbones. His mouth held her attention. The upper lip was narrow, the lower full, a wide mouth, firm and sensual. And he was still staring at her. Lauren pursed her own mouth. Jack Irving, who probably didn't have any idea he was training his eyes in her direction, would find her assessment funny.

"Dan." Christie came to stand with them and Lauren felt the arctic front that arrived with the woman. "We should circulate."

He blinked and turned to her. "Why?"

Christie pouted and Lauren studied dark overhead beams. "Because it's good for business, you know that. And we shouldn't leave Wednesday with the sitter for too long. You know how she misses you."

The last was delivered with a satisfied stare at Lauren who tried to banish evil thoughts. "How is Thursday?" she asked and immediately felt ashamed.

"Wednesday," Dan said absently. "That's the day she was born, remember? She's fine."

"Good. I'd love to come and see her again," she said of the little girl and meant it. "It's been six months and I bet she's grown inches."

"She has, and she doesn't like strangers," Christie said pointedly, slipping her arm through her husband's. "Dan?"

"Lauren isn't a stranger, dear. Come anytime. We'd love to have you."

She didn't trust herself to meet Christie's eyes. A longing to get away made her feel almost faint. "Thanks."

"Remember what we've been talking about," Dan said. "I'll call you later in the week."

"Why?" Lauren said.

"What about?" Christie asked sharply.

"I'm trying to get Lauren to look out after her own interests," Dan said. "The same as I always have."

For an instant she almost felt sorry for him. He actually believed what he said. "I won't be making any changes along the lines you suggest," she told him. "So don't call if that's what you want to talk about."

"You know—" he sounded aggrieved "—sometimes I think you forget that I did much more than I had to do when we were divorced. You couldn't have bought your business and an oceanfront town house if I hadn't felt you had the money coming."

Money that she'd helped him earn. But she said, "I know that," because he was right. He could have got away with much less.

"Dan, may I talk to you?" A tall, silver-haired man Lauren recognized but didn't know, tapped Dan's shoulder and he turned away.

Christie, shielded from Dan by the newcomer, pinned Lauren with her pale blue glare. "You think I don't know what you're doing, don't you?"

"I—"

"Well I do know and it won't work. You can't get him back by pretending to need him, so give it up. You can't give him what he wants. I can. I'm young and I can have children."

JACK HEFTED HIMSELF UP from the elegantly uncomfortable couch.

"Where you goin'?" Barney asked.

"Around. See you next week." He pushed back his jacket and slid his hands into his pants pockets. Lauren Taylor looked like a woman who'd been punched in the solar plexus and Jack didn't have to be clairvoyant to figure out that she'd just received a verbal blow from the retreating, smug-faced Christie.

He approached Lauren with as much nonchalance as he could muster. She appeared frozen in place, her face expressionless. The breeze blowing in across the lanai moved her sleek, shining hair.

"Hi. Long time—" He closed his mouth, totally disconcerted by her unfocused gaze.

"No see?" She'd heard him. The light returned to her almost opaque black eyes and she turned up the corners of her mouth. The comeback had been the right one, but delivered without spirit.

"You've got it," he said. Up close, she had flawless skin. Fine lines at the corners of her eyes and mouth stamped her as no stranger to laughter. Jack liked that. "I was trying to remember how long it's been since we actually talked."

She tilted her head and the dark hair swung away from her slender neck. "I'm not sure. Probably years. I don't go to parties usually—particularly on Sunday nights."

The fact that much had happened to change patterns in their private lives was unspoken between them.

"Neither do I," Jack murmured. Her black dress was of some soft stuff that draped. The bodice crisscrossed over her full breasts, plunging to a deep and alluring V. The skirt hugged gently curving hips and stopped just above the knee where black silk covered a long, long expanse of slender, shapely leg. Very high-heeled black pumps brought her to within a couple of inches of his own six-foot-two.

He was staring, but so was she. Jack smiled faintly. "You don't look as if you're enjoying yourself much."

"I'm not. I was just going home."

"I'm not enjoying it, either... or I wasn't."

She looked away immediately and he took a deep breath through his nose. Either his courting skills were hopelessly rusty, or he'd moved too fast or she couldn't stand the sight of him.

"Of course, we probably talk on the phone," he said quickly.

She frowned. "Really?"

"Irving Farms uses your service. We have for a couple of years."

"Oh, I see." Her smile lessened the tension around her eyes. "I don't usually answer phones at Contact. I hope you're satisfied with us."

"Very. Forgive me for the blunder. Of course you don't do the scut work."

"The phone work is the center of everything we do. It's essential."

Strike two. "Of course it is. I only meant that administrative work must keep you very busy."

"It does." She picked up a small black purse from a table. "It was nice to see you again."

"Yes." Not so fast, he thought. Rusty he might be, but he wasn't dead. "Have you seen the water from here at night?"

"My town house is on Ocean Street. I've got a great view. Please excuse—"

"I'd wager you don't spend much time gazing through the window at home." A waiter passed with a tray and Jack deftly removed two glasses of champagne, one of which he pressed into Lauren's unresisting hand. "Humor me. Brighten up a bored man's night for a while."

He stood back, inclining his head toward the lanai, and she walked out without a word.

They stood at the railing, separated by inches, looking at the night sky over the night sea. The breeze had dropped and the air was still. Palm trees rustled faintly and the sweetly exotic scent of shell ginger lingered. Jack glanced sideways. She didn't move. The hushed sound of unhurried surf on sand whispered in the distance. "I watched you in there," he said, never having planned to admit it.

"I thought you did."

"You look wonderful. The world of business agrees with you." The words came easily, but they still surprised him.

"Thank you," she said, sounding slightly breathless.

"The last time we talked was here, three years ago."

"You said you weren't sure how long ago it was."

"I lied," he said. "It was something to say."

She turned her face toward him. "Why?" Her eyes glittered in the silvered light.

Jack parted his lips, then paused. Yes, he was going to do something about Lauren Taylor. He still wasn't sure what it was, but the way he felt right now was too enticing not to be explored.

"I wanted to talk to you. You interest me."

"You don't know me." She laughed and the sound was soft, incredulous.

"Maybe we should do something about that."

"I don't think so."

"Why?"

She bowed her head and the smooth hair slipped forward. "I'm not at all interesting, Jack. I'm very dull, really."

"I doubt that. But why don't you let me find out?" If he stopped to think, he'd find his sudden approach bizarre, out of character and he'd retreat—and he'd regret it later. "Have dinner with me tomorrow night."

Lauren stirred. She tilted her head to sip champagne. The moon caught the glass, and the pale outline of her throat.

Jack swallowed. Every muscle in his body contracted as if he'd received a blow. "Lauren? How about it?"

"I don't have dinner dates anymore."

He narrowed his eyes. "Why?" Now he sounded like a record.

"Because my business uses all the energy I have and I like it that way." Her voice was low but clear. He'd like to hear it saying something personal, gentle to him.

"You know what they say about all work and no play." He moved closer and she held her ground, but she did stand a little straighter.

"I know what they say, and they're probably right. But I already told you I'm uninteresting, dull, if you like. How is your son?"

"Andy's great," Jack said, smiling despite his tension. "He's nine now. I enjoy every stage he goes through. We're into soccer at the moment."

He thought her shoulders rose a fraction. "Sounds wonderful. I probably wouldn't recognize him."

"Sure you would. He's taller is all. The face isn't so different from what it was three . . . three years ago."

"Don't feel awkward talking about my divorce. I don't. We have to get used to these things, don't we?"

"We sure do." And he had. And he wanted to spend time with Lauren. He wanted it more with every second. "Do you like Chinese food?"

"Yes."

"Good. How does seven sound?"

She handed him her glass. "Thanks, Jack, but I can't."

"Of course you can. Nobody works all the time. How about eight?"

"I can't."

"You mean you won't." Rather than defeat, he felt mounting excitement again. She'd barely seen the edges of his determination. "I'll have to find a way to change your mind."

Lauren moved around him toward the doors. "I'm known as a woman who doesn't change her mind. Good night."

He smiled. "I'm known as a man who can't resist a challenge. And I'm also known as a man who usually gets what he wants. Good night."

Chapter Two

Lauren rolled down the car window and stuck out her hand to signal a left turn onto Christianson Way.

"Jimmy Sutter says you're eccentric."

Clearly pleased, both with her precocious vocabulary and with having secured complete attention, Cara Flood smiled impishly at Lauren.

"Jimmy Sutter doesn't know me," Lauren said.

"Yes, he does. I tell him about you."

"So you think I'm eccentric, too."

"Nope. I think it's fine that you don't use turn signals because you used to have a car that had broken ones and now you like sticking your arm out the window."

"Ah. I see. But Jimmy thinks that's weird."

"Jimmy's weird."

"I see." As they approached Washington and the center of town, red lights flashed ahead, warning of an approaching train. Lauren braked. "Jimmy's your best friend, isn't he?"

"Yes." Cara nodded solemnly, turning her small, pointed face up to Lauren. Wisps of light brown hair escaped long braids and sprang into curls. Thick glasses made the girl's bright blue eyes appear huge.

"Why would you have someone you think is weird, as a best friend?"

"'Cause we decided."

Lauren digested that.

"We both wear glasses and wear no-name stuff. So we decided to be friends."

Lauren thought some more. "Do other children make fun of both of you?" Her heart beat a little faster. "Is that why you and Jimmy are friends, because you both have to stand up against the others?"

"Nah. We don't care about that." But the jerky movement of the thin hands in the child's lap caught Lauren's attention. "When Billy Smith pushed Jimmy down, I stomped on Billy's foot and he cried. Jimmy and me don't worry about them."

Lauren swallowed hard and felt tears of frustration and anger prickle in her eyes. "It's time you had contact lenses."

After a moment's silence, Cara twisted in her seat. "I'd like that, I think." Pink suffused her pale cheeks. When she was happy she was almost pretty.

"I'll talk to your mom and we'll make an appointment." She wished she could do the same for Jimmy but had no idea how to go about it.

Cara was silent again. The sound of the train grew. Shops were opening on each side of the street and scurrying clusters of people moved into their Monday-morning routine.

"Don't say anything to Mom about contacts," Cara said quietly.

"Why not?" The train rushed past—a blur of green and black and rows of silver containers.

Cara sank low in her seat. "No reason. I don't want them."

Lauren wasn't fooled or put off. "You just said you'd like them."

"Changed my mind."

"What are you worried about?"

"Jimmy and Mom," Cara said, so softly Lauren had to strain to hear.

"You mom won't mind. She'd have done it herself, only she doesn't have a lot of spare time." By the time Betty

Flood worked through the night and tried to catch up on some sleep during the mornings, her days were shot.

"She can't afford it," Cara said. "Anyway, if I had 'em, Jimmy and me wouldn't be the same anymore."

Lauren reached to squeeze a cold little hand. "You are a neat kid, Cara Flood. And I'll just bet you and Jimmy would still be friends." She'd leave the money angle alone until she could talk to Betty. They'd work that out between them.

"Maybe," Cara said. "We would still be no-names."

"You mean because you don't wear, what? Designer jeans and so on?"

"Yeah. Jimmy's folks don't have much money, either."

"I'll pick you up from school today and we'll go shopping." Even as she spoke she knew she was going too far, but she wanted to give this child everything.

"I don't want to," Cara said after some consideration. "Thank you, though," she added quickly.

"Do you want to explain that one to me?" The lights stopped flashing, the barriers rose and Lauren drove on.

"S'easy. Jimmy and me are different from the others. We like it that way. If we had designer jeans and stuff, we couldn't call ourselves the Out Group."

"The *out* group?" Lauren sputtered.

The school came into view. "Yeah. That's us. We put it on our book covers and everything. And when we grow up we're gonna show 'em all."

"I'm sure you will," Lauren said, a lump in her throat.

At the school gates, she drew to the curb and Cara unhitched her seat belt to throw open the door. "Bye. See you later."

"Have you got your lunch?"

"In my bag!"

Already Cara was in motion, running toward a skinny red-haired boy who waited near the fence. Jimmy Sutter, no doubt. Lauren had noticed him before but hadn't realized there was such a bond between him and Cara. The two children fell in step side by side, but Cara turned back to wave at Lauren.

The little girl was tiny for her age and Lauren doubted if she would ever be very big. All Cara's school reports showed her to be a bright student. In time she would go far, with or without help. Lauren felt strength in Cara. She wished the child were her own. Sighing, she made a U-turn and headed back the way she'd come.

Contact's offices were on Carlsbad Avenue, wedged between a florist and a bakery. The seven-day-a-week, twenty-four-hour-a-day operation kept Lauren and her staff of nine increasingly busy. And that was exactly the way Lauren liked it.

Once parked, Lauren pulled her briefcase from the back seat of her red Honda and hurried into the message center. Two of her employees, a man and a woman, sat with their backs to her, facing computer terminals while speaking into mouthpieces.

"Messages for me?" Lauren asked Susan Bailey, her office manager, who worked a third terminal and doubled as Lauren's secretary.

"On your desk," Susan responded, slipping off her headset and getting up. "Dan called. He sounded ticked you weren't here."

Lauren rolled her eyes. "Boy, he doesn't waste any time."

"What does that mean?" Susan followed Lauren into her cramped office.

"Nothing." A sheaf of pink memos was skewered to the cork globe that held an assortment of pens and pencils. Lauren retrieved the notes. "Well, you might as well know. It's the usual. Dan and I were at that charity bash at the Ocean Club last night."

"Was *she* there?" Susan, whom Lauren had inherited when she'd bought the answering service, was Lauren's self-appointed champion. She detested Christie Taylor.

"Yes," Lauren said, attempting to sound bored. "We didn't talk." Since last night she'd tried to forget Christie's cruel barbs—unsuccessfully—and she wasn't going to sharpen their impact by voicing them aloud now.

"So what was Dan's crusade this time? Or need I ask?"

"No. I'm sure you've already guessed. He still thinks Betty and Cara are out to divest me of my worldly wealth. How, he hasn't gotten around to explaining yet, but he won't leave the subject alone."

Susan shut the office door and sat on the edge of Lauren's desk. "Have you told the rat that he doesn't have a say in what you do anymore?"

"Yes. Many times."

"Have you reminded him that when he walked out, he blithely left you to rebuild your life from scratch and you've been doing that very satisfactorily ever since?"

"In those very words." She began to leaf through the memos.

"Then don't talk to him. If he comes to see you, walk away, or don't let him in, or whatever. And I won't put him through if he calls when you're here." Susan, thirty, glamorous and notoriously in control of her life, tossed back a riot of red curls. As invariably happened when she was outraged, a bright spot of color glowed on each cheek.

"Susan—" Lauren dropped into her chair "—I know I probably ought to be tougher, but Dan really does want the best for me. We've known each other since we were kids. He thinks of us as friends and we still are, I suppose. He goes about things the wrong way, is all. He only knows how to proceed in bulldozer mode. I think I'd rather you weren't rude to him. Let me be the one to tell him what he can and can't do."

Susan grunted. "You should tell him he can't do anything where you're concerned."

"I have. More or less."

"Sure you have. But you haven't told him firmly enough. Betty and Cara are good for you. They filled a great big gap when Joe went back to his dad. You know it and so do I. That little girl is a sweetheart."

"Tell me about it," Lauren said softly.

Susan eyed her sharply. "You love the kid, don't you?"

"I... Not really." If she made eye contact, the lie would be obvious. "I've always had a weak spot for children, we both know that. No one would find it easy not to care for Cara."

Susan let out a loud sigh. "You're right. But I do worry about what will happen when—"

"Don't." Lauren forced a laugh. "Don't worry about what will happen in the future. That can take care of itself. I knew when I took Betty and Cara in that it would be temporary. But they've been with me for a year and don't show any sign of leaving. Maybe it was fate that they made a mistake and thought I had rooms to rent. Maybe they will stay forever."

"Maybe."

Lauren didn't have to look at Susan to know there would be worry in those catlike green eyes. "Stop worrying about me. Any glitches around here I should know about?"

"Barnes, Cracknell Chiropractic wants a rate cut. Something about their high volume of calls being a good ad for Contact."

Lauren snorted. "Great. We work harder for less, huh? And we'll probably end up giving the jerks a break." She laughed. "Good pun, huh?"

Susan looked blank, then smiled disgustedly. "Jerks. Chiropractors. That's worse than your usual efforts. I thought you promised you wouldn't try to tell jokes."

"I didn't try. It happened. What's this?" She held up a memo for Susan to see.

"Irving Farms? Oh, yes. Mr. Irving himself called. They're delighted with our service." Susan wiggled her eyebrows. "Should have got that on tape for future replay. He's considering our switch-over service for whenever he's out of his office."

Lauren felt her color rise and kept her eyes down. "That's odd when he must have a secretary. We must have done some fantastic job on their after-hour calls."

"I guess so. He said something about wanting to give his secretary less to do. He also said he'd call back around one to talk to you in person about the idea."

So, Jack Irving was known as a man who couldn't resist a challenge and who usually got his own way. Evidently he'd set out to prove his words. "I won't be here at one."

Susan frowned. "Your sales call at that new medical/dental complex isn't until three."

"There's no reason you can't answer any questions he has," Lauren said, feeling both cowardly and defensive.

"I tried to tell him that, but no one except the head honcho around here will do for Mr. Irving." Susan smoothed an imaginary wrinkle from the thigh of her green slacks. "He has a sexy voice. Ever met him?"

Lauren kept her head bent. "Uh-huh."

"What's he like?"

"Okay." She shrugged. He was much more than okay, but so what? Romantic flings were a luxury—or, more accurately, a curse—she never ever intended to indulge in again.

What exactly *did* Jack Irving want from her? When she'd lived in the La Costa area they'd seen each other in passing as often as several times a week for years. They'd exchanged little more than pleasantries. He'd been divorced from that beautiful, but strangely silent wife of his before Dan dropped his little bombshell, and, by Jack's own admission, he'd known when Lauren was left on her own. He hadn't made any attempt to get to know her better then. Why now?

"Would you like me to try to get Mr. Irving on the phone now?"

"No!" Lauren cleared her throat and smiled sheepishly. "No thanks, Susan. I want to get through a few things then attend to some personal business before making the sales call. I'm sure Mr. Irving won't mind calling back again." In the meantime, she'd have more time to decide how to deal with him.

Silence forced her to meet Susan's surprised gaze. "Is something wrong, Lauren?"

"Nothing." Except that she had the most extraordinarily clear picture of Jack Irving hovering in her mind and he didn't belong there. No man did anymore.

JACK HUNG UP the phone. He pushed his chair back from his desk, hoisted his feet onto the blotter and frowned into the distance. If he didn't know better, he'd think a certain dark-haired lady was avoiding him. But, no, that wasn't possible. What unattached, almost visibly passionate woman would avoid a virile, handsome male prize like Jack Irving? He grimaced. Lauren Taylor was avoiding him.

He glanced at the clock on his office wall. One-thirty. Ms. Taylor was out and wouldn't be back today, her secretary had told him. No, it probably wouldn't be possible to reach her elsewhere because she would be going to her aerobics class as soon as she'd finished making her business calls. But he could try again tomorrow morning.

What had happened when he'd seen Lauren last night—the sensation that he'd been hit between the eyes and liked it—hadn't happened before. Not ever. He and Mary had met and married in college. Then, what had felt so right had ended so wrong. He didn't want to think about it and rarely did, except when he needed to remind himself that the rejection Andy suffered at the age of five must never be repeated.

He'd known Lauren Taylor was single but somehow she'd seemed to remain bracketed to Dan...until last night. Who could explain attraction? Once a guy got past the physical reasons, the whole thing hinged on opportunity and mood, the stars in the right place, he guessed. Whatever. Yeah, and "whatever" hadn't all been motivated by testosterone where Lauren was concerned.

He locked his hands behind his neck. His "nerve center," as he sarcastically dubbed the partitioned-off areas at one end of a storage shed from which he conducted business, pleased him. Like his father before him, Jack preferred to feel close to the action. Beyond dusty windows, fields of spring-blooming flowers stretched in undulating waves. Irving's was a multifaceted outfit of cut flowers in season year-round, an extensive poinsettia business and an exclusive brand of seeds and bulbs. And Jack loved it all.

The intercom on his desk buzzed and he reached forward to flip a switch. "Yes, Joyce?"

"Len wants—"

Before Joyce could finish, the door slammed open and Len Gogh, Jack's right hand, marched in. Thickset, ruddy and dressed in ancient overalls, Len looked anything but what he was: an ex-professor of Floriculture with a doctorate from New York State College of Agriculture Cornell University.

"Hi, Len. Problems?"

"Yes, problems." Len went to stare through the windows. His wiry gray hair stood on end. "There's something going on here, Jack, something insidious."

Jack got slowly to his feet. "Such as?"

"It's happened again."

Len was famous for expecting too much of his listeners, which was probably one of the main reasons he'd chosen to quit the lecture hall. "I don't follow you," Jack said.

"We're ready to place the dianthus."

Len had always been a man of few words. "I know that."

"You'd better start saying your prayers."

"Meaning?"

"Meaning that some damn fool played with the thermostat again. Jeffries just told me—after he'd finished his lunch, of course—that when he checked this morning, the settings were at seventy."

"Seventy!" Jack sat down again with a thud. "That's not possible. They'll be ruined."

"It is possible. And they may be ruined." Len paced back and forth with measured steps. "As I said, say your prayers. But I also want you to remember that we had that little incident of lights-out with the antirrhinum back in January. We came through okay because it probably didn't happen on more than one night before it was noticed. But both incidents smell like something other than accidents to me."

Jack chewed his lip. He ran the business as his father had, by being a hands-on part of the operation and only hiring the best. "There isn't a worker on this farm who would deliberately try to harm the business." Now he even sounded like his dad. And at this moment, as so often happened, he wished Denton Irving hadn't chosen to retire the moment Jack's mother had died, virtually divorcing himself from the operation.

"Suit yourself," Len said. "Think what you like. But I've done my duty by telling you I think something's wrong around here. And remember, Jack, Irving's is getting bigger every year. You've got one of the most thriving outfits of its kind on your hands. And that means things have changed. It isn't the cozy little family operation it was in your dad's time when everyone knew everyone."

Jack studied his hands. It might not be the cozy little family operation it had been, but this was still the driving force in his life—next to Andy. And it was for Andy that he intended to make sure the legacy continued to grow. "Point taken, Len. We'd better mount a more careful system for checking things out. Think about it, and I will too. Then we'll get together and put extra safeguards in operation. Do you feel comfortable with that?"

"I'm not comfortable with anything right now," Len said and his barrel chest expanded inside a frayed red plaid shirt. "But that'll do for a start. We can't waste time, though, Jack. Matt agrees with me. He's almost camping out with the Pearl." Matt Carson was Jack's hotshot poinsettia man. The Pearl, Irving's Lava Pearl, was a new mutant plant destined to become the hit of the next season.

"We're not going to waste time. Make sure Matt knows I'm on top of things. This has the makings of a big year for us—maybe the biggest ever—and nothing's going to interfere with that. I won't let it."

Len regarded him steadily. "If my hunch is right, you may have your hands full making sure of that."

He didn't wait for a response before leaving.

"LIFT THOSE KNEES, now! One and two, and one and two. And reach for the sky right, reach for the sky left. Everybody yell!"

Lauren yelled and laughed with the rest. The small aerobics studio bulged for the five-thirty session, the most popular of the day. The trick was not to miss a step unless you liked being elbowed or trampled.

"Come on. Let me feel that energy." The instructor, unruffled, makeup perfectly in place and not even shiny, threw herself into the routine, her smooth body gyrating in a silver spandex bodysuit. "Chicken walk forward, one and two and one and two and one and two. Flap those elbows. And back and two and back and two. Wow! Feel those little endorphins doing their thing?"

The thing Lauren felt was sweat coating every inch of her body, making her shiny pink-and-fuchsia striped leotard and matching tights stick to her skin. But she loved the feeling. Here she let the tension flow out and there was no time to think about anything else.

"Grapevine!" The instructor had one vocal pitch—high. Lauren smiled, exhilarated, and passed the back of a forearm over her forehead. For a thirty-nine-year-old lady, she was in pretty spectacular shape. Mirrors didn't lie. She knew the wrinkles were there, but they came with age and, as someone said, getting older was better than the alternative. Lauren grinned broadly and sashayed her grapevine with style. Life was mostly wonderful.

The music's heavy beat boomed, reverberating off the peeling white walls. The order came for the cool-down to begin. The group broke into a trot around the long room, past mirrored walls and the expanse of window that, as usual, afforded the laughing gallery on the sidewalk outside an unobstructed view. Lauren had learned to ignore the faces of people she characterized as jealous couch potatoes.

She jogged on, her eyes on the back of the man ahead. A great back and everything else. All men and women should take the time to make the best of themselves, she thought, even women like her who did so for purely personal reasons. Getting where she was hadn't been easy, but she was independent now, and liked it most of the time. She'd proven a woman didn't have to have a man to be complete. Never again would she be in a position where another human being could break her life into little pieces.

"March, kiddies. Slow it down, slow it down."

The customary chatter broke out. Lauren walked on, catching sight of her reflection, wrinkling her nose and looking away again. Strands of wet hair clung to her temples below a soaked headband and her face, devoid of makeup, was flushed and shiny. She'd always considered her breasts too big and the damp leotard emphasized that fault.

"Keep going. Five more."

What did Jack Irving want from her? Last night he'd looked terrific. The tuxedo accentuated his tall, lean build, the nonchalant grace of a confident man. But Jack Irving didn't figure in her life one way or another. He probably wouldn't try to contact her again, and if he did, she'd give him the brush-off. He was younger than her, too—something she didn't like.

But he *was* interesting and nice. And sometimes she wished she had someone to do things with. Men didn't want women just as friends.

Telling him to get lost might be tougher than she'd like it to be. On the other hand...

A tap on the window startled her and she broke a rule: Lauren made eye contact with a "watcher." He tipped the brim of the black Stetson he wore tilted low over his eyes.

His eyes and his broad, slightly crooked smile, the dimples on each side of his mouth, stopped her.

Jack Irving.

Chapter Three

The way out was through the front door or through the emergency exit into an alley behind the building.

Her car was parked in front.

Lauren backed away from the window.

And Jack walked toward the door, opened it and stuck his head inside. "Hi."

Hi. Just like that. As if they were comfortable old friends who "ran into one another" all the time. "Hello," she mumbled, aware of her ferocious frown, the damp pink-and-fuchsia leotard clinging to her body and her shiny face and mussed hair.

People filed past on their way to the showers and Jack smiled at her between the moving line. "Sorry I'm early." Taking off his hat, he stepped inside.

"I beg your pardon?" She had to raise her voice, but no way would she get an inch closer to anyone until she'd also had a shower.

"Early for dinner," Jack bellowed over the music and babble. "Sorry. I forgot to get your home address and had to track you down."

Passing faces glanced curiously from Jack to Lauren and heat flushed her cheeks.

Jack didn't appear to notice. "The woman I talked to at your office told me you'd be here now. I figured my only chance for a reprieve was to catch you before you left."

Lauren considered reminding him that they didn't have a dinner date, but he already knew as much and she wasn't enjoying her role as the afternoon's entertainment around here. Tomorrow, Susan would wish she hadn't been so free with details of her boss's personal agenda.

"I have to shower," she told him. And she wasn't fooled; her number and home address were in the phone book.

"Of course. I'll just wait here." Displaying another of his irresistible smiles, he sat on a chair by the windows, stretched out his legs and crossed his ankles. "Take your time."

Speechless, Lauren shifted her weight from foot to foot before turning and hurrying to the locker rooms. This was a calculated attempt to get his way by catching her off guard.

Marilyn Wood, owner of a copy shop close to Contact's offices, descended on Lauren as soon as she appeared. "Isn't that Jack Irving?" Marilyn knew everyone in town, and prided herself on being a reliable source of gossip.

Lauren opened her locker and took out a towel. "Yes," she said when it became obvious that Marilyn would wait as long as it took to get an answer.

"He's some hunk." Marilyn's blue eyes glittered avidly. "How long have you been dating him? He was seeing that Silky Harvey who models for some L.A. surfing equipment outfit. Guess that's over, huh?"

"I'm not dating him." She could almost feel listening ears all around. "And I don't know who he's involved with."

Marilyn smiled knowingly. "Defensive, aren't we?"

Lauren shook her head and stripped off her workout clothes.

"What do you call having dinner with a single, sexy and eligible male if it isn't a date?"

She wasn't having dinner with him, was she? "Excuse me," she said to Marilyn and hurried to the showers.

Within minutes she was deliciously clean, dry and dressed in the ancient faded jeans and sagging red cotton sweater she'd brought to relax in after her session. She combed her hair but left it wet and didn't apply makeup. One look at her—if he hadn't given up and left—should convince Jack that the only place she intended to go was home—on her own.

"Some people," Marilyn said, trailing back with a towel draped around her overly thin body.

"What does that mean?"

Marilyn wound her curly brown hair into a second towel and looked at Lauren in the mirror. "You," she said, turning the corners of her mouth down. "Old clothes, no makeup, wet hair and you look like a million dollars. Why don't sweaters look like that on me?" She held up her hand. "Don't answer that. I know why."

"You always look great," Lauren said honestly. Marilyn meant to be complimentary, but Lauren wasn't fooled. There was too much of her in the red sweater and her face might be described as striking by some, but she knew the lines were there. "See you Wednesday."

Jack sat where she'd left him, one ankle propped on his opposite thigh with the hat balanced on top. When she crossed the long room he made no attempt to move. Lauren felt his eyes on her and lengthened her stride. She wasn't a kid who could be embarrassed by a too-frank male stare.

"Ready?" he asked, standing as she reached him.

"I think we've got our wires crossed," Lauren said. A drop from her hair coursed down her face but she ignored it. "As you can see, I'm not dressed to go anywhere but home."

"Let's go outside." Jack eased the athletic bag from her hand and slung it over his shoulder before opening the door. "Come on. Live dangerously. Be led for once."

How did he know whether or not she ever allowed herself to be led? She went out onto the sidewalk and turned around, almost bumping into him.

Jack smiled. That darn smile. She stepped away, but he only followed, setting his hat in place and tilting it low over his eyes at the same time.

"Walk to the corner."

Short of making a fuss in front of people coming and going from the studio, she had no choice but to do as he asked.

"Look," she began when they stood under a striped awning a few businesses away, "this isn't going to—"

"I'd better quit playing games," he said. "I know you didn't agree to see me tonight, but I decided to try pushing my luck anyway. If you have time and you feel like it, I'd love to have dinner with you. If that isn't convenient, or you don't want to, say so and I'll get lost."

Lauren opened her mouth, closed it again and tried to think of a response. He stood, his weight balanced on one leg, a hopeful-boy look on his compelling face.

"Well—"

"I really will understand if it's no."

A man shouldn't look so good in well-worn jeans and a simple white cotton shirt. And a rough tweed sport jacket nonchalantly pushed back by the hand on his hip shouldn't make a woman want to stroke a wide shoulder, or feel her face there.

She was lonely.

"You want to say no, don't you?"

No, she didn't. "I'm a wreck."

"You look fantastic."

Before she could react, before she realized his intention, he stroked water from her cheek. Lauren lowered her eyes. This was a no-holds-barred attempt to sweep her off her feet and it had a chance of working.

"We could do something really simple if you'd feel more comfortable." He leaned closer and she looked up at him. "Fish-and-chips by the sea, maybe?"

His eyes were a tawny brown, warm and humorous. Maybe she could go for a quick meal. "Well..."

"Great. Let's go. We can walk, but let's stow your stuff first." He started toward a black pickup.

Lauren caught his arm. "My Honda's in front of the studio. It'll be easier to put my gear in there."

Without giving herself more time to think or to change her mind she walked ahead of Jack to her car, unlocked the trunk and let him put her bag inside.

A stiff wind had picked up, but the evening was warm. Strolling beside him along Elm Avenue, Lauren's senses were sharp to the scents of flowers, warm earth—and salt as they turned left on Carlsbad Boulevard and drew closer to the ocean, but she couldn't relax. With every step she was more aware that they were strangers with no reason to be together, and more aware that he, too, was silent, locked in with his secret thoughts.

What was he thinking?

"This is strange."

She glanced at him, taken aback.

Jack laughed. "You're going to think I'm nuts to say this, but you make me nervous."

Lauren looked at him again, her eyes narrowed in assessment. She made him nervous? "Really. Why?" She'd been out of circulation too long to know much about current rules of the man-stalks-woman game, but this sounded like quite a line.

"Not nervous exactly... Yeah, nervous. It's like we've known each other a long time without really knowing each other. And we've been part of another type of world where we never questioned being off-limits to one another, so this feels sort of...illicit?" He laughed and held her elbow. "Hell, what a lousy choice of terms. Forget I said anything."

"I know what you mean," she said, and she did. His honesty disarmed her. "We were both married and expected to stay that way. Or I did, anyway."

"Exactly. So did I. But my marriage is old history. Cross here."

The change in his tone suggested his openness about personal matters only went so far. And he'd reached his limit.

They crossed the boulevard at Pine and the ocean came into view. Lauren kept her eyes trained ahead but she could feel Jack, tall and solid beside her. A good feeling.

"Did you ever consider leaving Carlsbad?" Jack asked suddenly.

"No. Why would I?"

"You don't have family here, do you?"

"I don't have family anywhere. This is home now. Dan and I grew up in Laramie, but there's nothing there for me. My parents were older and I was their only child. They're both dead. I'm not aware of any other relatives." She let her eyes travel over the mix of European and Victorian buildings, interspersed with a heavy influence of romantic Spanish designs. Oddly, the architectural effect was charming rather than jarring. "I love this place."

"So do I. I guess I was wondering if you felt like getting away after your divorce."

"No. Did you?"

"My family has been here for three generations. Andy, my boy, had his routine here. And then there's my dad."

In other words, his situation couldn't be compared to hers? Lauren shrugged. He was only making statements.

Jack took her to a café near the beach and they both ordered fish-and-chips and beer. Sitting with him at a black wrought-iron table beside a frothy purple bougainvillea bush, Lauren ate and drank and found his silence more intriguing than disquieting.

"What else do you like to do?"

She started.

"Besides work and aerobics," Jack added.

"Grow flowers," Lauren said, caught off guard. How dull she sounded, but she had warned him.

"You have a garden?" Jack leaned forward. "What do you grow?"

"No garden. Just tubs in the courtyard and on the lanai." She felt foolish. "But I paint, too."

His gaze flickered and shifted away. "My son fills all my spare time. I like it that way."

Lauren frowned. His tone and face had hardened. What had she said? And if he preferred to be with his son, why had he deliberately tracked her down and virtually forced her to have dinner with him?

She looked at her watch. "Oh, no!" She hadn't realized how much time had passed.

"What is it?"

"I've got to be home by eight-thirty. That's ten minutes from now."

He got up immediately and dropped a bill on the table. "You should have said something. Am I keeping you from your painting?"

Lauren felt suddenly and unaccountably angry. This hadn't been her idea. "You're not keeping me from anything. I could have refused to come."

"But you did come, so why the hurry now?"

"I told you, I have to be..." She didn't owe him any explanations, but she believed in honesty. "Someone's expecting me."

He began to walk so fast that she had to jog to catch up to him.

"Who's expecting you?"

This was outrageous. "I've got a date," Lauren said. "I don't think I need to say more than that."

"How true." Jack inclined his head. "Forgive me for being rude."

They didn't speak until they reached her car and she let him take the keys to unlock the door. When she was inside, he dropped them into her outstretched palm and closed the door.

"Thank you," she said. "I enjoyed dinner." And she'd enjoyed him for a while.

"Thank *you*. And again, I'm sorry if I pushed. Have fun on your date."

He turned away and Lauren started the Honda's engine. Her throat ached. *Disappointment*. She'd turned him off and she wished she hadn't. Only it had been the right thing to do. Of course she'd have fun on her date. She always enjoyed being with Cara.

JACK GRINNED AND HELD his bottom lip between his teeth. "Mmm," he said into the phone, then, again, "mmm. I don't blame you, Charlotte. And I'm sorry Andy smuggled in his rat."

The phone had been ringing when Jack walked into the house. Charlotte Okita, mother of Andy's best friend, Rob, loved having Andy spend the night, but Jaws—as Rob and Andy knew—was not included in the invitation.

"Yes, Charlotte, I know you're afraid of rats." This wasn't the first Jaws emergency involving poor Charlotte. "I'll be right over to get Andy."

Jack listened while Charlotte insisted that Andy stay. The boys were asleep. She only wanted to be sure Jaws wouldn't "die of the cold" as the boys had insisted he would from being banished to a box in the Okitas' tool shed for the night.

"He'll be fine," Jack said. "Leave him out there. I'll pick him up in the morning." At home, Jaws spent most of his time entertaining himself in the elaborate play equipment Andy had devised for his pet.

Jack hung up, shrugged out of his sport jacket and tossed it across the back of the gray corduroy couch in his den. He picked up a photo of Andy from the desk. A face very much like a childhood version of his own smiled back, but the hair was dark, like Mary's.

She kept in touch sporadically, always tentatively signing off her calls from Paris with a request that Jack tell Andy she loved him. Mary usually avoided speaking to Andy in case she "upset him."

He replaced the photo and went to rest his forearms on the mantel. Love wasn't something you could switch on and off or put aside entirely to pursue a lackluster painting career halfway around the world, far from the responsibilities you had assumed and promised to honor. Not that he missed Mary. But Barney Middleton was right. A boy should have some feminine influence in his life on a regular basis. Dad was close to Andy. Jack sometimes felt he was competing with his father for his own son's time. But, with Mother gone, there wasn't a caring woman around Dad's place, either. Bernice, Jack's housekeeper, was kind but had a family of her own upon whom to lavish her attention. And the Silky Harveys of this world weren't interested in small boys who kept rats and anything else that crawled.

What about Lauren Taylor? And what about his unforgivable behavior tonight? She'd caught him off balance when she mentioned she liked to paint. Déjà vu. Was he wrong in assuming that because she'd never chosen to have kids, she didn't like them? He didn't think he was.

But he had been a boor, and he did want—more than he cared to examine too closely—to see her again.

He sat on the couch, then stretched out, his head on one arm. When he'd seen Lauren in that pink striped thing at the exercise studio his heart had almost left his body. She'd looked warm, and soft, and slightly mussed... and wonderful.

Jack closed his eyes. *What did he want?* She was dating.

He sat up. So she was dating. She wasn't married, or even significantly attached as far as he knew. A little competition had never stopped him from entering a race.

Before he could change his mind, he grabbed his jacket again and left the rambling single-story stucco house that sometimes felt too big, and pointed his pickup west, in the direction of the farm.

An hour later he nosed the Ford along Ocean Street. He'd taken Lauren's address from the phone book in his office. She lived in a town house, part of a two story Spanish-style complex with red tile roofs and an unobstructed view of the beach and sea. He remembered noticing and approving of the building.

When he parked, the dash clock showed eleven o'clock. The moon cast sharp white light and he was grateful the pickup was dark-colored.

Once out of the cab, he wrestled an oak tub of pink geraniums from the bed of the truck while he calculated which unit was Lauren's.

Staggering under its weight, he carried the planter across the street and puffed his relief at sighting the right number immediately. Intricate black iron gates stood open to a courtyard. On the far side a light shone through a glass panel covered by a metal grill in the center of the front door. Jack shouldered his way through the gates, making a mental note to find a way to tell Lauren they should be kept locked.

He placed the pot on her step, positioned an envelope among the blossoms and backed away. Was she back from her date yet? Probably not. She'd arrive and find his gift, and her "date," whoever he was, would get edgy. Great. Edginess could be a great advantage to an opponent.

Jack retreated. Tomorrow she'd call. Yes, surely she'd call.

The noise of the front door opening startled him. If he crossed the road his footsteps might be heard and the guy could decide to come after him. That would ruin everything. He pulled back behind a ginger bush near the gate.

"Yeah," a man's voice said. "Thanks, honey. Being with you always makes me feel good."

Jack stiffened and flattened himself against the wall. He should slip away like any decent human being would. He *was* a decent human being, but he had an interest here. Logic told him that was hogwash. But logic had very little to do with what he was feeling.

Lauren said something Jack couldn't hear.

"I'll remember that. But I'll call you about Thursday night. Hey, what's this?"

Jack leaned to see into the courtyard. A man bent over the tub of geraniums. He removed the card and started to open it. Jack opened his mouth to yell, but managed to close it firmly the instant before Lauren removed the envelope—from Dan Taylor's hands.

Chapter Four

"Lauren, I'm sorry!" Susan rushed through the front door, her red hair flying, her iridescent pink raincoat flapping open. "I overslept. Darned alarm. What can I tell you? I can't believe it."

Lauren held up a hand, continued speaking into her mouthpiece and watching the terminal screen. "Where can you be reached?" She typed in the number the caller gave. "Thank you, sir."

Susan took off her coat and pushed her fingers through her mass of hair. Lauren wished she wouldn't wear pink. "I'll take over now," Susan said, "unless you think I need forty lashes."

Twice in one week Susan had pleaded a faulty alarm as an excuse for her tardiness. Lauren glanced at the dark marks beneath her eyes and decided Susan must be enmeshed in a new heavy attachment that wasn't allowing much time for sleep.

Taking off the headset, Lauren stood. "It's all yours." Previous experience had taught her not to pry into Susan's love life. She was extremely private on the subject. "You might want to think about a new alarm."

"Yes, ma'am. I deserve at least that comment." Susan put her hands on her hips and narrowed her eyes. "You look . . . I do believe some would say you're glowing."

"It's a gorgeous day." Lauren laughed self-consciously and turned to catch the frankly curious stare of Jolene, one of five very good operators she'd inherited with the purchase of Contact.

Susan sat in front of the terminal. "Something tells me you've got more than sunshine and flowers on your mind."

"How did you—" A rush of heat to her face chagrined Lauren. "I've got a couple of calls to make. Try to make sure I'm not interrupted unless it's absolutely necessary."

The flower remark was a coincidence. But flowers were exactly what she had on her mind—beautiful double pink blooms, darker in the centers and with white rims.

Lauren shut herself into her office and sat on the edge of her desk. Pulling a scrap of paper from her pocket, she picked up the phone and punched in numbers.

A woman answered. "Irving Farms. Good morning."

In the second that followed, Lauren almost put the receiver down. Then she felt childish. "Good morning. This is Lauren Taylor. Is Mr. Irving in?"

"I'll see."

She waited. From her slacks pocket she removed the card Dan had almost read. The thought infuriated her. But Dan had his problems. He'd been an idiot, but, in some ways, he was paying a big price for that. Not that his frustration with a too young, too self-centered and rather foolish wife was her problem. And his apparent need to come to her for advice made her embarrassed for him.

"Are you still there, Ms. Taylor?"

"Yes."

"Do you want to keep holding?"

Lauren frowned. "Yes." He must be busy. She could have asked him to call her back.

She read the card.

Lauren.
If you need any instructions on caring for these, let me know. If I was rude earlier, I'm sorry. Amend that. I was rude earlier. Sorry.

Jack

She smiled. They'd both been awkward and he'd done all the reaching out. Now it was her turn. Her insides fluttered like a silly girl's, which she no longer was and hadn't been for a long time.

"This is Jack Irving."

"Jack, this is Lauren."

"Yes."

She opened her mouth and her mind blanked.

"Yes?" he repeated.

He sounded...ticked? "I found the beautiful geraniums." What was it with him?

"That's good." A muted tapping suggested he was using a computer keyboard while he talked.

"It was so nice of you." She should know what it was like to be interrupted at a bad time—and understood how difficult that could be.

The tapping continued and he said nothing.

"Anyway... Um, I'm very grateful." The bright bubbly sensation she'd felt on her way here this morning had definitely popped. "Um... I'll take really good care of them. I'm going to put them on my lanai."

"Good. You'd better get someone to move the tub for you."

Another furious blush rushed up her neck. "The gardener will be happy to do that." Why had she mentioned moving the thing? He undoubtedly thought she was hinting for him to come over.

"I'm glad you like the flowers."

Geez, he was prickly—and impossible to read. "I do." But he was kind and probably a little uncomfortable with her thanks. "Anyway, I won't keep you. I just wanted to tell you how touched I am, and surprised. It was a lovely surprise." She began to feel a gentling of the jumpiness in her stomach.

"It wasn't anything. Is that all you wanted?"

All she wanted? Lauren clenched her teeth. And he'd apologized for his rudeness of yesterday? "Yes, that's all. Except that I don't know why you bothered." He'd sought her out, not the reverse. None of this was her fault.

"I—"

"Goodbye," she said and cut off anything else he might have said with a smart smack of the receiver into its cradle.

"Temperamental ass," she muttered. "Men!"

Still muttering, cramming the card back into her pocket, she slid from the desk and yanked open a file drawer. She'd better figure out how much losing Irving's account would cost her if he was the type to bear grudges.

She located the folder and walked slowly to her desk. He'd been a customer for over two years. Minimal service agreement—after-hours switch-over only. But still she hated to lose the business.

A knock at the door was only a perfunctory courtesy before Susan came halfway into the room. "Finished with the phone?" she asked unnecessarily.

Lauren dropped into her chair. "Evidently." She couldn't summon a smile.

"Ooh, sudden mood change." Susan slipped all the way in, closed the door with a foot, and sidled closer, her hands behind her back. "What got to you? Or should I say who?"

Susan might be careful to keep her life outside the office mostly to herself, but she never hesitated to ask about Lauren's. "Nothing and no one," Lauren said. "Is there anything I should deal with before I get to my own work?"

"Ow. You're mad." Susan grimaced. "You are upset because I was late, aren't you?"

"No," Lauren said honestly. "You put in your time around here. I appreciate everything you do, Susan."

"Thanks." A smile softened anxious green eyes. "But something happened since you walked in. I know I shouldn't push, but maybe I could help."

"No—" Why not? Strong and silent wasn't anything she'd ever pretended or wanted to be. "Okay, yes. I am mad. I'm mad at the male of the species in general. Every time I try to treat one like a human being he turns around and stomps on my toes..."

Susan plunked into a chair and leaned forward. "Spill it. Dan again, I suppose."

"My toes are already pretty bloodied," Lauren said. Her lungs expanded hard. "I should call him back and give him some more home truths to think about."

"You should have done that a long time ago," Susan said. "And while you're at it, save a few for that sickening little airhead he's married to."

"He isn't married . . . not anymore."

"What! Dan got—"

"Not Dan." Lauren puffed and slumped. "Jack Irving. I'm talking about Jack Irving, alias Mr. Charm."

Susan raised delicately arched brows. For the first time in Lauren's memory, the ebullient Ms. Bailey seemed speechless.

"Anyway," Lauren said quickly, "enough of that."

"Jack Irving," Susan said, almost to herself. "I wondered why you behaved like a scalded cat when I tried to get you to speak to him on the phone. And then I wondered some more when he was so determined to track you down."

"I didn't behave any differently than I usually do when I've got a lot to do." Lauren felt defensive. She also wished she hadn't been indiscreet enough to mention Jack. "I had a lot to do yesterday, that's all. There wasn't time. And I meant to talk to you about not giving blow-by-blow descriptions of my itinerary to clients."

"I didn't talk about your private business. All I did was tell him why you couldn't return his call yesterday."

"And he tracked me down, Susan." Lauren bit her lip, remembering how frightful she must have looked. "There I was, leaping around in a leotard, sweating, thinking I was anonymous, when Irving's face appeared at the window. I didn't appreciate that." She wasn't being entirely fair but neither did she feel entirely rational.

"I'm sorry if I embarrassed you." Susan showed no sign of repentance.

"Forget it. In fact, forget it completely."

A determined set to Susan's features meant she had no intention of letting the subject go. "You just talked to him, didn't you?"

Lauren crossed her arms.

"Didn't you?"

"Yes, I talked to him. More's the pity." There, she was doing it again, letting her ire hang out.

"I knew it," Susan said triumphantly. "You can't fool me. Finally!" She got up and paced, grinning broadly.

"Finally?"

"Yes, finally. It's at least three years past the time for you to get involved with an interesting man."

"Do you know Jack Irving?"

"Never met him that I remember." The announcement didn't faze Susan's grin.

Lauren picked up a pencil and jabbed it into her desk calendar. "He isn't interesting."

"Yes he is. Dull men don't make women mad." She laughed. "Unless they're married to them."

Despite herself, Lauren smiled slightly. "Very funny."

"So?" Susan planted her hands on Lauren's desk. "What's it all about? Why are you angry with Jack Irving?"

The sooner she explained, the sooner they'd both get some work done. "I had dinner with him."

"Wow!" Susan tossed her hair back. "Wow! I can hardly believe it. That's terrific. Where did you go?"

"It was not terrific." As they'd sat above the beach, the breeze had ruffled Jack's hair, played with glinting traces of the sun's work. His eyes had taken on a curious, almost amber quality in the clear late-afternoon light. "Not terrific," she murmured. "We had fish-and-chips down on the boulevard. He's moody."

Susan breathed in, her eyes closed as if in ecstasy. "I *love* moody men. They're so sexy."

"Not to me." But she might as well get this subject over with. Susan wouldn't relax until she knew "all." Avoiding detail, Lauren filled in the picture of her encounter with Jack, finishing with finding the tub of geraniums on her doorstep late last night. Dan's visit was something she didn't mention. "So, I called this morning to thank him," she finished.

"And?"

"And he behaved like he'd just been kissed by a dog. He left me a gift with an apology for being rude, then turned right around and was even ruder. Now, let's get on with it."

"He's wild about you." Susan sat down again.

Lauren wrinkled her nose. "I don't follow you."

"I made some inquiries about him." Susan had the grace to appear uncomfortable. "Nothing direct. Just a word or two here and there. He hasn't had anyone serious in his life since he and his wife separated and divorced. There have been a few women, but apparently no one who held his interest for long."

Lauren regarded her coldly. "You're out of line—as usual. And, before you make any more brilliant observations, Jack Irving and I aren't even acquainted as far as I'm concerned, let alone 'serious' as you put it."

"Not yet, maybe." Smugness colored each word. "He's gun-shy is all. You mark my words. This is the start of something great."

"You sound like a mangled lyric. Go to work."

"I'm going. I'm going. But first I want you to promise me you'll go easy on him. Give him a chance to work his way through the shock he's feeling at having fallen in love at first sight."

Lauren rocked back and looked heavenward. "You're a nut. Jack Irving and I were a disaster from word one. The end. If he crawled through that door this minute and begged forgiveness, I'd stand on his fingers."

Susan laughed. "I knew it. You're crazy about him, too."

"I don't know the man," Lauren said, completely exasperated.

"But you want to. Give me that promise I asked for."

"What promise?"

Susan spread her hands and jutted her chin. "That you'll go easy on him. Give him a chance. Evidently he was badly hurt by his wife and he's been more or less in hiding ever since."

"In hiding? Most recently with Silky Harvey of the gorgeous bod?"

"Big deal. That was nothing. They went out a few times is all. Now he's seen someone worth getting involved with and he's scared. Men are like that."

"Sure." She knew what men were like. "Thanks for the benefit of your infinite wisdom on the subject. Not that I need it. I've made my peace with all of that."

"Meaning?" Susan asked.

"Meaning that women should learn at a very early age what their intended role is with the opposite sex."

"Really. Does that mean you've learned yours?"

"It sure does. The hard way." Lauren got up and walked to open the door for Susan. "As my marriage finally proved, the only thing I'm good at as far as the male's concerned is being a good buddy. With Jack Irving, there's never going to be a chance to get even that far."

WRONGLY PACKAGED SEEDS. Jack propped his elbows on his desk and scrubbed at his face. "Okay," he told Len Gogh. "I know how it looks right now, but we can't go to pieces on this."

"We could call in the police."

Jack snorted. "Like hell. A, they wouldn't do more than send a man out to take notes. Then they'd do nothing because there's nothing they can do. B, I don't want this getting out."

"It already is out," Len said, his hands tucked inside the bib of his overalls. "If it weren't, we wouldn't know about it."

"Damn," Jack said. "It had to have happened months ago. And it could have been an accident. Don't forget that."

"I'm not forgetting a thing. I just want to know what we're going to do."

Jack got up and went to stare through the window. "Nothing. That's what's so damned frustrating. All we can do right now is watch and wait and pray the whole thing goes away. Until something overt happens—and I hope to God it doesn't—but until it does, all we have are a bunch of isolated, potentially damaging incidents that could be explained away as accidents.

"I'll arrange for replacement stock to be sent to the locations where the mismarked product showed up and we'll send complimentary packages to any customers who are identified. This isn't widespread."

Len grunted. "Yeah. Not yet. I've got old hands in every area keeping an eye open for anything out of the norm."

"Great. Thanks, Len."

"Never mind the thanks. Keep up the prayers, and anything else you can think of."

Len left and Jack turned back to the room. If these incidents were deliberate, they were also clever. They left him with nothing to pin a real investigation on.

The phone kept pulling at his attention. He wished he could have a second chance at the conversation with Lauren. "Damn it all," he said through gritted teeth. What right did he have to censure what she did or who she saw? None. There could be a dozen explanations for Dan Taylor's presence at her town house last night.

Yeah, like he was married to a second wife and having an affair with his ex-wife. Jack rammed balled fists into his jeans pockets. Regardless of the fact that he had no right, he hated the thought of Dan and Lauren together. A flash of pale skin, dark hair, black eyes, passed through his mind. He must be losing it. Why else would he suddenly get a wild crush on a woman who'd been available for three years? Not that he'd had an opportunity to get close to her in those years.

He didn't have an opportunity now, unless he chose to make one. And for that to happen, he was going to have to do something he didn't like doing—grovel.

Damn. He picked up the phone, hit the button for a line out and dialed her office number.

"Contact. May we help you?"

They were prompt and efficient, but he'd expect that from anything she was involved in. "Is Lauren Taylor in, please?"

A breathy voice he recognized from the previous afternoon said "May I tell her who's calling?"

"Ah—" He thought a moment. "Look, this is an old friend and I'd like to surprise her. Do you suppose you could do me a favor and just put me through? It's okay, I promise."

What sounded suspiciously like a snicker came from the phone, then the clearing of the woman's throat. "It'll be my pleasure. One moment, please."

A moment passed, and another, before Lauren's voice came clearly to him. "Yes, Susan? Give me the figures."

Jack hunched his shoulders, hitched at the knee of his jeans and perched on his desk. "Please don't hang up, Lauren."

Silence greeted his request.

"This is mean Jack Irving, fastest mouth in the west—or south, I mean."

"Hello, Jack." And the frost was in that tone.

"We haven't exactly gotten off to a roaring start, have we?"

"I wasn't aware that we'd gotten off to a start of any kind."

The door opened and Joyce peered at him. Jack shook his head and she retreated. "Look, crass jerk isn't my preferred mode of approach. Again, I'm saying sorry and asking you to forgive me."

"Consider yourself forgiven."

And the ball was back in his court. She wasn't giving an inch. "Thanks. I don't deserve your kindness."

"Forget it."

Say thanks and hang up, Jack. "I can't forget it." He couldn't. It was as simple as that. For some reason it was becoming increasingly important to him to know this woman better.

The door opened again and this time his father put in one of his rare appearances in the office. "Just a minute, Lauren. Don't hang up, okay?" He covered the mouthpiece. "Great to see you, Dad. Take a pew. Unfortunately, this probably won't take long." To Lauren he said, "Are you still there?"

"Yes, but we will have to cut this short, I'm afraid." None of the cold front had left her voice.

"Look. I feel like a louse and I'd like to wave a white flag, okay?"

"That isn't necessary."

"It is to me. I—" he glanced at his father who was quietly regarding him "—I was a louse this morning. Unforgivable. When I see you I'll explain some of what's behind that. Things have been a bit tense around here. I'm sure you know how that can be."

"With business you mean?"

Jack relaxed at the slight softening he heard in her voice. "Exactly. But that doesn't excuse my taking it out on you and I want a chance to make up...clean the slate. Any chance of that?"

"Well..."

"That sounds hopeful. How about Saturday? At my place? Andy will be there to chaperon you and I'm told my cooking isn't so bad, especially if the pizza's delivered."

She laughed and he felt his shoulders drop. "Is that a yes?"

"You don't have to feed me. I really do understand getting uptight about the job. Let's forget the whole thing."

"I won't if you don't come and eat. In fact, if you don't come, I'll probably go on a fast until you do." He avoided his father's eyes. "You wouldn't want a thing like that on your conscience."

"Mmm." She was bending, bending.

"Is that a yes?"

"Oh, I guess so. Okay, yes. What time?"

"I'll pick you up at, oh, six-thirty." The damndest feeling of exhilaration flooded him, like a sophomoric kid.

"That'll be fine. See you then."

"See you then, Lauren."

She'd hung up before he finished speaking and he was left looking at the receiver. He put it down slowly, softly.

"Who is she?"

He jumped at the sound of his father's voice. "Just a friend, Dad."

Denton Irving had taken up his favorite position near the windows overlooking the fields. "You sounded... determined. Like you weren't taking no for an answer."

"Did I?" The thought made Jack strangely pleased. "I was afraid I sounded uncertain."

"Well, since you obviously aren't volunteering, I'll have to ask again. Who is she?"

"Lauren Taylor."

His father, tall and rangy with thick white hair and beetling brows that were still dark, fixed him with a piercing brown stare. "Dan Taylor's wife? The real-estate people?"

"His ex-wife. They've been divorced three years. She's a nice woman, Dad. Not that this is anything major. Just someone I like."

"Sounded like more than that to me."

Had it? He guessed it probably had. Was it? Couldn't be. "I've reached a point where I'd like some intelligent female company. Someone to take to dinner, or to a show, who can manage more than a one-word answer from time to time."

"Like that Silky whatever her name was?" His dad dislodged himself from the windowsill and prowled the room, looking at framed show prize certificates.

"Exactly. Silky's a nice kid. But that isn't exactly what I need."

Denton stopped prowling. "But you've decided you need something, huh?"

Jack felt irritated at his own careless comment. "No, I haven't. Don't make anything out of this."

"Okay. Forget I pried. I was hoping you'd let me take a look at the new mutant. This is still going to be the rollout year, huh?"

"Lava Pearl is as much yours as mine," Jack said of the mutant, orange-red and white poinsettia they'd been cultivating. "The same as everything else around here."

"Not anymore. Too many bosses spoil things. And I don't want the responsibility anymore. But we won't flog that subject again. I'd just like to see how the project's going."

"Sure. Matt Carson loves a chance to show off our baby." Jack took a key from a drawer. He discarded the idea of talking about the problems around here. "Let's go take a look." He was picking Lauren up for dinner on Saturday. He couldn't help grinning.

"You like her, don't you?"

He looked up sharply at his father. "You drive me nuts with the mind reading."

"What's she like?'

"Nice. Really nice and good to look at in a different kind of way."

"Sexy?"

He shook his head at his father's faint grin. "That, too."

"Can I give a few words of, er, advice before we go?"

Jack sighed. "If I said no, would it make any difference?"

"It might. But you aren't saying no." He gripped the front of the blue plaid wool shirt he wore over a red T-shirt. "You won't forget Andy in all this, will you, son?"

Jack stood very still. "Andy? What the hell do you mean?"

"I mean Andy. He was five when Mary decided her so-called painting career was more important than her husband or son. You might make an argument for his having been too young for that to make a big impression on him. But don't bet on it."

"I won't," Jack said slowly. "I don't. I put in my time thinking about it regularly. What happened isn't something I can erase and I know it's likely to be something that may cause him a few problems in the trust department in the future."

"As long as you know that."

"We've already had this conversation. Many times."

"Yes. So you'll be careful, won't you?"

Jack narrowed his eyes. "Careful?"

"I know a man's interest in a woman when I see it—real interest." His father's mouth came together in a firm line. "What I just heard was a man who could be winding up for a shot at a major involvement."

"You're exaggerating." But Jack frowned and chewed the inside of his mouth.

"Maybe. Only make sure you don't get into something that's likely to hurt that boy again."

Jack met those wise eyes and had to look away. "I don't know what you mean."

"Yes you do. Andy gets attached to people, maybe too attached. He's a special kid and he probably needs a woman around. But if he gets used to one and then things don't work out for you and whoever she is, Andy'll have another strike against his confidence. I don't want to see that."

Holding his temper wasn't easy. "Neither do I, Dad. And it's not going to happen. This thing with Lauren Taylor is purely casual. Believe me."

HUMMING, LAUREN CLATTERED down the stone steps from the third-floor studio where she took her Wednesday evening oil-painting lessons.

The old Victorian house where Mrs. Laphagia lived, taught and sold her own works stood like a dilapidated older relative between low-lying stucco buildings on the edge of the business district.

Mrs. Laphagia liked the seascape Lauren was working on. Or she said she did. The elderly lady needed her class fees to keep solvent. Lauren could never quite shake the notion that many of the compliments Mrs. Laphagia dispensed were to ensure students didn't lose heart and drop out of her class.

As she searched in her pocket for her car keys, her wooden paint case bumped against her knee. On Saturday she was having dinner with Jack Irving. The same thought had intruded dozens of times since his call yesterday. She smiled and felt nervous at the same time.

"I'd like a few words with you."

Lauren jumped and looked into Christie Taylor's blue eyes. Beside her, dressed in pink and white polka dots—shirt, jeans and even tennis shoes—Wednesday hopped up and down, her blond hair a soft curly mop.

"Hi," Lauren said when she'd recovered. "Were you looking for me?"

"This won't take long if you listen carefully," Christie said, ignoring Lauren's question.

"How did you know where to find me?"

"You keep my husband informed of your whereabouts. All I had to do was look in the back of his journal."

Lauren held back the temptation to say what she thought of snoops. "He always did that. It doesn't mean a thing, Christie. Old habits die hard, right?"

"I wouldn't know about anything old."

Lauren sighed. This type of nastiness sickened her and she wouldn't play games with a woman Susan aptly described as an airhead. That should probably be amended to vindictive, insecure airhead.

"Hello, Wednesday," Lauren said. She dropped to one knee, set down her paint case and smiled at the little girl. "You've grown since I saw you last. And you're even prettier."

The child leaned against her mother's leg and stuck a finger in her mouth. "I'm three," she mumbled.

"Yup," Lauren said. Before she could stop herself she touched the soft hair. "Getting to be a big girl. Do you like to color?"

"Uh-huh."

"Me, too. That's what I've been doing. Next time I see you I'll try to remember to bring you some new crayons."

"She's got all the crayons she needs." Christie swept the child into her arms and pressed her face into her shoulder. "Stop encouraging Dan to spend time with you. Stop giving him a shoulder to cry on. I know all about women like you."

Lauren turned first hot, then very cold. "Women like me? That's rich." If Wednesday hadn't been present she would have told Christie a few truths about her own opinions on the subject of scheming women.

"Dan's been seeing more of you," Christie said. "Telling you our private business and letting you worm your way into his confidence. It's going to stop. He told me you wanted to baby-sit Wednesday tomorrow night."

Wednesday on Thursday. Poor kid. "That wasn't my—"

"I'm going to tell him you called to say you had other plans. Understand?"

Lauren ached to lash back, but nothing would be gained. Dan had amazed her by asking if she'd baby-sit his daughter. She'd refused, and he'd begged, saying Christie didn't trust anyone they hired, but she would feel comfortable with Lauren. How little poor Dan knew about women.

"Are we finished?" she asked.

"Almost," Christie said. "If Dan asks you why you changed your mind about baby-sitting—"

"I didn't. I never said I—"

"I don't believe a word you say. You'll tell him not to come around. Got that?"

"Oh, you bet I've got it," Lauren said, wanting only to get away from this silly woman.

"If you don't get out of our lives you'll wish you had." Christie backed away, turned, and said over her shoulder, "Remember this the next time you feel like interfering in my marriage—I've got influence in this town now."

"Meaning?"

"Meaning nothing," Christie said. "Except that I'm a winner, Lauren. I get what I want—one way or another."

Chapter Five

Jack looked upward. Lauren followed his glance and saw Cara's small face drawn quickly back from her bedroom window.

"Who's that?"

"Cara Flood. She and her mother rent rooms from me."

His brows shot up. "Really?"

She laughed. "Uh-huh. It's a long story, but not very interesting." To anyone but her.

"I see," Jack said in a tone that let her know he wasn't a man to quiz. "That jumpsuit looks great. Black is definitely your thing. You look wonderful."

The warmth of pure pleasure suffused her. "Thank you. So do you," she told him and grimaced.

This time he laughed, tipped back his head to show strong teeth and deep dimples in his cheeks. "You're something. *I* look wonderful. That's a first for me."

Lauren couldn't think of a response.

She almost expected him to drive a different vehicle, but the big black pickup waited at the curb. Lauren liked him for that, for his lack of pretention. And when he helped her up the high step into the cab she was grateful she wore pants.

He walked around, his head bent over his keys. The late sun picked out those glints in his hair again. He was rangy but lithe in gray pleated pants and a white shirt, open at the neck and rolled up over his tanned, leanly muscled forearms.

"Off we go," he said, climbing in beside her and switching on the ignition.

Lauren, her stomach doing somersaults, steadily regarded the ocean. Gentle waves rolled in to curl along the state beach. No surfers were evident today. Even the usual motley assortment of mostly junker cars sporting boards on their roofs was missing.

"No surf today," Lauren said, for need of something to say.

"Do you surf?"

She shook her head. "I don't even swim," she admitted and regretted the confidence. "Not well, anyway." *Not at all* was the truth.

"I'm damned. You never learned?"

More golden hair covered his arms and the backs of his broad capable hands resting loosely on the steering wheel.

"Swimming isn't big where I grew up."

"Nevertheless you should be able to, just in case." He drove with relaxed ease. "You ought to learn."

"I'd be embarrassed."

"No you won't. I'll teach you."

She swallowed and concentrated more intently on the sea. Again there was nothing she could think of to say. Looking ahead, she was aware of his leg close to hers, his thigh flexed. This man had too strong an effect on her or maybe she was too vulnerable to any attractive male who showed interest in her.

This was just a dinner date with his son present because he felt obligated to make up for his earlier rudeness. There'd been no prior rudeness to explain his turning up at the aerobics studio, however.

"You're quiet." He inclined his head until she was forced to meet his tawny eyes. "Are you afraid of the water? I'll teach you in my pool."

"I don't have a swimsuit."

He splayed fingertips over his smile and she bowed her head.

"People always say I have a way with words," Lauren told him. "That's an example of why."

"I find you delightful. You say the first thing that comes into your head, thank God. Pretty rare in a female."

"Equally rare in a male," she said before she could stop herself.

He laughed. "See what I mean? Natural. That's marvelous. But now you think I'm a chauvinist."

Now she didn't know what to think, especially about this different, very charming, very confusing side he was showing. He was probably playing with her. Why, she had no idea.

Once beyond the main development of the town, he followed the route from Carlsbad Avenue and inland on Palomar Airport Road. The vegetation became scrubby—a straggle of bushes and shrubs growing despite the rocky terrain. But, beyond the scattering of red-tiled roofs, a forest lined the horizon below a pale blue sky.

Minutes passed before Jack spoke again. He turned his face briefly toward her, then faced the road once more. "Do you think I'm a chauvinist?"

"I don't really know you," she reminded him.

"True."

Silence sank between them again. The low-lying buildings of Palomar Airport came into view on their left. As they drove by, a sleek white Learjet swept in for landing.

"And the great golf game goes on," Jack remarked.

Nearby La Costa, one of the nation's ritziest clubs, drew wealthy and famous players from all over the world.

"Do you play?" Lauren was increasingly aware of the awkwardness between them.

"Not if I can help it. Racquetball's my passion."

"Mine, too!" She instantly regretted her outburst.

Jack smiled at her. "You really are into fitness, aren't you?"

"It's good for the nerves as well as the body."

"And your nerves need lots of things that are good for them?" A right turn onto El Camino Real had them heading south again.

"I was only making conversation."

He thought about that. "Do I make you uncomfortable?"

"A bit."

"That's the thing about trying to know someone, isn't it? The getting past the awkward stage. Feels a bit like fencing, testing."

He was open with his thoughts himself. "I guess." Impetuously, she added, "I'm rusty at this anyway."

"Why's that?"

Lauren swallowed. "I've been busy."

"Too busy for people?"

"Too busy for men is what you're asking, isn't it?" She rested her head back. Another plane passed overhead.

"Mmm. You're right. That is what I mean."

"Dan was my first real boyfriend. First boyfriend—period. We were in grade school when we met. There were brief times when we went our separate ways, but not for long. I never really learned the dating dance." This man engendered frankness. "And now I don't want to."

"Why?" He turned his face toward her. "Do you like being alone that much?"

She took a deep breath that seemed to go no farther than her throat. A glance from Jack Irving had the unwelcome effect of searing the air around her. "Maybe. Maybe I just don't like the odds against having a successful relationship."

"What constitutes successful to you?"

This was a conversation she'd never had with anyone. With herself many times, but never aloud. "I'm not sure. Maybe it would be a friendship where I never had to doubt that I was . . . wanted for myself. Maybe there isn't such a thing as a successful relationship. Knowing the other person would never change, or would always put you first would do it. Being sure that you would never wake up one morning to find the bottom had dropped out of everything you believed in.... If you knew that whatever happened, the other person would never even consider letting you down, that would be a successful relationship, wouldn't it?" She laughed and the sound was hollow in her own ears. "I think my interpretations belong in a fairy tale. And no one cares what I think anyway."

"I care."

Lauren looked at him sharply. The lines of his face had hardened and his hands were no longer relaxed on the wheel. His knuckles were white.

"Your interpretations as you call them should be written on stone—in blood—before people make promises to one another."

"Yes." Her throat constricted. "But that isn't likely to happen, so the best thing we can do if we tend to wound and not heal too quickly is to steer clear of potential disaster."

"How right you are."

She felt the lightness go out of the moment. He was closing up. The startling realization came that he was probably still in love with his ex-wife. What Lauren couldn't figure out was why he'd decided to hold out a tentative hand in her direction. Friendship seemed the unlikely motive. And the other possibility... Her chest expanded uncomfortably. Surely she hadn't given off vibes that suggested she'd be a willing candidate for a casual affair.

There could never be any question of that. Not for her. She made up her mind. She liked him, might be capable of really liking him, but this would be the last time she'd say yes to an invitation—not that she expected another. Obviously he'd acted on a whim.

The houses they passed became very familiar.

Lauren felt Jack's eyes on her again. "Does it bother you to come out here?"

"No," she said, and was pleased to realize she meant it. "It would have a couple of years ago, but not anymore."

But she didn't look to the right when they drove past the turn to Arenal Road.

"It's a striking house," Jack said as if seeing into her mind again. "I always admired the lines. Very clean."

He didn't mean to upset her. "Yes. We had it built," she said of the multilevel, flat-roofed white house where she and Dan had lived for ten years.

Jack turned sharply right, then left onto quiet Caleta Court. Evening jogging had often taken Lauren along this short street lined by tastefully expensive stucco ramblers with tiled roofs.

"Here we are." He drove up a sloping red brick driveway and parked before wrought-iron gates in a white stucco wall that shielded a courtyard in front of the house. "Stay put until I can help you."

She did as he asked, aware of a thudding in her chest. What was she doing here?

Jack squinted into the sinking sun. A compelling man by any woman's standards. She couldn't, must not, allow any fantasies about him. But the fitted shirt showed off a well-toned body and he moved with sure power that brought goose bumps to her arms and a tightness to her jaw.

He opened her door and smiled up at her. And the sensation that hit her now was as old as mankind, but too rare in Lauren's recent memory. She took the hand he offered and looked away, certain that if he saw her eyes he'd know what she'd felt.

When she stood beside him in the driveway, he continued to hold her hand until she turned her face up to his. He was still smiling.

"What?" She inclined her head. "Why are you smiling?"

"I don't know. Maybe I'm glad you're here." He shrugged his wide shoulders. "And maybe I'm surprised you are."

"And maybe you can't figure out why you asked me at all," she said more tartly than she'd intended. Somehow she had to get through this experience unscathed and make sure she never allowed another potentially destructive encounter with Mr. Irving.

"Dad!"

One half of the black metal gates swung inward and a boy ran out. He threw himself at Jack. Lauren would never have had any difficulty figuring out who he was. Though in the gangly stage with curly hair that was black rather than light-colored, the boy's eyes and bone structure were too similar to Jack's for him not to be the man's son.

"Hey, let up, Andy. Here's our guest."

The boy immediately separated himself from his father. A frank, assessing gaze pinned Lauren before he smiled politely. "Hi."

"Lauren Taylor." She held out a hand and immediately wondered if she'd lost her mind, but he shook hands without hesitation, his skin slightly powdery from the layer of dust she noted on his fingers. "You must be Andy."

"Yeah. Hi. We're havin' lasagna. Bernice made it up."

Lauren looked quizzically at Jack.

"Our housekeeper. She's a gem."

"She's a pain about some things," Andy retorted. "Yesterday she put Jaws—"

"That'll do," Jack said quickly, but he laughed. "Andy and Bernice get along very well most of the time. Let's go in. I expect Lauren's ready for something to drink."

The smell of the lasagna was the first impression Lauren had when she passed through the lushly planted courtyard and into Jack's cool house.

"Would you like to sit on the patio?" Jack asked.

"Um."

"We don't have to. Are you chilly? I could turn down the air conditioning. I tend to keep the house pretty cold." He moved a step behind her and she felt him at her shoulder. "Andy, did Bernice lay the table?"

He was almost chattering, Lauren thought. Her next thought surprised her. He was as nervous as she.

"Bernice did *everything*." Andy sighed audibly. "She made me tidy up my room."

"Good for Bernice," Jack said. Lauren could hear anxiety in his voice.

"I'd love to sit on the patio if you would," she said, smiling back at him.

His glance shifted fractionally, from her eyes to her mouth. "I'd like it very much." He caught his bottom lip in his teeth.

Lauren swallowed and found herself mimicking his action, pulling her own lip between her teeth. Aware of the beginning of a flush, she turned to Andy. "Lead the way to the patio, Andy. You're going to join us, aren't you?"

"What will you drink?" Jack asked.

"White wine would be lovely," she said without looking at him.

"White wine it is. Take care of her, Andy."

He touched her back before walking away across the terrazzo floors. Lauren watched him go. His fingers had left a tangible print on her shoulder. Letting out a slow breath, she smiled at Andy.

The rooms he led her through were airy. Pale shades predominated—cream and pearl gray with touches of black or brilliant blue. Not Jack's choice, she thought with certainty. Somewhere there must be a room that would be distinctively his. These austere spaces, attractive and tasteful as they were, and appealing to Lauren on some level, had to be left over from his beautiful, artistic and supposedly self-absorbed wife.

"Don't sit in the striped chair," Andy said as they emerged onto a flagstoned patio. "It falls down sometimes."

"Thanks." Lauren sat in the white chaise Andy indicated. "This is great." No austerity here. This was an area that had to belong to a lover of color.

Hanging baskets, tubs, planters on scattered low tables, flowers sprayed and sprouted everywhere. Jack had geraniums of a dozen varieties captured in small planting areas and clustered amid billowing purple lobelia in two wooden wagons.

Suddenly aware of being watched, Lauren gave Andy her attention. "Do you like flowers?"

"'Course."

Of course? Most nine-year-old boys might not be so quick with that answer. "Do you help your dad at the farm sometimes?"

"Yeah. A lot." He looked at the sky, then at his worn sneakers.

Lauren cleared her throat. Jack seemed to be taking a long time with the drinks.

"You like flowers?" Andy asked.

"Very much."

He strolled around the patio, his hands in the pockets of his jeans, scuffing at nothing in particular. "You used to live near here, Dad said."

"Yes. Just a couple of streets away. I remember you as a little boy." That wasn't entirely true. She remembered a small boy with Jack at the store, or outside in the yard when she jogged by, but he'd been more an impression than a presence.

"I don't remember you."

She almost laughed. It was too bad adults learned to play polite games. Being honest would be so much easier.

"What time do you have to get back home?"

The question jolted her. "I hadn't thought about it." She sat straighter and tightened her hold on the small purse she'd brought.

Andy circled some more. "Where'd you meet my dad?"

"Well, we first met years ago—sort of."

"Yeah. But now, I mean. He doesn't invite... He doesn't usually have people to dinner."

Lauren felt tempted to ask if Silky had come to dinner but thought better of it. "We, er, talked at a party. And I have an answering service that does work for him."

"So you work for him." He paused an instant, thinking. "Lots of people work for him. He doesn't ask them for dinner."

Glancing at the door, willing Jack to arrive, Lauren considered what was happening. "Maybe you'd better ask him about that." The beginning had seemed promising. Now a cold front was moving in and she didn't need child-psychology classes to figure out that she made the boy feel threatened.

A scratching sound distracted her. She tried to smile at Andy and leaned to look beneath the chair. The wooden box with holes in it had escaped her notice.

More scratching.

Lauren returned her attention to Andy and found him watching her intently. "That's Jaws," he said. His slender, freckled face had turned pink.

"Jaws?" She pursed her lips.

"One of my pets." Andy planted his feet wide apart. "Want to see him?"

Lauren smelled a setup but decided to play along. "Sure."

Andy approached, dropped to sit cross-legged beside her, and reached to pull a string that raised one side of the box.

The first thing Lauren saw was a long, twitching, gray-and-white nose adorned with stiffly sprouting whiskers.

Lauren's heart did a neat flip and settled back in place. Not so much a setup as a test. Well, rodents weren't high on her list of favorite things, but she'd never been squeamish.

The animal slid carefully from his hiding place and into his master's lap, where he peered sideways with a beady black eye. He endured the captivity of Andy's hands with apparent resignation.

Andy's attention was on Lauren. His narrowed eyes, the now-what-are-you-going-to-do smirk amused her.

Suppressing a rise of sickness, she fixed her own smile in place and held out her hands. "Does he go to strangers?"

"You wanna hold him?" Andy wasn't quite up to camouflaging his disbelief.

"Sure." No, she didn't, but neither was she about to be outmaneuvered by a nine-year-old.

The scratch of small pointed claws on her palms almost undid Lauren. Jaws's long sinewy body tensed in her hands but he held still, his head darting this way and that. His pink tail, like a cold, dull-skinned snake, wound about her wrist.

"He's... he's really something. Very tame." Her heart gradually stopped jumping. The creature seemed clean and he hadn't bitten her—yet.

"You like him!" Andy's grin was sincere. "Geez, you're the first girl who didn't scream. You shoulda seen Rob's mom the other night."

"Come and get your Coke, Andy."

Jack emerged through the open French doors, a wine-glass in one hand, a highball glass in the other.

Andy didn't move.

"Hop to it, kiddo," Jack said, approaching. At Lauren's side he stopped and stared down. "What the—Andrew! What do you think you're doing?"

Lauren suppressed a giggle at the age-old parental reaction. "Andy said I could hold Jaws," she said. "One of the best, nope, I'd say the very best rat I ever held." The only rat she'd ever held.

"She's the only girl I ever met who likes him." Awe hung on every word. Andy turned to her and his smile was genuine. She was being silently thanked for not selling him out.

Jack's eyes met hers and she saw humor sparkle there. "Sorry I took so long. The wine was in the basement."

Lauren kept her face straight. "Don't worry. Andy's been looking after me." *And trying to scare me off.*

Jaws moved, whipping his body in a semicircle. Andy removed him, sidled past his father and across the patio. "I'll get my Coke," he said as he went into the house.

"You really are something," Jack said, giving her the glass of wine.

Lauren swallowed a large gulp and let her muscles go limp. "No big deal. Andy's proud of his pet. He wanted to show him off."

"Wanted to see if you frighten easily is more likely."

His frankness took her aback. "Why would he want to do that?" She had a perfectly good notion why but wondered if Jack, who must know the reason, would admit it.

"Just kidlike, I suppose."

No, he wasn't comfortable enough with her to say exactly what he thought.

"This is beautiful," she said when she couldn't bear the silence any longer. "Wonderful flowers."

"Thanks. Since they're my business it would be funny if I didn't have a show at home."

"Of course."

"Do you bring on your own starts?"

She stared at him blankly. "Starts?"

"For your containers?"

"Oh. No, I buy plants when I'm ready for them. I don't really have a place to keep things like that."

"Doesn't take much room. You could do it in a window."

He wouldn't relate to her dislike of clutter. Boxes of seedlings would fill needed spaces and look messy.

"Come and see the pool," he said abruptly, taking her glass and setting it on a table with his own.

Without waiting for her response, he walked on stepping stones leading from the patio, behind the planting areas to one side of the house. The pool was oval. On the far end stood a small building of stucco that matched the house and had its own tiled roof.

Jack continued around the pool with Lauren in his wake. Outside the building he stopped. "Poolhouse," he said. "There's a shower and sauna. Bar. Small lounging area. Get a suit when you can and I'll teach you to swim."

His voice was almost toneless, but why would he repeat the offer if it wasn't sincere? Lauren's stomach clenched. "Thank you. Maybe I'll take you up on that one day." The thought of entering that warm blue pool, of her body and Jack's being close, skin to skin, did amazing things to her brain... and other areas.

She was thirty-nine. A few months and she'd be forty. Jack had undoubtedly seen Silky Harvey's flawless mid-twenties body in a swimsuit—or less. Lauren turned away. She was happy as she was and intended to stay that way. Being compared to a woman fifteen years her junior wasn't something she planned on going through. There would be no swimsuit competition, or any other competition for any man.

"TIME YOU HIT the hay." Jack reached to ruffle Andy's hair. "Your grandfather's coming for you early in the morning."

"I'm not tired yet," Andy said. "Lauren, would you like to see the gym I built for Jaws?"

Jack propped his elbows on the table and regarded his son. This behavior was out of character. Usually the boy was quiet around strangers, particularly women. Not that Jack had brought more than one or two home, and never for dinner.

"You bet I would," Lauren said.

He looked from Andy to Lauren. She'd eaten well. He appreciated a woman who didn't pick at her food as if she disdained anything as earthy as a good appetite.

"I think you should run along, Andy. Lauren can see the gym another time."

Andy frowned. "I picked up the stuff in my room."

It also wasn't like Andy to persist once he'd been given an instruction.

Lauren got up and turned so that Andy couldn't see her face. "You stay here with your coffee. I really want to see the gym. I won't be long." She gave him an exaggerated wink that looked so odd he almost laughed.

"Okay, but do make it quick, okay, son?"

Andy nodded and left the room with Lauren. She glanced back at Jack before going through the door, then went from sight.

Jack leaned back in his chair. What had made him feel he wanted to see Lauren at his table, and with his son?

He sat up again and drank not coffee, but brandy, taking a long swallow from a snifter. That was it. Of course. It wasn't how she reacted to his home, or even to him. He'd wanted to see her with Andy.

And she was passing the test with flying colors. The brandy burned all the way down. What test? And what was the prize for passing? He flared his nostrils. He was certainly no prize. So far his record for choosing the right woman was a great big zero. Mary was supposed to have been it, the one and only. Some judge of character he was.

Lauren was something special.

Hell, what did he know? He *thought* she was something special, but he couldn't risk... His mouth dried out. He wanted to know Lauren, to know her better, whatever that would mean.

Andy had reacted positively to her.

A coldness crawled into his belly. Andy must not be hurt again by learning to care for someone who could walk away without looking back. No, that must not happen again. A polite dinner was all this was.

Her flat sandals made a clipping sound on the hall floor. "This boy's got talent," she said, coming back into the room with Andy grinning at her heels. "Jaws is one lucky rat."

Jack regarded the two of them and the coldness inside him intensified. "Some gym, huh?"

Andy's face glowed. "She likes Strangler, too."

Jack closed his eyes and shook his head. "You set that snake of yours on her, as well?"

"Strangler's got a lot of personality," Lauren said.

"For a snake," Jack muttered. Andy was taking out all the stops. Jack knew only too well that his boy judged his friends by their reactions to his creepy menagerie. "To bed with you."

"Okay, okay. I'm going." At the door Andy paused. "I play soccer."

"Oh." Lauren's smile showed interest. "Soccer's a good game."

Hers was a face he'd never get tired of, Jack decided.

"I've got a game next Saturday. Would you like to come?" Andy looked at Jack. "You'd bring her, wouldn't you, Dad?"

"Ah, yes." He'd made a horrible mistake here.

"Well, I don't know." Lauren's tone had changed, subtly, but had changed nevertheless.

Jack looked at her alertly. The smile on her face had lost its brilliance.

"It'd be fun. Wouldn't it, Dad? Rob's mom and dad always go. Lauren could talk to Rob's mom. Maybe she could tell her how Jaws isn't anything to be scared of. Then we could all go for pizza like we usually do."

"Hmm." Jack listened to Andy's rapid fire delivery, but watched Lauren. She'd laced her fingers tightly together.

"What d'ya say, Lauren?" Andy asked.

She reached behind her, found a chair and sat down. "That's so sweet of you, Andy. I'd like to come, but I'd better take a rain check this time. I... I've got something I have to do next Saturday."

"Oh." The animation fled Andy's features. He shrugged. "That's okay, then."

"I would like to." Lauren appeared to take short puffs of breath through her mouth like a woman drowning. "It just wouldn't work out next Saturday."

Jack flexed the muscles in his jaw. She'd been putting on an act, pretending to like Andy. He'd been right; Lauren didn't particularly care for children... not if they threatened to take up too much of her time.

"Night then," Andy said.

"I'll be in to say good-night shortly," Jack told him.

"Good night, Andy," Lauren said. "Thanks for showing me the gym."

Once they were alone, Jack returned his attention to his brandy glass. He was being irrational. There was no reason for him not to enjoy the company of a woman who appealed to him even if she didn't instantly fall for his son.

This was a casual date, not an audition for a lifelong commitment. He'd probably never make another one anyway.

"You're quiet," Lauren said softly.

He looked up into her dark, gentle eyes and every nerve in his body leaped. "I was thinking."

"What about?"

She'd never know. "About how nice it is to sit here with a beautiful woman." It probably sounded phony, but at this moment it was true.

A blush did great things for her. "You don't have to be so nice," she said.

He studied her speculatively. "Don't you know you're beautiful?"

"You ask funny questions. You embarrass me."

"Maybe I want to. I like it when you blush."

"I don't." She drank coffee and grimaced.

"Cold? I'll make some fresh."

"No. I'll drink more wine." A laugh softened the strain that had tightened her mouth. "I'm not usually a lush, but this is very good."

There was something between them, something growing more intense with every second. She was rusty at the dating dance, she'd said. Jack swirled the liquor in his glass. Could Taylor have been the only man in her life—really in her life? Had she completely kept to herself since the divorce? He raised his eyes. Was she ready to take a lover? He shifted in his seat, felt his thigh muscles jerk.

"Perhaps it's time I went home."

He started, realizing he hadn't responded to her previous comment. "Drink the wine. And no, it's not time for you to go home. Do you play table tennis?" The instant he'd asked he felt foolish.

Her "Yes, I love it," was delivered as if the question couldn't have been more normal.

Jack searched for the next comment. "Would you like a game?" From lover to table-tennis player. None of this felt like anything he'd ever experienced.

"Now?" Lauren asked. "Where?"

"There's a game room in the basement. But you don't have to if you don't like the idea."

"I do like it." She was on her feet.

The basement was his favorite spot in the house. A big paneled room furnished with comfortable tan leather, this was where he came to listen to music and read.

Lauren walked slowly past his overflowing bookshelves, turning her head sideways to read the titles. "This is a neat room," she said and pointed at the stove. "I'd curl up by that with a book and forget the rest of the world."

"That's what I do." So, they had that much in common.

The paddles lay on the tabletop. Lauren picked one up and flipped her wrist in a way that gave Jack pause. She hadn't said whether she considered him a chauvinist. In fact, he wasn't. But he hated to lose at anything, especially to a woman.

"Warm-up?" he asked.

She nodded and started a rally. Seconds later she said, "Let's just play." Catching the ball she waited for his response. When he took up position, she served. An ace....

Jack opened his mouth to say he hadn't been ready, but changed his mind.

Lauren served again.

Another ace.

Jack couldn't bring himself to look at her. He must be out of practice or going too easy on her.

"Just a minute." Hopping, Lauren took off first one, then the other sandal. "They get in my way," she said, tossing them aside.

She could have fooled him. "More comfortable now?" He smiled inquiringly and missed her third serve.

The first game went to Lauren, twenty-one to ten.

"I didn't realize how rusty I was," Jack said. "My turn to serve?"

"Uh-huh. How long is it since you played?" She returned the ball with a vicious rolling forehand that sent the ball to Jack's backhand corner. It rose vertically, but this time he was ready.

Jack leaped, smashing the ball for a short angle shot she'd never get.

The ball hit the net and dropped back on his side of the table. Furious, he gritted his teeth. "It's been weeks. Where do you play?"

Lauren frowned. "Nowhere really. Dan and I had a table, but I don't think I've played since then."

He laughed. He had to. "And you're creaming me? I've gotta concentrate here." He pointed his paddle at her. "Not a word about this massacre to Andy."

"Not a word. Serve."

Their play evened out, but she was obviously a competitive player.

Lauren reached and ran, stooped and bounced in place. Maybe if she weren't so irresistible to watch he wouldn't keep missing shots. As it was he couldn't help mentally cataloging the magnetizing things all those moves did to her body encased in the simple black jumpsuit.

"This is fun," she said breathlessly. Her hair had become mussed, her cheeks flushed.

"Mmm." It was fun. How long had it been since he'd felt as he did tonight? "Are you thirsty?"

"Are you?"

"I asked first."

She smiled and laid down the paddle. "I'm thirsty if you are."

Her voice, the breathy quality, singed some deep part of him. "Pop, or more wine?" He went to the refrigerator behind the bar.

"Pop. Coke if you've got it."

"Sure." And she didn't say "diet."

He gave her a glass of Coke, poured one for himself and went to light the wood stove.

Lauren chose a chair and curled up on the seat with her feet beneath her. "This is so nice."

When flames flickered up the stovepipe, Jack sat on the floor. Nice it might be. Relaxed, he wasn't. "There's something I need to say."

She tilted her head. "Okay."

"I really am sorry for the way I spoke to you the other morning."

"You already apologized. I understand how edgy business problems can make you."

For some obscure reason he didn't want her to make this easier on him. "I brought the geraniums over the night before."

"I know."

He raised his face. She regarded him steadily. In her throat a pulse beat visibly. Her full breasts rose and fell as if she were still slightly out of breath. Yet again his gut reminded him sharply that he was a man in the company of a woman he found incredibly sexy.

"I was in the courtyard when Dan left your place." All week he'd told himself he wouldn't do this. No way would he broach a subject that was none of his business.

"Why didn't you..." Her lips came together in a line that trembled slightly.

Jack felt as if his insides had been ignited. "I couldn't interrupt." He curled his fingernails into his palm. "Do you and Dan still see a lot of each other?"

"More than we should." She rested her head back. Her skin was very pale, all the way down her slender neck, and all the way to the top button on the jumpsuit where a shadow hovered. "More than I want to, now. I already told you we've been friends most of our lives. When Dan's troubled, I'm the first one he turns to, the same as he always did."

"You could tell him you don't want him around."

"I more or less have."

More or less. Why did it bother him that she still spent time with her ex-husband?

Lauren jerked upright and leaned forward. "Was that why... No, of course not."

"Why what?"

"Nothing."

He breathed deeply through his nose. "When a woman says 'nothing' she always means something and it's usually something that bugs her."

"Not this time. And it was a stupid thought. I suddenly wondered if seeing Dan had anything to do with the way you spoke to me when I called the next morning." Her pale skin turned that fascinating shade of deep pink he was coming to like.

"No, nothing like that. Why should it?" He hated to lie. "Well, yes. Now that I think about it, it did bother me. You told me earlier you had a date and then you were with Dan. I immediately thought you two must still be... Well... Forget it."

"Still... You mean you think there's still something physical between Dan and me?"

"That's your business."

"He's married to someone else."

It was his turn to feel very hot. "I know. But you see how it looked, don't you?"

She took her time before answering. "Yes, I guess so. You don't know me well enough to realize that wouldn't be something I'd do." Her short fingernails ran along the side seam in her pants. "Why would it matter to you?"

"It doesn't," he lied. "I was only speculating."

The next silence was uncomfortable before he said, "You do aerobics and paint and you like to do container gardening. What else do you like?" Changing the subject had become imperative.

"Jogging. I love to jog."

"Where?"

"All over the place. The beach is good."

Jack studied her. "Who do you jog with?"

"Me." Her eyes slid away.

"You make sure you go in daylight?" Now he sounded like an anxious parent.

"Not always. It's safe down there."

"The hell it is. Why don't you jog with me?" He hated jogging, but maybe with her he'd become a convert.

"One day perhaps. Thanks."

"You said you like racquetball." A spark flew to the hearth and he deadened it with the base of his glass. "Do you have a regular partner?"

"No." Her lashes lowered, thick, casting a shadow on her rounded cheekbones. "I just play pickup games with anyone who's around."

"I like to play a couple of times a week. Play with me."

"What about your regular partner?"

"I play pickup, too." Another lie. He and Jess Parker, a local accountant, had played together for years.

When he looked at Lauren, the intensity of her gaze disconcerted him. "What is it? Am I being pushy?"

"Maybe. What is it that you want from me, Jack?"

Her directness rendered him speechless.

"Jack?"

"I . . . I'm not sure."

"Try and figure it out." With her nose in her glass, her dark hair fell forward to shield her face.

Jack scooted closer and touched her knee. He let his hand rest there. "I can't be that cool. I like you. Isn't that a good reason for wanting to be with someone?" Some of the other feelings he had couldn't be voiced; not now and probably never.

"If you want—" She tossed back her hair but didn't meet his eyes. "I don't have a good record with the men in my life."

He had the vague feeling that this was a landmark conversation, and that this woman was totally unlike any other he'd known. "I got the impression there hadn't been so many."

"It doesn't take many failures to get the message about what you aren't good at."

"Could we agree to give one another a chance? We could do something nonthreatening, like jog, or play racquetball, and just see what happens."

"You're hedging. I'm hearing another message, Jack. Or I think I am. And that one won't work—not for me."

"Tell me what you mean."

Footsteps on the stairs were an intrusion Jack resented. His father came into view but didn't come farther than the bottom step. "I need to talk to you, Jack," he said, his attention on Lauren.

Jack stood up. "Lauren, this is my dad. Denton Irving. Dad, Lauren Taylor."

His father nodded perfunctorily. "May I have a few words with you, Jack?"

"Now?" He checked his watch. "It's after eleven. Can't this wait till I see you in the morning?"

"If it could, I wouldn't be here."

"Couldn't we have talked on the phone?"

"I tried that. Andy was using it. I got through on call waiting."

Jack narrowed his eyes. Did his father think he was slow-witted? Sure he'd talked to Andy and Andy had said Lauren was with Jack. So Dad had hotfooted it over here to make sure Jack didn't forget the warnings about Lauren. And as long as she was in the room there was nothing he could say to set the old man straight.

"Mrs. Taylor," Dad said with more formality than Jack ever remembered hearing from him. "A little family matter has come up that Jack and I need to talk about. Would you be offended if I called a taxi for you?"

Jack swung toward his father, fury whipping along every vein. "Dad! What the hell—"

"It's all right," Lauren said from behind him. "The taxi's a good idea. That way you don't have to drive all the way back to town then out here again."

"I'll take you home," Jack said forcefully. "When you're ready to go."

She retrieved her sandals and slipped them on.

"We need to talk," Denton said, giving Jack a meaningful glare.

"Then talk. Now."

"When we're alone."

Lauren patted Jack's arm as she went to the stairs. "I'm going to call a taxi. Please don't give it another thought."

"No way." He couldn't believe his father would pull something like this.

Denton stood aside to let Lauren pass. "This is important, Jack."

"Good night, " Lauren said.

Jack started for the stairs but she held up her hand. "Relax. I'm used to doing things for myself. This is the way I prefer to go home. Really."

"Lauren—"

"I wouldn't do this if there was any other way," his dad said. "Mrs. Taylor's obviously a sensible woman. I need your attention now, son."

"Talk to your father."

With a sense of total disbelief, Jack watched Lauren climb the stairs and go into the hall.

"You'd better have one damn good reason for this," he told his father through gritted teeth.

"The best," Denton said evenly. "Trust me."

Chapter Six

Betty Flood had something on her mind, and whatever it was, she clearly had no intention of sharing it with Lauren.

"Tomorrow's Monday," Lauren said. "What about school for Cara?"

Betty, thirty, of average build and height with a pleasantly unremarkable face and light brown curly hair, stopped going through her purse and looked at Lauren. "I'll call the school first thing in the morning and tell them she won't be in."

"I see." Lauren stood near the sliding windows that opened onto the living room lanai. Outside, an uninviting gray sky pressed into a matching sea. Wind buffeted the glass. "Who did you say you were going to visit?"

Betty's bright blue eyes, the pattern for Cara's, met Lauren's. "I didn't. I said I was taking Cara away overnight." She stopped replacing items in her purse. "Look, I know I owe you openness for all you've done for me, but this is something I'm not ready to talk about."

Lauren's stomach turned. She made fists at her sides. "You don't owe me anything." But she wanted something anyway, she wanted to know what was going on and how it would affect Cara.

"Yes, I do. But you'll have to trust me this time."

Betty was planning to take Cara away. Lauren could feel it. It would be like losing Joc all over again: the empty days and nights after he left, the house silent except for the sound of her own footsteps, her own breathing.

"I'll call the school if you like," she said with forced brightness. "Then you won't have to worry. Shall I tell them she'll be back on Tuesday?"

"I'll call," Betty said gently. "And I'll tell them she'll be back on Tuesday."

Lauren let out a long breath. "Okay." She swallowed. "Do you have everything you need? Enough money?" The suitcase Betty had packed already stood in the hall.

"I don't need a thing," Betty said, bowing her head and snapping her purse shut. "You're too good to us. Lauren, I wish you'd find someone to love...." Her eyes, when she raised her face, were filled with tears.

I love Cara, Lauren wanted to shout. But Cara wasn't hers and she had no hold on the child. This oppressive Sunday should be a lesson to her, that the child was only hers on loan.

Years ago she'd been able to accept that there would be no babies of her own. She'd moved on, slowly at first, so very sad at first, but she had grown stronger with time. If sharing someone else's child was something she couldn't do without falling apart when the inevitable time to part came, then she must never share again.

The door from the kitchen opened and Cara, pushing it with her bottom, entered the room. Wisps of hair escaped her pigtails and her blue-and-white striped T-shirt was torn on one shoulder. Two brown bags filled her arms.

"Cara," Betty said, "I told you to bring the sandwiches I'd made and two cans of pop. Not everything in the refrigerator."

"I didn't. I brought my animals, just in case."

Lauren had to turn away. On that afternoon, a year ago, when the Floods had turned up on her doorstep mistakenly thinking she had rooms to rent, Cara had carried a pillow slip filled with stuffed animals. They had been the first things she'd arranged on the bed in her new room; her way of making the space her home. Something within the girl was giving her the same premonition Lauren had that she might be about to move on. Cara would never leave her animals behind.

"You don't need to take the toys," Betty said quietly. "Put them back in your room."

"But, Mom—"

"Put them back," Betty insisted. "Hurry. We've got to go."

The girl did as she was told and within minutes, after Cara had given Lauren a quick hug, the front door closed behind mother and daughter.

Someone to love.

Lauren wandered along the hall and into the small dining room with its round teak table and its pinky beige wallpaper sprigged with vertical lines of tiny blue flowers. A door on the other side of the dining room led to the kitchen. Spotless, with a center island and white appliances, the space was well utilized and convenient. A vaguely cloying sweetness perfumed the air. The hoya plant, its vines climbing from a hanging pot toward the skylight over the window, was in bloom. Clusters of flowers, pale pink, hung like waxy, upside-down umbrellas.

All empty...and silent.

A restless night, passed in a state of half sleep, half dreamlike wakefulness, had ended with this colorless morning. Lauren went to sit on a high stool near the scrubbed wooden top of the cooking island. The night had been filled with vague expectancy. She'd expected Jack to call. Now that she was alone she could admit as much. But there had been no call, no word. His father's face had told the story. Like Andy, in his first moments with Lauren, Denton Irving had seen her as a threat and, unlike Andy, he'd shown no sign of changing his mind on the subject.

This was ridiculous. Sitting here feeling sorry for herself was out of character and totally unproductive. Betty would bring Cara back tomorrow. And she'd banish Jack Irving from her mind immediately.

Coffee was needed. And a bagel with cream cheese. And maybe some ice cream. Or maybe a good hard run instead of all the above.

Jack Irving had been mildly and fleetingly interested in her and his reasons were undoubtedly all the wrong ones from her point of view. If she got involved with him she'd get involved with Andy. Then she'd start to care for the boy, and possibly even for the man.

Out of the question. She'd had a narrow escape.

So why did she feel like crying?

She'd run.

When she was halfway up the stairs, on her way to change clothes, the doorbell rang. Slowly she turned and retraced her steps.

The bell blared again. Beyond the amber glass in the door and the pattern of iron grillwork, a shadow moved. Whoever stood there was tall.

Lauren reached the door, opened it, and looked up into Jack's eyes and down at a flapping black T-shirt and black running tights slashed with winding red bands.

He spread his arms. "I was running in the area and thought I'd stop by."

"That's not very original."

"I know. What is?" He smiled and sank his teeth into his lip.

She wasn't going to attempt an answer. "I was just getting ready to go running myself."

He glanced at her jeans and sweatshirt.

Lauren shook her head. "Not like this. I was going to change."

"D'you suppose I could come with you?"

She crossed her arms and rolled onto her toes. "It's possible."

"That sounds promising. Shall I wait out here?"

"Don't be ridiculous." Moving back, she opened the door wider. "Come in. Wait anywhere you like. Kitchen, if you want. There's cold coffee and a microwave. I won't be long."

She left him and didn't look back. By the time the bedroom door closed behind her, the thudding in her chest was suffocating. This was pointless. They could have nothing together. But she couldn't stop thinking about him or wanting to see him.

The front door slammed.

Quickly she crossed to the window and peered down, half expecting to see him leaving. Outside the courtyard, Jack's black pickup stood at the curb. There was no sign of Jack. He was in her home, downstairs, waiting.

She was a mature, capable, self-supporting woman who should be able to deal with attention from an occasional male. Evidently she'd become a passing interest to the male in question today and that should make her feel good.

Rapidly she stripped to her bra and panties and donned bright yellow tights and an electric-blue tank top. Overheating while exercising had always been a problem for Lauren. With shoes and socks in hand, she went back downstairs.

She found Jack in the kitchen taking a cup of coffee out of the microwave. "You follow instructions well."

"As long as they're easy to follow," he commented and sucked a noisy mouthful from the steaming cup. "I tend to get in a lot of trouble when I misread signals." He looked at her squarely.

"I haven't given you any signals at all that I'm aware of."

"Did I say you had?"

Lauren sat on the floor and pulled on her socks. "Let's drop it."

"Fine with me."

But it wasn't fine with her. In the act of tying a shoelace, she peered up at him. "Dinner was great last night. I forgot to tell you that." She ran her tongue over her dry lips.

"You hardly had a chance. That was my fault."

His mouth held her attention. How did he kiss? Was he a man who moved slowly with a woman, thinking and feeling his way while he matched his pace to hers? Or did he proceed quickly, spurred on by his own arousal, sweeping his lover along and into his need until there was no place for thought, only a dark, obliterating heat?

"Lauren? Are you okay?"

She started. "Yes." Bending her head to hide her face, she finished tying her shoes, then bounced to her feet and pulled a rubber band from her wrist. Gathering her hair at her crown, she captured it in a thick ponytail and smoothed back strands that tried to escape.

Jack's eyes were on her breasts.

Lauren's knees felt weak. She dropped her arms and turned away. He was a man, with a man's reactions—nothing more.

"Let's go. Slam the door behind you. It'll lock." Snagging a door key from the hook by the phone, she pinned it to the waist of her tights and led the way from the house, across the road, and down to the beach.

They fell into stride, side by side, their feet scrunching on the shingle bar at the tideline.

"I wanted to call you last night."

Lauren glanced at him. He was a pace ahead and she automatically studied the movement of his back and shoulders under the thin T-shirt and the way other parts of him flexed and stretched under their spandex second skin. His body would be unlikely to go without notice from any red-blooded woman.

"Did you hear me?" he asked, raising his voice over the wind that sang in her ears.

"Yes."

His hair whipped around his head. He was younger than she, but she had no idea how much. In broad daylight, seeing her without makeup as she was today, he'd be bound to make comparisons with Silky, and whoever else had filled some of his needs. He needed someone solid, stable, unthreatening, an ear that listened without making demands. That had to be the explanation for his seeking her out.

But she still couldn't figure out why he'd chosen her for the job.

"I was afraid I'd wake the whole household if I phoned."

She wished he'd called anyway. "Don't worry about it." Sprinting, she caught up.

"Aren't you cold?" He glanced at her tank top, plastered to her body.

"No. I get hot easily and I hate that." She was acutely aware of how little the top camouflaged. Flattened to her, it rode up, baring her midriff and clinging to her breasts.

"I'm sorry about last night." Jack jogged easily, clearly holding his pace down to hers. "I don't know what got into my dad."

A wave broke and foam rushed up the beach. Lauren veered away and Jack followed.

"He obviously had something important to say. And he didn't want a stranger as an audience."

"He wanted to discuss his latest concerns about my parenting techniques. That and a few other issues. And you're not a stranger."

"Aren't I?" Light rain joined misty spray off the ocean and she blinked.

"Not to me," Jack said, keeping his gaze fastened ahead.

"We've only known each other a few days—if you can call it knowing each other."

"I can and I do. And it seems longer than a few days." He jumped over a piece of driftwood. "Gulls coming inland. A storm won't be far behind."

Lauren lifted her chin. The gulls wheeled and wailed overhead. "I love being down here when it's like this."

"I never have been before. But I think I'm addicted already." He laughed. "The company helps."

Lauren's heart thumped. "Andy's a great kid. You must be very proud of him."

"He's the center of my life. The best thing I ever did."

"And you did it right," she said impulsively.

He slid to a stop and caught her arm. "You mean that?"

"Yes, I do. He's happy, Jack. And secure. It shows and you did that for him."

"Thanks." His eyes moved beneath downcast lids. "That's about the nicest thing anyone ever said to me."

What must it be like to be a parent? Lauren took a slow, deep breath and wiped moisture from her face. No matter how hard she tried to fill every corner of her life, the empty space left by not having a child was always with her.

"Run," she said tightly. "I don't want to cool down yet."

"The rain's getting heavier." Nodding skyward, he squinted. "It's just a shower. We could sit in the lee of the wall and wait it out."

Without answering, Lauren took off in the direction he indicated. They arrived neck and neck and plunked down, cross-legged on a triangle of dry sand in a sheltered corner.

"Did you and your father get things sorted out?" She felt she had to ask.

Jack shrugged and rested his elbows on his knees. "As I said, apart from wanting to talk about Andy, I'm not sure what he came about really. We've been having some... I guess you'd say some incidents out at the farm."

"Problems, you mean?" she shivered.

"I guess you'd say that. Dumb little things that could cause total disaster. Like thermostats being changed. Sprinkler timers tampered with... whole batches of seeds mismarked. A real pain and a real potential headache for us."

"You think these things are deliberate?"

He shrugged again, glanced at her and put an arm around her shoulders. "You look cold. Hold onto me."

It was said and done so naturally that she moved closer and slipped her own arm around his waist almost without thinking until the heat of his solid body struck through the thin fabric of their shirts.

"You love your business, don't you?" she asked.

"It's the only thing I ever wanted to be involved with...as a career, I mean. My dad before me—and my mother before she died—were both totally committed to the farm and so was my grandfather before them. Back then it wasn't more than a seat-of-the-pants operation with Grandpa doing everything himself. Now Irving's is a big outfit, but I still have the feeling that family involvement is the heart of the thing."

"That's nice." She liked what he said, and the sensation his honest enthusiasm brought. "Andy sounded as if he's going to follow right on after you."

"I hope so. But that'll be his choice."

They fell silent. Jack's rough fingers stroked her shoulder absently. Heat flashed beneath Lauren's skin...and desire. She'd identified any involvement as a potential disaster and she was allowing it to stalk her.

"How old are you?" She gritted her teeth, horrified at her bluntness.

Jack laughed. "Thirty-seven. Why?"

"I wondered."

"And I already know you're thirty-nine. Is age an issue here?"

Here? What did he mean by here? "I was only asking."

"And now you know. Any more questions?"

She felt foolish. "I guess not. Yes. Why do you want to spend time with me? Or why do you seem to want to spend time with me?"

His rhythmic stroking of her shoulder continued. "I like you. Is that good enough?"

"You didn't know me at all when you walked up to me at that party."

"We'd met before. Sort of. But that was the first time I'd had a chance to study you and I decided I'd been missing something important."

She let herself be drawn nearer. "What were you missing?"

"Getting to know a fascinating woman," he said without hesitation. "And you were missing getting to know a fascinating man, so I decided to put us both out of our misery."

She had to smile. "I guess I should thank you, huh?"

"That would be a good start."

"I like you." This conversation couldn't be taking place.

"I like you, too." Jack looked at the sky. "But I already said that. Shall I count the ways?"

"Please," she couldn't resist saying.

"An ego that likes to be stroked? Thank God you're normal. I like the way you say what's on your mind."

"The way I can be horribly rude, you mean?"

"That's it. And I like how natural you are. You aren't a primper. You just know you look terrific."

Her blush was instant and furious.

"And I like that." Jack laughed. "The way you turn red and look horrified."

"Thanks."

"And I like your appetite."

"My appetite?" She screwed up her eyes.

"Yeah. You eat well and never talk about dieting. Do you know how rare that is in a woman these days?"

"I can't say I'd considered the question." Another thought came. She glanced down at herself. "You probably think I'm overweight."

"I think you're perfect." And his appraisal, the slight sensual flare of his nostrils, swamped her with a dozen unwelcome responses.

His hand had become still on her arm, and his eyes fixed on hers.

"We should run some more." Her bones felt formless.

"Should we? Are you sure that's what you want to do?"

Lauren sighed, and scrambled to her feet. Jack held out a hand and she took it, leaned back against his weight as he pulled himself up.

"I think we should get one or two things straight," she told him in a rush. "Don't you?"

Jack frowned. "What things?"

"We're two needy people." She shook her head impatiently. "That doesn't sound right, but you know what I mean."

"I'm not sure I do. Why don't you explain?"

He gathered strands of hair that had escaped her ponytail and hitched them behind her ear. Lauren stared at him, her train of thought lost. She wetted her lips.

Jack's attention was there now, on her mouth. "What does needy mean?" he asked.

He was thinking about her mouth, as she'd thought about his earlier. He was probably also wondering about how they would kiss—if they kissed—which they never would. It was like sinking into a dream, a soft, sexy dream, and Lauren slowly pulled her hand away.

"You and I seem drawn to one another," she said, aware of the huskiness in her voice. "All I meant was that maybe it's because we both need a friend."

"Just a friend?" His golden eyes darkened.

"We've got a lot going on in our lives. I say that without really knowing if it's true of you. It is of me and I'm guessing in your case."

"It's true." He reached for, and captured, both of her hands.

"A lot of that stuff—in my case—isn't so easy to talk about. I may not be what you want even in a friend, Jack." If only she didn't long for him to tell her he wanted her to be much more than a friend.

"Why did you look so trapped when Andy asked you to go to his soccer game?"

It took an instant for her to switch gears. "I didn't realize... I don't know." She couldn't handle talking about this.

"Don't you like kids?"

Her teeth came together hard. "Why would you ask something like that? Of course I like kids."

He looked at the sand. "Of course you do. Everyone's supposed to, aren't they?"

She didn't understand his point. "I suppose so."

"Don't give it another thought. I think it was a call from Andy that brought my father rushing over last night. Andy really fell for you."

Lauren smiled, pleased. "I fell for him, too."

"Evidently he told my dad he thought you were great and that got him worrying, so he came over to make sure you weren't about to cause his favorite, only grandson any grief."

"I don't understand."

"No, of course you don't." With a hand on her neck, he turned Lauren toward the sea and they began to walk. "It's tough on a five-year-old to have his mother walk out. My father worries that I'll introduce another woman into Andy's life who'll repeat the process."

Lauren's stomach turned over. "I don't blame him. But you wouldn't, so he should trust you."

"Yes he should."

"You would never expose Andy to anything that could hurt him, I can tell that."

Jack stopped again. "You're right. I never would do that."

Lauren looked into his eyes and read his message as clearly as if he'd spoken it. He was telling her that all he wanted from her was a casual relationship, nothing that could become important enough to eventually make his son unhappy.

"I've already told you Dan and I've been friends forever."

"Yes." His wrists came down on her shoulders. Their faces were inches apart.

Lauren breathed with difficulty. "One of the things I've learned through a failed marriage that left me with an ex-husband who's still on good terms with me is what I do best with men."

Jack regarded her intently but said nothing.

"What I'm best at is being a friend."

He continued to study her.

"So, I think that might be what I could do for you. And what you might do for me, if you want to."

"Be a friend?"

"Yes. We're both working our way through heavy stuff. If something bothers you, or doesn't go well and you need a sympathetic ear, I'm a great listener."

He tipped back his head and looked down at her. "And if I don't believe you, ask Dan, right?"

"Right. He talks to me about things all the time."

"And sometimes you wish he wouldn't. Didn't you tell me that?"

She nodded. "Yes. But with you and me it would be different. We were never—" Her skin heated. "You know what I mean."

"Oh, I do. I do, indeed." He pursed his mouth sagely. "We were never lovers is what you're trying to say?"

Lauren's knees felt wobbly. "That's exactly it. And it makes things so much simpler. It's a myth that men and women can't be friends, don't you agree?"

"You definitely seem to have this all worked out."

She took a shaky breath. "So that's what we'll do...if you ever decide you need to, that is?"

"Do?" He glanced away. "Oh, yeah. That's exactly what I'll do. In fact, regard yourself as engaged."

She stared, nonplussed.

"I'm definitely going to need your friendly services. Thank you for being so understanding. I'm engaging you as a permanent buddy."

Chapter Seven

"I'm sure you understand this is purely a business decision," the woman on the other end of the telephone line said.

Lauren wrinkled her brow, searching for an appropriate response. She felt confused and vaguely sick. "Mrs. Wakefield, are you telling me you've decided Contact is too expensive for We Serve U? If so, perhaps we should see if there's some way of negotiating terms we can both live with." Mrs. Arthur Wakefield—the woman introduced herself just that way—ran a gourmet meal delivery service.

A delicate cough preceded a short pause. "I think we should simply agree to part company," Mrs. Arthur Wakefield said. Lauren didn't miss the ice in her tone. "Maybe you'll learn something from this."

Lauren sat very straight. "Learn something?" She wiggled a pencil between her fingers, thinking rapidly. "Are you suggesting we've done something wrong? Failed to give you good service?"

"I think you know what I'm suggesting. Goodbye, Lauren."

"Mrs.—"

The line went dead. And Contact had lost the second client in two days, the second client to make veiled references to dissatisfaction with the company's service.

The buzzer sounded on the intercom and Lauren pressed the button. "Yes, Susan?"

"Just give me the word and I'll tell him to get lost."

Lauren rolled her eyes. "Is Dan trying to reach me?" Later she'd get together with Susan to try to figure out the possible cause for the recent client defections.

"He sounds irate."

"Put him through," Lauren said testily. She was in no mood for one of Dan's so-called helpful diatribes.

The line clicked, and clicked again.

"Lauren?" A diatribe was on its way. "Why didn't you just come out with it to me?"

She sucked in her cheeks. "I don't know what that means, Dan."

"Oh, yes you do. I've been through pure hell for the past week."

"I'm sorry to hear that."

He barked a short laugh. "I'll just bet you are. It took me until this morning to get Christie to tell me what happened."

Lauren leaned back in her chair. This promised to be maddening, but she'd hold her temper.

"Are you listening to me, Lauren?"

"I won't be if you continue to shout."

She heard him breathe out hard through his nose. "I thought you were above this kind of thing."

Lauren tossed the pencil on the desk. "Spit it out. I don't have time for riddles."

"You told Christie I came to see you. And you told her I cried on your shoulder about the problems we've been having."

"Did I?" How could a so-called mature male be such an ass?

"You know you did. You stopped her in the street—with Wednesday there, mind you—and told her that if she knew how to be the kind of wife I needed, I wouldn't have to come to you."

"Christie told you that?"

"Yes. She was very upset."

"Hmm." And it took a whole week for her to tell Dan this little myth. Lauren wondered why the wait. "Does she know you called me on Monday, too? And yesterday?"

"Yes. I told her. I don't believe in keeping secrets from her."

"That's commendable. Are we finished?"

"What hurt her most was the way you said you weren't interested in sitting with Wednesday for us. I'd hoped we could eventually put the past behind us and you two would be friends."

Lauren's blood began a slow boil. "I didn't tell her that, Dan." And she would choose a pit bull as a friend over Christie.

"Did you say you wanted to look after Wednesday?"

"No-o." This was all a waste of time.

"Exactly. I thought you loved kids. I thought you'd really enjoy getting to spend time with Wednesday. You can't get enough of that kid who lives at your place. And she isn't anything to you."

"Neither is—" She shut her mouth and bowed her head. "Goodbye, Dan."

"Lauren—"

She hung up and covered her face with her hands. Irritation value was all Dan spelled these days. And his doll of a wife made her sick. Jealous, insecure, vindictive—and all because Christie knew she'd been wrong in the first place and assumed every other woman was capable of the same kind of underhanded tactics she'd used to get Dan.

The intercom buzzed again.

"Yes, Susan."

"Dan again. He says he's sorry and would you please talk to him again."

And he'd managed to sound pathetic enough to catch even Susan's hardened sympathy.

"Tell Dan I had to go out. And please don't put any calls through until I tell you it's okay."

She had two sales calls to make this afternoon. The thought of putting on a serene, confident face for strangers made her tired. But if she was going to start to lose clients for no good reason, she'd better step up her recruiting efforts.

The tap she recognized as Susan's came an instant before the door opened. "Is it safe to come in?" Susan peeked at her.

"Only if you're wearing a bulletproof vest."

"Firmly in place." Susan closed the door behind her and plopped into a chair. "Kick me out if you like, but I'd like to know what's going on with you. All week you've been snapping. When you haven't been totally silent, that is."

"I've got a lot on my mind," Lauren said shortly.

"Anything you want to share?"

She looked up sharply. "I don't know. Is there anything about your life outside this office that you'd like to share with me?"

Susan's eyes widened. "You are uptight. If I had something I needed to say, I would. I trust you. I thought you trusted me."

Guilt overtook Lauren. "Forgive me. It's more of the same and a few new twists. Dan irritates me. Christie's a bitch. We've lost two clients for reasons they say we know, when I don't have any idea what they're talking about. And I think I'm getting a case on Jack Irving." She closed her eyes. The last had definitely not been something she had planned to say.

Susan's broad grin promised to make sure Lauren regretted her indiscretion.

"You've been seeing Jack?"

"I saw him."

"When?"

"Saturday and Sunday."

"*Both* days? Wow. Fantastic." She leaned forward. "What's he like?"

Lauren looked away. "He's a nice man." And he'd "engaged" her as a buddy.

"Nice?" Susan wrinkled her nose. "He's a dish. Why haven't you seen him since Sunday?"

Because he seemed to find cozy, general telephone conversations adequate. Late at night he called to ask how she was and share a few details about his day. Then he signed off with some cheerful nothingness.

"You don't want to talk about this."

Lauren had forgotten Susan for a moment. "It doesn't matter," she said lightly. "We talk on the phone. He's got a lot on his mind these days."

"Like what?"

She told Susan something of the incidents Irving Farms had been suffering.

"That's too bad. What are they doing about it?"

"There's not much they can do, evidently. But Jack says they've got a trusted hand in each area keeping close watch on what goes on. Then, after the men go home, someone goes back to check everything again."

"What a nuisance for them." Susan spread her hands on the arms of the chair as if to get up. "Did you find out where Betty and Cara went last weekend?"

A heaviness formed in Lauren's chest. "No. I can't ask Cara. That wouldn't be right. And Betty must have told her not to say anything." She turned up the corners of her mouth. "But they seem settled back into our normal routine, so maybe it was all nothing."

"I'm sure that's right." Susan didn't look any more certain than Lauren felt. "So, you've got the hots for Jack Irving."

Lauren's blood seemed to drain to her feet. "Susan! I didn't say that."

"Don't sound so shocked." Susan stood up and plunked her fists on her hips. "There's nothing wrong with wanting to go to bed with a man—particularly if he wants to go to bed with you."

"Well, he doesn't." She was no prude, but Susan's bluntness made Lauren squirm. "Drop it, please. Any theories on why we've lost We Serve U and the beauty-supply place both in the same week?"

"Whew." Susan raised her brows. "Was that why frost was on the Wakefield?"

"Mrs. Wakefield," Lauren corrected while she mentally selected one or two much more satisfying names for the woman. "Yes. She said we might learn a lesson from losing her account."

Susan shook her head slowly. "Makes no sense. We've done good work for them. More than they've been worth, really."

"I don't suppose—" As fast as an idea formed, Lauren dismissed it.

"What?"

"Oh, you don't think one of our people might have made any comments in places where they'd have been reported to Mrs. Wakefield, do you?"

"Not a chance!" Susan's eyes flashed. "You know as well as I do that nothing we hear goes anywhere but to the person who pays for the information and has a right to it."

"Sorry." Holding up her hand, Lauren stood. "I'm puzzled, that's all. It could be a coincidence and there may be no more defections. But if there are, I'm going to have to take a hard look at things around here."

"And I'll be right behind you." Susan cleared her throat and tossed back her hair. "When do you think you'll see Jack Irving again?"

Throwing up her hands, Lauren marched to the door. "Never, as far as I can see. Forget the whole thing, will you? I shouldn't have mentioned him."

"Because you really aren't all that interested?"

"That's correct." Lauren gripped the door handle.

"Good. I like to see a woman who isn't bowled over by a guy with a to-kill-for face and a body to match. It sickens me when a woman can be turned to putty by a pair of soft brown eyes, and a mouth that looks wasted if it's not being kissed, and curly blond hair you want to run your hands through."

Lauren realized her mouth was open. "Susan—"

"Wouldn't you think a mature woman could resist a pair of broad shoulders and a muscular chest and lean hips and long, powerful legs? Disgusting weakness."

"Stop it! I thought you hadn't even seen Jack."

"Hah!" Susan gripped her waist and laughed. Tears escaped the corners of her eyes and she covered her mouth. "I—I—"

"You, what? Did you drive by his house, go to the farm, what?"

With obvious effort, Susan sobered. "No. I asked Marilyn Wood at the copy shop what he looked like. She said he had brown eyes and dark blond curly hair. And that he was tall." She snickered again. "I made the rest up. But you recognized him, didn't you?"

Lauren's mouth twitched. "Get back to work. There's nothing between Jack and me and there won't be. And don't talk about it to gossips like Marilyn Wood."

"Yes, ma'am. Anything you say."

"And no interruptions that aren't imperative. Don't forget that. I'm very busy."

Alone again, Lauren tipped back her head and closed her eyes. It would be so much easier if a woman who didn't arouse a man sexually or emotionally could feel equally ambivalent about him.

She didn't have time for this. Paying Mrs. Wakefield a personal visit might be a good idea.

The buzz of the intercom exasperated her. She leaned over the desk. "*Yes,* Susan?"

"I know the answer, but he insists I ask anyway."

"No. Tell him no, and don't even tell me the next time he calls."

"You've got it. Would it be all right if I ask him if I'll do instead?"

Lauren paused in the act of flipping off the speaker. "What?"

"If you don't want Jack Irving, is it okay if I say I'm available?"

Hot, then cold, Lauren walked around her desk and dropped into her chair. "You and I will talk later. Put him through."

Her heart broke into double time before she heard Jack say, "Hi, Lauren. Am I interrupting at a busy time?"

"Er, no. Not at all."

The muted click of Susan switching from the line made Lauren bare her teeth.

TO MAKE SURE he didn't run into Jess, he'd booked the last available court time of the night. Having backed out of their regular match earlier in the evening, Jack didn't want to risk having to explain why he was available to play racquetball later as long as his partner was Lauren Taylor.

Advice from a friend was what he needed. That had been his persuasive excuse for inviting Lauren to play tonight. He underhanded a ball against the front wall, sidestepped and slapped another idle stroke before turning to watch through the glass back wall for her to come down the stairs to the lone basement court.

The only advice he needed was how to concentrate on the rest of his life when all he could think of was Lauren.

Silver striped court shoes appeared at the top of the stairs. Then came long, long shapely legs topped by very brief white shorts that curved into high cut slits at the sides. Her red-and-white striped tank top was even briefer than the one she'd worn last Sunday, and this one, tucked into the formfitting shorts, was tight over her full breasts.

Jack rolled his tongue back inside his dry mouth, smiled and held the door open for her. "Hi. I thought you'd decided to take a sauna or something."

She gave him a cool glance. "All you have to do is change. This coiffure takes time." She flipped her ponytail.

He noted her clean-scrubbed face with approval. That took a little time, too. No makeup to sweat through for this lady.

"Is something wrong?"

He'd been staring. "No." But from the moment she'd roared up to the club in her Honda—"I'll drive myself, thanks"—he'd wanted to ask what had upset her. A second question might have been, why had she come at all if she was in such a foul mood?

"Ready to warm up?"

He was already warm—and getting warmer. "Yes, ready."

"We don't have to do this, Jack. Maybe you'd rather go somewhere and talk."

Maybe he'd just rather go somewhere else—period. "I'm looking forward to this match and you're not going to wriggle out of it."

When she smiled she touched a part of him he didn't remember having. She made it impossible for him not to smile back. He relaxed a little. Her initial coolness didn't necessarily have anything to do with him.

"It's been a couple of weeks since I played," she said. "I hope you won't be bored."

He groaned and slapped a hand to his brow. "I see it all in living color. This is going to be a repeat of the famous table-tennis game. Please be kind to me."

She shrugged and pulled a red terry headband low over her brow. "I'm a lowly amateur. Almost a novice." With her racquet between her knees, she adjusted sweatbands on her wrists and pulled on a glove. "You're bigger and stronger and you'll probably wipe me out in two games, if I don't collapse first."

Sure. He swung his racquet and studied the way she went through a series of stretches. "A novice, huh?"

She ignored him and dropped to the floor to bend over her legs.

Jack leaned on the wall. Her legs were smooth, all the way up to the hint of very white lace where what there was of her shorts had hiked even higher.

"Aren't you going to stretch?"

And miss looking at her while she did? "I already have," he lied.

His father was still harping on the evils of getting involved in a relationship that could hurt him all over again—and Andy. And Jack had told him not to worry. Even if he were considering another marriage, which he wasn't, Lauren had given clear indications that marriage was the last thing she wanted from a man.

"Are you about ready?" Watching her threatened to destroy any hope he had of concentrating.

"Almost."

He shouldn't be here with her. But he'd been helpless, unable to think of not seeing her and this seemed the safest activity he could come up with.

She pulled on her toes and bent low over her knees.

Jack looked away. This wasn't working and it probably never would. He wanted her, mood swings and all. End of self-examination.

"Okay, let's go." Lauren hopped up. "You can serve."

"Ladies first."

She glanced around with mock surprise. "Yeah, well, how about men first, in the absence of ladies?"

Jack sighed and served. Jogging in place, Lauren let the ball go by without moving her racquet.

He caught the ball. "I thought you were ready."

"Just giving you a head start." She smiled grimly.

"I see. Second serve coming up."

He served again, deliberately easing up.

Lauren was a red-and-white streak he saw from the corner of his eye.

He never saw the ball until it ricocheted off a side wall for a second bounce.

Innocently checking her strings, she sauntered past him, retrieved the ball and took up position.

Ten minutes later he made a conscious decision to pull out all the stops. The lady was a vampire and he was scheduled to be her special of the night if he didn't get his act together.

He missed the next two balls.

"Game!" Her grin glittered. "This is fun."

"Glad you're having a good time," he muttered. "My serve?"

She nodded, snapping her hips from side to side.

Jack subdued a shudder. He was allowing sex to get in the way and that wasn't what this was about... was it?

He played in earnest. *The other body on this court is good old Jess. Fix the thought, Jack. That flash of red and white and skin is Jess. And you're going to blow him out of the water.*

The play took on first a furious, then what felt uncomfortably like a violent flavor. Lauren stopped meeting Jack's eyes. She was good, extremely good—he'd hand her that—but he had the uneasy sensation that each time she slammed the ball she saw something he didn't see, some enemy she punished.

Another sickening thought came. Was she punishing him? That couldn't be. She had no reason.

The pace increased even more.

After a long fight, Jack took the second game. "Want to rest?" he asked. "You look like you could use some water."

She ignored him and walked to the opposite side of the court.

"Did you hear what I said?" He narrowed his eyes and stayed where he was.

"I'm not thirsty. Serve."

"What's the matter with—"

"Serve. That's what we're here for, isn't it?"

"By all means." He did as she asked, but muffed the shot and watched her take the point, and line up for the next serve.

It was a bomb, but angry people dealt well with bombs. And he was getting angrier by the second. Skidding, ducking for a volley, he lunged to take the ball on the fly and stumbled into his opponent.

He caught her arms and stared into her black eyes. Expressionless eyes. Sweat coursed down the sides of her face and her lips were parted. Her breath came in short gasps.

Jack let his gaze linger on her mouth.

"My serve, I think." She shrugged away and the play continued, but only for one more point.

"Watch it!" Jack stretched and ran for a shot before he saw her coming at him.

Too late. They hit again, hard this time, and he couldn't stop the fall.

"Oof." Lauren gritted her teeth and grabbed for him.

They went down in a jumble of arms and legs, and red and white, and slick skin.

The face that stared up at him bore no resemblance to Jess Parker. Nor did the sleekly voluptuous body he felt all too acutely.

Breathing hard, he propped his weight on his elbows. "Are you all right?"

"Yes, damn it. I'm great."

"What's with you?" He narrowed his eyes. "What the hell's eating you?"

"Nothing." She pursed her lips and tried to squirm away. "I'm competitive. Does that hurt your ego?"

Jack pushed their racquets away and pinned her by the wrists. "My ego isn't at stake here. And you aren't even playing me. You're using that ball to beat the crap out of something that has nothing to do with me."

She rolled her head away and attempted to shift again. The motion did things she'd undoubtedly had no intention of doing. His body leaped and a dull heat inflamed his brain.

"Let me go."

"Look at me."

She struggled and he felt a violent surge of desire.

"Look at me, Lauren."

"All right." Her eyes, when they met his, brimmed with tears.

"Oh . . . Oh, Lauren."

He brought his mouth carefully down on her trembling lips. One wrong move and he'd lose control. Then it would all be over. Jack forced his mind into neutral and gave his all to feeling her mouth gradually soften beneath his.

Her breasts, an insistent pressure on his chest, rose and fell and dark fire pierced his belly, his groin.

Slowly, brushing, touching, tasting, he moved her face from side to side. Wrenching against his hands reminded him he still held her captive. He released her wrists and she wound her arms about his neck, sighing softly with each short breath she took.

He felt her fury ebb. Rolling sideways he brought her with him. Lauren stared into his eyes, pushed him, and sent him to his back. Straddling his hips, she took control, holding his wrists as he'd held hers, and staring down into his face.

"Lauren—"

"Don't talk." Her skin glistened. Bent over him, she studied his face, then ran a hand from his wrist, down his arm, to his chest. Resting her fingers lightly on the side of his neck, she kissed him again, parting his lips with the tip of her tongue.

Jack groaned, and shifted against his arousal. Lauren closed her eyes.

"We're on the floor of a racquetball court," he whispered in a brief second of lucidity.

Her mouth moved again, a whispering, featherlike caress that started a burning pulse.

Lauren raised her head, and used her hands on his shoulders to push herself up. He panted, watching her through slitted eyes. Moisture shone on every inch. A shining line disappeared into the cleavage between her breasts.

He had to touch her.

She bowed her head, swung from him and sat on the floor.

Jack got up slowly and knelt beside her. "Lauren." He kissed her neck and she tilted her head to give him better access. "We need to go somewhere else."

Her lips parted but she didn't say anything.

With one finger he slid a track from her jaw, over her slick skin, down to the swell of her breasts where the tank top gaped.

She shuddered and turned into his arms. "Kiss me again."

He did as she asked, pulling her to him, letting his hand slip farther inside the tank top until she shuddered again and jerked away. "No," she said quietly. "This is no good."

"You're so right."

He stood and pulled her up and they came together again in another brief, searing kiss that made him pray for privacy—now.

"We'd better go." Lauren put distance between them and held him off when he tried to catch her once more. "I'm going to shower and change."

"That wasn't enough, Lauren. Not for me."

She stroked his cheek. "Not for me, either. But I think we'd better stop this, Jack. We don't have any place to go from here."

"Why?" The anger began to return. "I want you. You want me. We're both free."

"That's not enough and you know it."

He wasn't letting her get away, not that easily. "Andy's spending the night with his grandfather. Come back with me."

"No."

"I'll behave myself."

She smiled grimly. "Why don't I quite believe you?"

"Because you don't want to?"

"Maybe."

He pressed her. "Come anyway. I won't force you into anything you don't want."

Her eyes said she was afraid she wanted what she didn't think she should have.

"Come, Lauren. There's too much between us to just walk away and pretend it doesn't matter."

"No."

"Lauren—"

"Okay!" She smoothed back escaped hair in that way that made it hard for him to keep his eyes on her face. "Okay, Jack. I'll come. But we're going to talk and that's all."

"Whatever you say." He'd take what he could get, no matter how unsatisfactory. But he knew he would pursue her one way or another.

In the locker room, he showered quickly, lathering down, rinsing with cold water which did nothing to cool his blood. From the women's locker room next door, came the muffled sound of another shower. His teeth jarred together. She'd be washing her hair, her arms raised in that posture she struck so often. And her body would be naked. He locked his knees.

Half an hour later, Lauren joined him in the balmy darkness outside the club. She wore a loose sweatshirt and jeans. Her hair had been dried and fell softly about her face. Jack rammed his hands into his pockets to keep from seizing her and kissing her again.

"We could leave your car here," he said. "I promise to get you back at a reasonable hour."

She appeared to hesitate. "Well...okay." She smiled and his heart pounded in his throat.

"I'll throw my things in my car."

As she opened the door of the Honda he was startled to hear a ring.

"What—"

"Car phone," she said matter-of-factly, reaching in to pick up the instrument. She dropped to sit on the passenger seat. "Lauren Taylor."

Noncommittal noises punctuated silences as she listened. Jack moved closer and she looked up at him, a frown drawing her brows together.

"What is it?" he mouthed.

She shook her head. "I'm sorry, Dan, but this isn't my problem."

Jack scrutinized her closely, cursing Taylor for his rotten timing.

"Look," she said. "It'll all blow over. It has before. She's young. Don't forget that."

Good grief. The guy was calling his ex-wife to complain about the current one. "Lauren!"

She covered the receiver. "This won't take long." Into the phone she said, "I really don't think it would do any good for me to talk to her. She hates me, Dan."

Jack crossed his arms.

"*You* tell her," Lauren said. "Tell her there's absolutely nothing between you and me and hasn't been..." Her chest rose sharply and something like pain passed over her features. "Dan, remind Christie that the two of you were sleeping together for months before we split up.... I'm not throwing it up at you. I'm stating facts."

He couldn't believe this. If he didn't think she'd be furious, he'd hang the phone up for her.

"Dan, you told me the reason you no longer wanted sex with me was because I couldn't make you feel alive the way Christie could. I believed you. Tell her that if she's having doubts."

Jack rubbed at his jaw. An almost uncontrollable urge to do Dan Taylor damage rocked him. "Lauren."

She shook her head again, but her eyes were closed. "Yes, we did make peace," she said in a low voice. "For old times' sake. But you're asking me for too much."

Seconds of silence passed.

"She won't listen to me. If she wants to believe there's still something between you and me there's nothing I can do to change her mind." Lauren swung her legs into the car and rested her head against the seat. "Okay, yes. Please don't say anymore. I'll talk to her, Dan. But this is it. The last time."

Jack ground his hands into fists.

"Tomorrow," Lauren said and hung up. She got out of the car, evaded Jack's hand and walked around to the driver's side.

"Where are you going?" He slammed the passenger door. "Lauren, answer me."

"Home," she said. "I'm going home."

"Because of *him?*" He pointed to the car phone.

"Because of what I almost forgot." She opened her door. "I almost forgot I'm too old for this, and too tired. Take my advice, Jack. Forget me."

Chapter Eight

"Yes, I'm going to make a police report, Dad. And no, I don't want to talk about Lauren. Not to you. Not to anyone."

"Good." Jack's father settled his big, rough hands on the table. He appeared neither relaxed nor mollified.

Jack frowned. Across the restaurant he could see Barney Middleton talking to another patron. Dining out had been Dad's idea, a surprising one from a man who preferred to eat at home. The thought came to Jack that Denton Irving was a smart man who knew his son well, knew he was less likely to make a scene in a public place. Here there was a better chance that Jack would be forced to listen with apparent attention to almost anything his father decided to say.

"That night when Lauren was at my house, did you call Andy or did he call you?"

"I thought you didn't want to talk about Lauren." Dad eyed an approaching waiter.

"I don't," Jack muttered.

"That's what I was hoping to hear. You're coming to your senses."

Before Jack could respond, the waiter arrived and Barney's voice boomed across the room, "They're having the eggplant, Colin."

Jack gave Barney a wave. Barney always decided what his friends would eat. "I'll have a beer. How about you, Dad?"

They ordered and his father sat, stolidly waiting, until they'd both been served drinks. "I talked to Len Gogh and Matt Carson."

"And?"

"They're worried."

Jack slid his glass back and forth over the red-and-white checked tablecloth. "And you think I'm not?" This renewed interest his father was showing in the business would have pleased him if he didn't think it was a cover for something else, a means to oversee all of Jack's life more closely.

"I think a woman can get in the way of a man's thinking."

"Coming from you—" Jack closed his mouth and averted his face. What was getting into him? He'd almost reminded his father that his mother had mattered more to him than anyone or anything.

"Your mother wasn't like any other woman, son."

His father wouldn't get an argument on that. "I know. We were lucky."

"You've said it. And then some." Dark brows drew together. "Got any idea who's behind this nonsense at the farm?"

Saying that "nonsense" was mild for the kind of dangerous tampering they'd suffered wouldn't help. "No. Len and I can't make anything add up. It's starting to look as if the bum seed labeling was a one-time shot, but there was enough product involved to make plenty of trouble for us."

"Anything else happen? Since you found out about the seeds?"

"No. We've got a watch system going and as far as we can make out everyone's lily-white. Making the police report is just covering bases as far as I'm concerned."

His father swallowed some beer and leaned back to let the waiter put a plate in front of him. "I know I haven't spent much time around the farm in recent years. Doesn't mean I'm not interested."

Jack sampled the eggplant. "You don't have to explain. Any time you feel like—"

"I'm retired," Dad cut in. "Maybe I'd enjoy coming out a little more often. Nothing more. Andy called me."

"What?" Jack set down his fork. "When?"

"You asked if I called him or he called me. He called me. Had a lot to say about that woman."

"I see." For several minutes, Jack ate in silence. Getting angry would accomplish nothing. "That woman is Lauren, Dad. Lauren Taylor. And she's a friend of mine." He'd like her to be a great deal more. In the week since he'd seen her, a week when he'd replayed the episode at the club over and over, he'd barely managed to get her to speak to him on the phone.

"Andy talked a lot about her."

"He likes her," Jack said.

"What do you think I'm getting at here?"

Jack sighed. In bed at night he saw her . . . as good as felt her, damn it. He thought about her a dozen other times a day, too. And she'd made it plain she'd just as soon he went away and stayed away. Only, he wasn't giving up—not yet. Regardless of what the future held for the two of them, if anything, he knew what he felt and he wasn't finished with Lauren.

"Are you listening to me, Jack?"

"Listening, and hearing. Do you think this is any of your business?"

His father showed no sign of offence. "What happens to my grandson is my business. He's—"

"So how's the masterpiece?" Barney arrived, pulled up a chair and rested his elbows on the table. He beamed, his round face shiny. "Best Italian food in town, huh?"

Jack concentrated on his plate. "It's good, Barn." He'd like to be just about anywhere but here.

"Too long since we saw you, Denton," Barney said in a tone that spelled cheerful oblivion to the antagonism in the air.

"Got to make an appointment to see my own son these days," Jack's father said. "Figured the offer of a good meal might get to him."

"Good thinking. Good thinking." Barney chortled. "Guess the boy here's got other things on his mind, these days."

Jack looked up in time to see Barney give Dad a meaningful wink.

"What would that be?" His father's eyes were innocently lowered.

"Ah, don't give me that." Barney elbowed Denton, who dropped a forkful of food. "Sorry. Our Jack's got pretty good taste in companions, wouldn't you say?"

Jack aimed a narrow-eyed warning at Barney, who didn't notice.

"Plays a mean game of racquetball, huh?" Barney laughed and repeated the wink, this time in Jack's direction. "One of the regulars said he never saw anyone look the way Lauren does in shorts."

Jack glowered and caught his father's eye. "I wasn't aware the whole town knew Lauren and I had played a game."

"Hah! You know how this town works. We're all interested in our favorite people."

"All gossips, you mean," Jack muttered.

Barney laughed again. "Bet racquetball isn't the only game she plays well, hey, Jack?"

Jack pushed his plate aside. His father's face was cast in a mold that belonged on Mount Rushmore. "Barn, Lauren's a friend of mine. Cut the personal crap, okay?"

"Okay, okay." Barney held up his palms. "Didn't mean to step on any toes."

"Forget it." Jack felt cornered.

Barney's smile was quickly back in place. "Bit touchy about a simple friendship, aren't we?"

Sometimes, like now, it was hard not to tell Barney to get lost. "End of subject" was all Jack said.

"Maybe not." His father had been observing, his eyelids at half-mast. "What I'm going to say isn't for general consumption. Got that, Barney?"

"Got it." Barney shifted in his chair and studied his fingernails.

"I mean it. I'm only talking in front of you because I know Jack trusts your judgment. He knows the 'crap', as he puts it, is all a cover—"

"I—"

"Shut up and listen."

Jack looked sharply at his father. "Dad—"

"You, too. I may be old, but I'm not senile."

"I know that." This had definitely been a bad idea. He caught Barney's eye and saw discomfort and sympathy there—and apology.

"Some men can afford to make mistakes with women. You can't, Jack. Not when you've got a son who's obviously ready for someone he can think of as the mother he never had."

"Dad, aren't we getting ahead of ourselves, here? Lauren and I—"

"Are just friends. Yeah, so you keep telling me. Only I know what I'm seeing in you. And it isn't anything I've ever seen before. Not even with Mary."

"Dad—"

"No. I'm pulling rank. I'm your father. You'll listen while I talk. Then, since you're no kid, if you want to forget every word, there isn't a damn thing I can do about it. Right, Barney?"

"Er, right." The normal ruddiness of Barney's face turned to puce. He picked up a glass and drank, obviously forgetting that the beer was Jack's.

"You thought you loved Mary, didn't you?"

"I *did* love her." He felt the heavy throb of the pulse at his temples.

"Do you remember how it felt when she took off to Paris to do her damn fool painting?"

"Er, Denton, maybe I should—"

"Maybe you should sit right where you are and listen, Barney. Then you won't be so likely to encourage what's wrong."

"Wrong!" The word exploded from Jack. He made fists on the table.

"Wrong," his father said calmly. "I know the signs, my boy. You're ready to take a big fall."

From the corner of his eye, Jack caught sight of Barney's miserable expression. There was nothing to be done about that. "How many times do I have to tell you you're making a big deal out of nothing?"

"That may be." His father appeared serene now. Now that the damage was on a roll. "I just want to be sure you've looked at all the angles and that you don't run blindly into the biggest mistake of your life."

"This is... I'm not talking about this anymore."

"That's good. You be quiet and I'll talk some more. I know what it's like to love someone so much the rest of the world can go to hell. And I know what it's like when you don't have that person around anymore. You've gone through it once. I saw how you hit bottom, boy. I couldn't go through that again and I don't think you can, either. And I know damn well your boy shouldn't be put through another piece of business that tells him he's replaceable."

Jack stared. "In other words, you think it would be better for me never to try for another real relationship with a woman in case it doesn't turn out?"

"In case she hurts you like you've already been hurt. Don't risk it. That's my advice."

Barney cleared his throat.

"Sit where you are," Denton snapped.

Jack felt tired. "For God's sake, Lauren's a friend, nothing more. Now, can we leave it at that?"

"Sure—" his dad picked up what was left of his beer "—once I've said one more thing. Can you tell me you don't look at that woman and think about taking her to bed?"

Blood rushed to Jack's face. "For—"

"Can you?"

"Well—"

"Exactly. I shouldn't have to tell a man of your age this, but I guess I'm just going to have to." Pulling himself very upright in his chair, his father drummed the table. "A man and a woman attracted to each other. A man and woman capable of doing what men and women do together..." He let the sentence trail.

"Dad—"

His father waved a hand. "That man and woman can't be just friends."

LAUREN PRETENDED to be engrossed in her newspaper. She was very aware of Betty moving restlessly around the kitchen.

Since the mysterious weekend trip, Lauren had tried to believe nothing had changed, but there were too many signs to the contrary.

"Business good at the service, is it?" Betty asked.

Lauren had known the other woman needed to talk but was afraid of what she wanted to say. "Generally. We've lost several customers for reasons that escape me."

"Isn't putting you in a bind, is it?" Betty was making conversation, skirting whatever was on her mind.

"Not yet. It will if it continues. I get the feeling there's something going on I'm not aware of. But it could just be that the cancellations have come in a bunch and I'm making too much of them."

"That's probably it."

Betty turned away and clattered pots in the sink. She'd be late for work if she didn't leave soon, but Lauren wasn't about to tell her so.

She rattled the paper. "How's the job going?"

"Fine!" The pots banged some more, and Betty ran water too hard into the sink. Spray splattered the window. "Darn it all anyway."

Lauren's heart thudded unpleasantly. "Leave it. I'll clean up after Cara goes to bed." The girl had been upstairs when Lauren got home and had still to put in an appearance.

"I'm on edge," Betty admitted, turning to smile sheepishly. "I've got a lot on my mind."

Lauren sensed this was supposed to be her opening to ask questions. "I know how that can be." Whatever was wrong, she had an increasingly strong hunch she didn't want to know. "Shall I call Cara down to say goodbye?"

"I'll run up before I go. She's got a bunch of homework—"

The door swung open and Cara trailed in. "Dumb math." More wisps than usual sprang into curls around her face.

"Problems?" Lauren folded her paper and put it on the table. "When your mom leaves I'll give you a hand."

Cara mumbled something about multiplication and Lauren prayed she'd be able to handle whatever new ways the school system had now found to accomplish the process.

"I suppose I'd better leave." Betty hovered.

"It is after seven." Lauren could feel Betty's indecision, feel her wanting, but not knowing how to say what was on her mind.

"You be good for Lauren," Betty said finally, sweeping the child into her arms and squeezing. "Be very good and get to bed early. And don't take up a lot of Lauren's time with your math. You can work it out yourself. You're a clever girl, thank goodness."

"Nobody else thinks so." Cara's bright eyes were cross behind her glasses. "Mrs. Beaman says I'm a dreamer."

"Oh, Cara." Betty pulled on a parka over the sweatshirt and jeans she wore for work. "You've got to learn not to spend your time gazing out the window. Your father never knew how to concentrate long enough to make something of himself."

Lauren bit her lip, holding back her irritation with Betty.

"Yes, Mom," Cara said, her small face pinched.

Be a dreamer, Lauren wanted to say. *Be who you are. You're wonderful.* And, beneath it all, seethed the longing to be able to call this child her own. That couldn't be and she had no right to the thought.

Betty gathered her purse and pulled out her car keys. "Tidy yourself up," she said to Cara. "You look messy."

Lauren felt a rush of sympathy for the woman. She was troubled and pressured and she'd had hard years since she'd been left with only rusty working skills to support a child. The previous day, Lauren had finally found the courage to broach the subject of contact lenses for Cara. Betty had looked instantly worried and cornered and Lauren decided she wouldn't mention the topic again.

"I'm off, then." Betty ran her fingers through her curly hair and smiled. "You two will be all right?"

"Of course." Cara scowled. "We're always all right. We look after each other, don't we, Lauren?"

Her stomach dropped. "We sure do."

"Yes, well—" Betty shoved the handle of her purse over her shoulder. "It's just I feel guilty sometimes."

"Guilty?" Lauren raised her brows.

"You've done so much for us."

Before Lauren could respond, Betty rushed from the house.

"Don't mind Mom," Cara said, too loudly. "She's been like that lately. Ever since . . ."

Lauren held her breath, waiting for the girl to say more, but Cara didn't continue. She scuffed into the living room and Lauren followed.

She was reading too much into too little, Lauren decided.

"Is school going all right?" Deliberately affecting nonchalance, she settled into the soft blue love seat that faced a matching couch. "Did your teacher like the story you wrote?"

"Yeah. And you don't have to worry about the math," Cara said. "I've got it figured out now. No sweat."

"I'm not worried about it. I like to help."

"Yeah." Cara flopped into her favorite chair, cream-colored corduroy, with a swivel base that allowed her to hook a leg over one arm while scooting herself in circles.

"Shall we watch TV?"

"If you want."

Lauren fidgeted. "Only if you want to."

"I don't want to." With one sneakered foot, Cara thumped the floor rhythmically, shoving the chair around and around.

"Is something wrong?" Lauren couldn't miss the serious set of Cara's features.

"Nah."

But there was something on the child's mind. School, home, the kids, her mother. Lauren mulled over the possibilities and felt helpless.

"Oh—" she remembered the bag beside the couch. "—I've got something for you."

The chair stopped revolving.

Lauren leaned over and retrieved the brown sack she'd substituted for the store bag. "Not much, but I thought you might like them."

Cara sat upright, her hands trapped between her knees, her shoulders hunched. Lauren could feel the girl's anticipation.

"What do you think?" She pulled out a neon green sweatshirt.

"Wow." Cara's loud breath held delight. "Awesome. That's my favorite color."

"I know."

The smile disappeared as quickly as it had come. "Mom says I'm not to let you buy me things."

"This is different," Lauren said quickly, but her heart raced. "I had some shirts made up for the service—to give out as promotional incentives." Lying didn't come easily, but this was a special occasion with extenuating circumstances.

"What does it say on the front?"

"Contact." That had been an inspiration and who knew, maybe she would get some more, for employees perhaps. "I thought it would be...well, you know...meaningful?"

Cara's blank glance said she didn't see anything meaningful; not in the way Lauren meant. "Contact. Yeah, I'll—" She frowned and pursed her lips. "It's okay."

Lauren smothered a grin. "I had two of them." She produced a second, identical shirt. "D'you suppose Jimmy would like it? I kind of thought you could add it to your club, or whatever you call yourselves. No name but Contact, maybe?"

"Yeah," Cara whispered. "Jimmy'll like it a lot. He never gets anything till his big brother's finished with it." She took the two shirts, spread them along the back of the couch and smoothed the rubberized letters Lauren had had applied. "You don't think Mom'll say we can't have 'em?"

"I know she won't." Let her try. Betty would find herself no match for Lauren at her most persuasive. "They're just leftovers, so I had to find someone to give them to."

Cara turned to Lauren. Her face was pink, her eyes glittering.

Without warning, the girl launched herself, wrapped her thin arms around Lauren's neck and buried her warm face. After an instant's hesitation, Lauren returned the hug, breathing in the scent of soap and dust and feeling silky hair on her cheek.

"I guess you really like them," she said, swallowing against the lump in her throat.

"They're totally awesome. I love you. I'll love you for always, no matter what."

Lauren's heart seemed to pause. She closed her eyes. "I love you, too." And she did. And it was worth the way she felt now for as long as she was given to enjoy it.

As abruptly as she'd thrown herself at Lauren, Cara extricated herself and gathered up her treasures. "I'll take them upstairs and put them in my bag for tomorrow."

"Great. Then a snack? Popcorn—"

The phone rang.

Cara ran, grinning, from the room while Lauren picked up the receiver and said, "Hello."

"Lauren. This is Susan. I hope I'm doing the right thing by calling, but I thought you might like to know."

Lauren's scalp tightened. "What is it? Problems?"

"Not really. At least, not the kind you mean. You probably don't want me bothering you with this."

"Susan, tell me. Now." Lauren stood very straight, every nerve on alert.

"Okay. Irving's packing plant is on fire."

A DULL RED GLOW SHIVERED in the night sky. Lauren slammed the accelerator to the floor. She'd called Jack's home and had gotten no reply. Arranging for a teenager from one of the neighboring town houses to stay with Cara had taken precious moments when all Lauren had wanted was to rush to the farm. Now she drove much too fast, but she had to get there.

Glaring pink lights hit her rearview mirror and a siren wailed. She pulled to the side of the road to allow an engine to race by, followed by another, and a third.

Trembling, she traveled in their wake. She'd driven past the farm's huge acreage before without as much as a thought for what it represented: an old and very successful enterprise. Parked opposite the entrance with its illuminated swinging sign, Lauren peered toward the chaos she could see in the distance.

Why had she come?

The answer wasn't comfortable. Jack Irving would be there and she wanted to be here; not only as a concerned friend, but because she cared about him as a man.

In her mind she saw the way his upper lip curled away from his teeth when he smiled, the deep dimples that formed.

There was nothing she could do to help.

In the white glare of the searchlight she saw men running. Jets of water arced over flames.

She could be there, just be there—let him see her. Every day for the past week he'd called and she'd been polite but deliberately short because she was afraid, not of him, but of herself. He'd been fair enough not to mention her response to him at the club. He didn't have to. The scene replayed and replayed in her mind, in vivid color, complete with sensations.

The jury was still out in the case of Jack Irving and Lauren Taylor.

Stuffing down her doubt, Lauren got out of the car and ran across the road. Inside the farm gates a wide drive curved between the greenhouses. She ran on, toward the fire.

On her right, a shed loomed. Lights showed in windows at one end. Lauren hesitated.

"North corner, Frank," a voice boomed over a bullhorn.

Lauren shrank back. A blast of heat shivered through air laced with acrid fumes and bursts of red sparks. But the flames seemed lower... didn't they?

The men were more distinct now. Fire fighters slipped rapidly back and forth, swift in their movements as they seemed to follow hand signals and nods from each other's masked faces more than the few commands barked. Their yellow hats and suits were ludicrously cheerful splashes against the charred and crumbling outline of a disintegrating building.

A hand, closing on her arm, jarred her to the bone.

"Lauren?"

She swung around and looked into Jack's soot-streaked face. "Jack. I'm so sorry, I—"

"Get back from here." In the ghastly flicker, his eyes shone dark and angry.

"Yes. I'm sorry. I only thought you might need—"

"I do," he said. His hand moved from her arm to rest heavily on her shoulder. "The bastards. They've got what they wanted now."

"No," Lauren whispered. She cleared her throat. "Jack, come away."

"I can't."

"Then I'm staying, too."

For an instant, his stare slid to the scene behind her. "Andy's in the office. I didn't want my dad to see this so I couldn't take Andy to his place."

"Where is the office?"

Jack looked at her again and nodded over his shoulder at the shed.

"I'll wait with him," she said.

Without responding, Jack moved past her. Lauren caught his arm. "Be careful."

He nodded, studied her face for a long moment, and strode away.

Lauren watched him go, a tall, lean man in a gaping cotton shirt torn at one elbow and jeans splotched with oily black smears.

But his back was straight and he walked with purpose.

Lauren smiled, a small, tight smile. Whoever had taken on Jack Irving had started a fight that wouldn't be one-sided.

She found Andy in the shed with lighted windows. The windows were in an unpretentious office at the end of the building overlooking what, in daylight, would be flower fields.

"Hi, Andy." She approached the boy who stood, staring toward the fire.

He turned. "Hi." The corners of his mouth pulled in. "Did my dad call you?"

"No." Smiling with effort, she slid her car keys into her jeans pocket and pulled off her jacket. "I heard what was happening and came out to see if there was anything I could do."

"Boy, is my dad gonna be mad."

Lauren's smile came more easily. "You bet he will be. And I don't blame him. He's going to need you to talk to after this."

"Yeah." With a huge sigh, his chest rose and fell. "He's been...well, you know... Anyway he's gonna get even worse after this."

Lauren went to stand beside Andy at the window. "How has your dad been?"

"Grandpa would say like he had a bug...." The boy looked straight ahead but his pale face had begun to turn pink. "He's been kinda cranky for days."

So Jack had been in a bad mood for days—about a week, maybe? Just about the length of time she'd been snapping at everyone at the office and pounding the floor at the aerobics studio like a possessed woman. And it was no coincidence.

"Your dad's had a lot on his mind. I expect he's told you there have been some problems with the farm." She hoped she wasn't speaking out of turn.

"Yeah. Grandpa talked about it, too. And he's mad, too."

"Well, he spent a lot of years working here himself. He's bound to feel tied in to whatever happens to the farm."

Andy held onto the windowsill and put his nose on the glass. "I don't think it's the farm he's mad about. He seems angry with my dad about something."

Lauren felt awkward. "Fathers and sons have differences. I expect you and your dad disagree sometimes." She sighted a coffee maker and a box containing packages of hot chocolate. "Would you like something hot to drink?"

"Okay. I wish Dad would come back."

So did Lauren. "I'll heat some water."

"You like my dad, don't you?"

Startled, at a loss for words, she pushed back her hair.

"He likes you." He turned his head toward her. "Know how I know?"

"Tell me."

"He had you over for dinner and I ate with you. We've never done that before." His shrug was elaborate. "Not since my mom. That was when I was just little."

Lauren couldn't think of an answer. She swallowed. His posture was rigid, belying the unconcerned words.

"Do you like him?"

"Of course I do," she said in a rush, making much of switching on the burner under a pot of water. "I like him very much. He's a nice man. That's why I came out when I heard about the fire and he said he'd like me to come and keep you company." *A nice man.* How silly it sounded.

"You saw Dad?"

Lauren felt the child's anxiety. "Yes. Outside. I told you he asked me to come and stay with you."

"Mmm. The fire isn't so big anymore, is it?"

She glanced at the window and tore the top off a packet of hot chocolate. "Not nearly so big. They'll have it out soon. What is that building?"

"It's where they put seeds and bulbs in packages and stuff. They get shipped out from there. And plants."

"I see." She was afraid she saw too much. *They've got what they wanted now,* Jack had said. "That must be pretty important."

Andy didn't appear to hear.

Lauren emptied the chocolate powder into an old brown mug, poured hot water over it and took the drink to the boy. "Here. This'll warm you up."

His hands, when he took the mug, shook. "He wouldn't let me go with him."

"That's because he worries about you. He wants to be sure you're safe." After a moment's hesitation, she smoothed back tousled black curls. Joe's hair had been dark. Lauren dropped her hand and stared through the window. There had never been as much as a few written words since she'd said goodbye to Joe, but she thought of him often and prayed the world would be kind to him.

"I want to be sure Dad's safe," Andy said in a small voice. "I'm scared."

Lauren chewed her lip. It was happening again: the subtle pull of a child. "He'll be okay. The firemen won't let anything happen to him." Please let that be true.

"He doesn't listen to people sometimes," Andy whispered. "Not when he's mad."

Lauren looked sideways at the boy. Tears stood in his eyes. "Oh, Andy." She caught the cup the instant it would have slopped chocolate, set it down and gathered Andy into her arms.

Gradually the rigid body relaxed. He held onto her shirt and sniffed.

Minutes passed. Lauren closed her eyes and felt a trembling inside. Jack wouldn't do anything foolish, would he? She wanted to see him walk through the door.

"Do you want some of that chocolate now?" She peered down into Andy's face. "If we watch, we'll see when Jack—your dad—comes."

They stood, side by side, Lauren's arm around the child's shoulder, his around her waist, for what felt like hours. The flames steadily diminished to an occasional burst that was quickly extinguished. Shouts came to them even through windows that didn't open.

Eventually all the engines left but one. Water continued to arc over what was now a smoking hulk. The sounds of axes and falling debris joined the other noises.

"Are you two okay?"

Lauren jumped and turned. "Are you all right?" She hadn't heard Jack come in. "We've been waiting," she added lamely, searching his blackened face and clothes for signs of injury. She found none.

"I'm terrific," he said, his eyes narrowed on her and Andy. "You looked after each other, huh?"

She managed a smile. "Andy looked after me."

The boy slipped from her and went to look up at his father. Silently he walked into the man's arms and they hugged one another.

Either she had to look away or cry at the special picture they made.

She looked away. "It looks bad," she said. "Andy explained what the building was for."

"I'm glad you put it in the past tense," Jack said. He scrubbed at his eyes. "God knows what we'll be able to save. Some of the equipment may be salvageable. That'll take time."

"Does it mean—" There was so little she knew about his business. "Will it make a big difference?"

His laugh was short and bitter. "You might say that. Irving's seeds and bulbs are going to be a memory for some time. And God knows how we're going to get the cuttings ready to go out."

Lauren wound her fingers together. "You'll pick up again."

"You bet your boots I will," Jack said in a tone that made Lauren lift her chin. He was aggressively confident. She'd hate to be Jack Irving's enemy.

"It, er... Do you think it could have been something to do with faulty wiring...? Something like that?"

Jack's smile was grim. "This was no accident." He held Andy tight against his side. "The fire chief agrees but he doesn't expect to come up with a culprit. Arson gets proved all the time, but finding the creep who set the fire doesn't happen often. An attempt's being made to take us out of contention in this business. But it's not going to happen."

"You should get home," Lauren said, quietly reveling in his determination. "You're going to need all the rest you can get to deal with what's waiting for you."

"Isn't that the truth." He raised a hand and let it fall heavily to his side. For an instant Lauren saw a shadow glaze his eyes. Confusion? Frustration? Probably both and so much more.

"Is there anything I can do for you, Jack?" She knew the answer and felt so helpless.

"I've got to wash some of this filth off. You did come in your own car, didn't you?"

"Yes." Disappointment sent Lauren's stomach plummeting. He was anxious for her to go. "You will let me know if there's anything I can do to help?"

He regarded her intently. "Yes, Lauren. I'll do that. Would you mind running Andy and me home? I came with Len Gogh, my overseer. He'll be here a while longer to answer any more questions and make a report for me. I'd like to get Andy home, though."

The pleasure his request caused was absurd. "I'll be glad to drive you." She suppressed a bubble of delight that threatened to make her grin.

Jack excused himself and returned ten minutes later with damp hair and a more or less clean face.

Outside the shed, the heavy odor of burned wood drifted on the wind. Gritty particles hurt Lauren's eyes.

Jack settled one hand on the back of Andy's neck, the other at Lauren's elbow and walked purposefully toward the road without looking back.

At the car, she pulled out her keys and gave them to him. "You drive." It would give him something to think about and she felt too tired to concentrate.

Jack sent her a grateful glance as if he guessed she was trying to do some small thing to help his state of mind. She climbed into the back seat and Andy sat beside his father.

They drove south until Lauren saw the dark shimmer of Batiquitos Lagoon. Jack, silent since they'd left the farm, turned the Honda left onto La Costa and headed inland.

"It was good of you to come," he said finally.

"No problem."

The quiet in the car felt thick. Andy slipped sideways against the door. Jack glanced at him. "He's tired out, poor kid."

"He was worried about you."

"I don't like doing that to him."

Lauren scooted forward and rested a hand on each of Jack's shoulders. She drove her thumbs into knotted muscle. "Calm down," she told him. "Andy's fine and so will you be. This'll blow over."

He took a hand off the wheel to cover one of hers. "I'm not sure it will. Not without one hell of a fight. Having you with me makes it feel possible, though."

She bowed her head, closed her eyes. "Good." It would be too easy to really fall for this man, fall badly in the way that ended up leaving you with the kind of wound no one with a brain would self-inflict.

"Andy thinks you're something."

"I think he's something." And the net closed a little tighter.

"Here we are." Jack drove the little car into his driveway and Andy jerked upright. "Home, son. Get yourself inside and into bed."

Andy was slow to react. Lauren leaned forward and rubbed his back. "You okay, Andy?"

"Uh-huh." He sounded sleepy. "Are you coming in with us?"

Lauren was glad to be in the back seat, in the dark. "Not tonight. It's too late. You get to bed."

"Will you come by soon?"

She hesitated, not answering.

"I'll make sure Lauren visits us soon, son," Jack said. "Take the door key and run along. I'll be right behind you."

Lauren climbed from the car behind Andy and watched him go into the house. Jack stayed where he was. Her heart thudded slowly and hard.

Slowly she turned back. In the pale wash of a yard light, with his chin atop his crossed hands on the steering wheel, he stared at her through the windshield.

Deliberately avoiding thought, Lauren climbed into the passenger seat beside him and closed the door. "I should get home. I have to start early in the morning."

"So do I. But I'm not going to sleep anyway."

She rested her head against the back of the seat. "I doubt if I will, either. It doesn't help, Jack, but I really am so very sorry."

"I know. And it does help. We've got big trouble that could make this a losing year. But we'll get things together. This is when diversification helps and we've got that over most other operations like ours." He sighed. "Damn, this hurts. The same question keeps going around and around in my brain. I'm fair, I'm good for this town—who would want to destroy me?"

"Don't torture yourself with questions. These people are never rational." She rolled her face toward him. "I know you'll get it together."

Jack stared back at her. "I really want to kiss you, Lauren. Is that okay?" As he asked, he leaned nearer. "I think I'm going to have to even if you say no."

Every moment she spent with him spelled danger, and more danger. Without bothering to reply, Lauren shifted, slipped her hands around his neck to tangle in his hair. Breathing softly, she brought her face close to his until she felt his breath, warm and clean, on her face.

The subdued light drew a slim line of dark shadow along the firm lines of his lips, shaded his sharp, straight nose and etched the dimpled grooves beside his mouth, the cleft in his chin.

"You smell like soot," she said quietly.

"I know. Do you kiss sooty men?"

"Only one sooty man." Her eyes lowered to study his mouth, then closed as her lips brushed his.

Carefully, letting her sensitive skin, the tip of her tongue, test and taste every nuance, she gradually deepened the kiss. Jack's sigh became a groan and he urged her closer, ran his hands around her waist and over her bare back beneath her shirt. His hands, firm yet gentle, moved again, coming to rest with his thumbs stroking the sides of her aching breasts.

When they were breathless, he pulled back, looked down into her eyes, kissed them both shut and cradled her face into the hollow of his shoulder. "My timing was never brilliant."

"Seems fine to me."

He gave a short laugh. "My son's in that house. My packing plant's a pile of rubble and ash, and what I want most is to stay right here with you."

What she wanted most was to be with him somewhere much more comfortable, like in his bed, or in hers. Her body throbbed.

"I'd better get going, Jack." But she didn't want to.

"Please don't leave until you make me a promise." He pulled the keys from the ignition and pushed them into his pocket. *"Please."*

Lauren stroked his face, kissed the corner of his mouth, and made herself sit, facing squarely forward. "What's the promise?"

"That you'll see me again soon."

She looked at sticklike hala fronds silhouetted against the sky. "I don't think I can make a promise like that. I don't think I should."

"You don't have a choice."

Unable not to, she smiled at him. "Why's that?"

He patted his pocket. "I've got the keys."

Sighing, she opened the door, got out and walked around the hood. By the time she reached his side he was out of the car and towering over her.

"Give me the keys, Jack."

"Will you see me again?"

"I don't know."

Gently he used his hips to push her against the car. "We'll have to work on that." With a finger and thumb he tilted up her chin and smiled into her eyes. The look flickered to her mouth and he lowered his lips slowly until they barely touched hers. Grazing back and forth, so lightly

Lauren's legs weakened and tingled, he teased her mouth open with his tongue.

The kiss was tantalizing. Holding her with his fingers and his lips, Jack balanced her nerves on the edge of wildness before he raised his head again.

"Jack, I—"

This time he pulled her close, so abruptly she let out a small cry. "I'm not taking no for an answer." His next kiss was so thorough she was left panting. "Do you believe me now?" he said when he finally raised his head.

"We'll talk about it when we aren't both exhausted and overemotional."

"No. I mean it, Lauren. This time you aren't getting away without telling me when I can be with you again."

"Why do you want to?" she asked and suffered a moment's shame at her own need to hear him tell her over and over that he desired her.

"Today's Wednesday," he said. "That means you'll have two days to get ready."

She leaned back to see his face. "Get ready?"

"Buy a swimsuit."

"I don't know what you're talking about."

"Of course you do. You and I have a date on Saturday. Between now and then we'll both concentrate on the very serious pressures of our businesses. But on Saturday, I'm yours . . . and you're mine."

A chill worked up her spine. "I may be missing something, but I don't see what a swimsuit has to do with any of this."

Jack locked his hands around her waist, held his hips to hers and swung her gently back and forth. "I'll pick you up in the middle of the day. Say noon?"

"To go swimming? I don't swim, remember?"

"Exactly." His body, where it touched hers, was unyielding. "I'm going to teach you. Do *you* remember that? Only first we're going to lay around and do nothing. I've decided that what appeals to me most is being with you in the water when it's very, very dark."

She tingled all the way to her toes. "Jack—"

"Shush," he said against her lips. "Maybe we'll both learn something."

Chapter Nine

Candace Lane presided over her boutique with an air that suggested she'd consider it a deathblow to discover she didn't have what a potential customer desired.

"*Why* would you want to cover it up?" She rolled her eyes and tweaked the plunging neckline of the one piece coral-colored swimsuit Lauren wore even lower. "Most women would give their eyeteeth for a fraction of what you've got."

Lauren tried not to notice how much of her breasts were revealed between and on the sides of the stretched contours of the suit's top. "I wish I only had a fraction of it," she muttered grimly. "This won't do it, Candy. I'm not comfortable."

Candace puffed, sending her long blond bangs flying. Gracefully slim herself, she favored animal prints and sparkle but always managed to appear like a *Vogue* model. "Are you going to swim at the club, or what?"

"I don't know yet." The more tight-lipped she remained, the better in this town.

"If you're going to try for a tan," Candace rolled her eyes again, "though how you'd do that around here at the end of a May like we're having, I don't know. But if you are, why not go for a bikini? I've got a terrific little black number that has your name on it, darling."

"No way." Lauren shook her head emphatically, longing to get out of the coral suit.

Candace splayed long, pale peach-colored fingernails over her full mouth and appeared deep in thought. She hummed, running her eyes over Lauren. "Stay right where you are. Get that off and I've got something coming right up."

Lauren went into the dressing room, stripped, donned the robe hanging there and waited.

The door flew open and Candace triumphantly brandished a handful of what looked like black lace. "This is you. I don't know why I didn't think of it before. When I took it I thought, 'there isn't a body in this town to wear it.' I must have known you were coming in and then forgotten."

"Candy—"

"No. I won't listen to arguments. Put it on now."

The door slammed shut and Lauren held up the wisp of black stuff. If it didn't stretch a whole lot it was probably intended to be worn as panties with suspenders and a shirt underneath.

Grumbling, she tossed aside the robe and slipped into the suit. It did stretch and grow thinner and thinner until it covered, or almost covered, the essential parts like a black net body stocking. Clusters of polka dots, artfully placed, were scattered on gossamer thin Lycra that showed much too much skin beneath.

"I'm waiting," Candace sang out. "You've had plenty of time."

Wincing, Lauren stuck her head around the door. When she was sure she was still the boutique's only customer, she sidled out and stood, arms crossed, her weight on one leg.

"Oh my God." Candace dropped into a chair and stretched out her leopard-clad legs. "There's no justice in this world. I'd sell my soul—even my Porsche—to look like that."

"No way," Lauren said. "I'm not auditioning as a tabletop dancer."

"In that suit you could audition for anything you wanted and get it. It's yours and I'm not taking any arguments."

"Candy!"

"Have I ever steered you wrong?"

"Well." In fact, Candace had always sold her clothes that Lauren ended up enjoying. "I guess not."

"Exactly." With a satisfied grin, Candace got up and pulled Lauren's arms to her sides. Then she tweaked and molded the suit, pulling it higher at the hip, farther apart where the top angled down from thread thin straps. "Jack Irving, eat your heart out."

"Candy! What did you say?"

But the woman sauntered away, a knowing smile on her lovely face. "I'll just ring that up for you."

Lauren returned to the sidewalk, a small, shiny pink *Candace* box in hand and feeling slightly stunned. This whole town knew she'd been seeing Jack Irving.

She hurried across the street, checking her watch and silently berating herself for what she'd agreed to do next. After several attempts, she'd made contact with Christie Taylor and they were meeting for lunch at Garcias on State Street.

Lauren drove through town, dread mushrooming with every block she passed. The silver Mercedes she recognized as Christie's was already parked outside the restaurant.

She could drive on and pretend she'd forgotten the date. No, she couldn't. She'd promised Dan this one last favor and she'd do it to make sure he had no more excuses to badger her with. And anyway, it had begun to suit her to think of him as well settled in his marriage, hadn't it? Lauren wasn't sure she wanted to examine the question too closely.

Inside the cool, stucco building with its exposed beams and bright splashes of color, a pretty waitress in a peasant blouse and full skirt smiled and ushered Lauren across exposed wood floors. "Mrs. Taylor's waiting for you," the girl said and Lauren registered then quickly discarded the thought that Mrs. Taylor was waiting for another Mrs. Taylor. She'd once thought of changing her name back to

Erickson, her maiden name, but never got around to the paperwork that entailed.

She slipped into a chair opposite Christie who leveled a hostile and slightly unfocused stare in her direction. The large margarita in front of her was almost drained and Lauren came to the uncomfortable conclusion that it might not have been Christie's first.

"How are you?" Lauren asked politely.

Christie lifted her chin. "Short of time."

"Oh." Lauren declined a drink from the cocktail waitress and asked for coffee. "We could order lunch if you're ready."

"I won't be eating. Let's get this over with. I'm only here to please Dan."

Which made two of them. Odd how one not-very-honorable man could command so much obedience. Lauren reminded herself that she was doing this for old times' sake, nothing more.

"How does it feel to be the one who lost out?" Christie's voice was slurred.

Lauren sighed. She bowed her head. "You and Dan have been married three years. My marriage to him is old, worn-out and not very interesting history."

"But you haven't forgotten, have you?" Christie tossed back her blond hair. "You'd still like to find a way to come between us if you could."

"No," Lauren said, striving for patience she didn't feel. "I've gotten to the point of thinking of Dan as someone I've known for a very long time—nothing more." Just when had that point come? Years ago? Maybe even before he'd said he was leaving?

Christie pouted. "And you think you can hold that over me. All the years you two have known each other. You use that to keep him running to you every time he decides he needs a shoulder to cry on."

"According to Dan, you made that suggestion before—to him. And you told him I was the one who let you know he'd been talking to me. It isn't true and you made up a lie because you're insecure. And now I think I'll go."

"You're jealous," Christie said. She tipped back her head and drained her glass. "You know Jack Irving's only after what he can get out of you and then he won't want you any more than Dan did. So you want to try to get Dan back again."

Lauren's cheeks burned. "What a horrible thing to say." And how was it that everyone in this town, a town where she hardly socialized at all, knew about the attention Jack had shown her?

"It may be horrible, but the truth hurts, doesn't it?" Christie gave a smug smile.

"Okay." Lauren took her wallet from her purse. "Dan asked me to tell you there's nothing between us. So I'm telling you, there's nothing between Dan and me. I'm not interested in him anymore. I wouldn't be here if I didn't believe he's basically a nice guy who gave in to an overdose of mid-life crisis—with a lot of help from you."

"You bitch."

"Be quiet. The people in my life don't talk like that." Lauren stood up and tossed down enough money to cover the price of coffee. "My advice to you is to examine what it is that makes you so insecure. Then see if you can't make something worthwhile of your marriage—for your child's sake if not for your own."

"What do you mean, for *my* child's sake? Wednesday's Dan's, too."

Lauren sighed. "Yes, so you make a point of telling me whenever you get the chance. And I meant that, as well. Excuse me, but I've got a business to run."

"Really? Still?"

"Yes." Lauren stopped and frowned. "What did you mean by that?"

"Nothing." Christie signaled the waitress who was already approaching with Lauren's coffee. When the girl had put down the cup, frowned at Lauren and taken Christie's order for another margarita, Christie added, "I meant that for someone with a business to run you seem to have a lot of free time to meddle in other people's lives."

"Goodbye."

"Stay away from Dan. Don't even talk to him. If you do, I'll make things even worse for you."

Lauren hesitated. There was something that began to niggle here. "How would you do that?"

"Isn't there somewhere else you'd rather live? You don't have anything to keep you in Carlsbad really, do you?"

Setting her mouth in a firm line, Lauren walked out and got into her car. She was barely aware of driving through sunlit streets and her heart didn't settle back into a normal rhythm until she was safely inside her office.

Predictably, Susan gave her only a few minutes to settle in before presenting herself on the other side of the desk, a stack of memos in hand.

"Don't tell me," Lauren said wearily. "Someone else wants to quit."

Susan sat down. "As a matter of fact, two of them. Small Talk, the kids' clothing shop, and Sabina's. That's the tanning salon on—"

"I know where it is." Lauren sank back in her chair, deep in thought.

"Well," Susan said when the silence grew long, "what are you thinking?"

"That there's a certain pattern in all this. Put it out of your mind. I think I can deal with the problem as soon as I can decide on the right line of approach."

"If you say so." Clearly, Susan ached to ask what Lauren meant but sensed the timing was very wrong. "Would it be okay if I left a few minutes early today?"

Lauren looked up. "Hot date?"

"Well—" Susan visibly battled with her natural reticence over her private life "—as a matter of fact, yes." Her ivory skin turned bright pink.

Lauren grinned. "This has to be serious. I've never seen you look like an excited kid over anyone before."

"I don't now," Susan said crossly, getting up.

"Okay, okay. Have it your way."

There was a tap on the door and Yolande, one of Lauren's newest operators, poked her head into the office. "A gentleman to see you, Lauren. Mr. Irving. Shall I show him in?"

Susan made owl eyes and went toward the door.

"Er, yes." Lauren's stomach made a complete revolution. She ran her fingers through her hair, moistened her lips and gripped the edge of her desk.

"Thanks for seeing me. This won't take long." Denton Irving came in and closed the door firmly behind him.

When Lauren recovered from her surprise, she stood up. "Hello, Mr. Irving. How nice to see you."

"Hmph."

"Sit down, please."

"That won't be necessary. I understand you were out at the farm the other night. When that damn fire was going."

"Yes," Lauren said. "It was awful. I'm so sorry it happened."

Denton Irving straightened his shoulders inside a blue plaid shirt. "So am I. My son's had enough hard knocks in the past few years. He didn't need that."

"Of course not. No one needs that kind of thing."

"I'm not interested in anyone but my son. And my grandson." The man's dark brows were a startling contrast to his thick head of wavy white hair. His brown eyes bored into her. "I'm sure you have some idea why I'm here."

She didn't. "Is there anything you think I can do to help?"

"Four years ago my son's wife left him. She left him with a five-year-old boy to bring up. Did you know that?"

"I knew some of it. Not any details, though." Crossing her arms, Lauren willed her heart not to skitter.

"The details aren't something you need to know. Jack's very private about that part of his life and he wouldn't appreciate my telling you things he hasn't told you himself."

"Of course." So why was Irving here at all?

"Jack's a good man. He's also a vulnerable man—although he doesn't think so. He thinks he's immune to being swept away by... You know what I mean."

Lauren cleared her throat. Her answers weren't something she thought Denton Irving wanted. She was supposed to listen and agree.

"It would be too bad if Jack got involved with someone who didn't share his values." Those piercing brown eyes impaled her.

"What exactly are you trying to say?" Lauren said when she couldn't wait any longer. "Are you suggesting I'm pursuing Jack and that I'm bad for him?"

Irving half turned toward the door. "I'm suggesting whatever you want to think I'm suggesting. And by the way, Jack and I are very close. He wouldn't take kindly to you trying to put me down."

"I wouldn't do that," Lauren said heatedly. Her temper was wearing thin. "Get to the point, please."

Irving looked at his big, work-worn hands and cleared his throat. "It was good of you to go out to the plant the other night."

"I wanted to." His change in tactics bemused her.

"Awful lot of women stay away from the first hint of trouble."

She sucked in her bottom lip. He was trying, as best he could, to say something nice.

Producing a large and wrinkled red handkerchief, he mopped his brow. "Andy said you were kind to him."

"Andy's easy to be kind to."

"I think so." He glared at her again. "Spunky little kid. Deserves the best. So does his father."

"It's nice to see someone who really likes the members of his own family," she said softly. "You'd take on any fight for them, wouldn't you?"

"That's neither here nor there," Irving said gruffly. "Thank you for being there for my son and my grandson. I appreciate it."

"You're very welcome." Lauren turned up the corners of her mouth. "I hope this is going to be the last of their bad luck."

"Yes, well, look, young woman, I've got to say the rest of what's on my mind."

Lauren took a deep breath. She wouldn't be able to stop him if she wanted to.

"Even if Jack can take care of himself, which I'm pretty sure he can, Andy can't. He's got some buried scars that I want left that way—buried. Are you getting my drift?"

"No, I'm not." But perhaps she was. He was suggesting she had the power to hurt Andy.

"Then I'll make it clearer. Playing with a man for your own ends might be all right if there wasn't someone else who stood to suffer. When there is, it isn't all right. Think about it. That's all I ask."

Something near pain stole around Lauren's heart. Denton Irving thought she'd encourage Jack for nothing more than sexual reasons and not care if Andy got hurt in the process. "I resent the suggestions you're making, Mr. Irving. I'm not a woman on the hunt for a man I can use and then throw away when I feel like it."

"Maybe," Irving said. "But I had to say my piece just the same."

"No you didn't." Lauren walked to the door, opened it and stood back. "What you've implied is an insult. Thanks for the tip of the hat for what little I was able to do the other night. Now I'd appreciate it if you'd leave."

"Gladly." But when he drew level he stopped. "You will think about what I've said?"

"Oh, I doubt if I'll be able to avoid it." She turned away and repeated in a whisper, "I doubt if I'll be able to avoid it."

Chapter Ten

Jack regarded the outside of the aerobics studio with distaste. In the sports bag he carried were a pair of shorts, a T-shirt and the closest thing he could find to the appropriate shoes the woman on the phone had insisted he should have.

There was no point in waiting.

Tipping his Stetson lower over his eyes, he pushed open the door and walked in behind the rows of gyrating bodies. He was going to hate this but he couldn't think of another way to show her he wasn't accepting her brush-off—no matter what the effort cost him.

He found his way to the locker rooms, quickly changed and returned to the studio. What a lousy way to spend a Friday evening.

"Are we having fun yet?" a woman in a shiny yellow bodysuit yelled from her position facing the group.

"Yes!" came the roar over a pounding beat from the music sound system.

Jack sidled to the back, jogged in place and began searching for Lauren. There she was, in the second row, dressed in red tonight: red leotard and tights and a red sweatband around her brow and beneath a bobbing ponytail.

He studied the man in front of him and tried to copy his movements. If the things his muscles started to do meant anything , the instructor's warning to get here for the warm-up had been valid. But that might have given Lauren a chance to leave before he could talk to her.

Every time the steps changed he fell behind. Like a damned overseas telephone call, he thought. An echo.

"One and two and one and two," the instructor called. "Swing those elbows, saw and saw and lift those knees, to the left, to the right."

He began to get the hang of it as long as he didn't think of anything else.

Between Jack and Lauren were three rows of bodies in violent motion. Sidling, trying to concentrate on the moves, he worked his way to the end of the back row. A step took him one line forward, another step a second, and then he was behind and a short space to the left of Lauren.

The woman to his right turned.

He didn't.

"Ouch." She hissed the word as she continued moving.

"Sorry," he responded, trying to catch up.

"You're going the wrong way," the woman said, glaring.

Jack smiled weakly, turned, and took the opportunity to slip more or less between Lauren and a man beside her.

"Circles in the air and strut your stuff!"

Facing forward, Jack attempted the hand moves demonstrated while trying, not very successfully, a hip-clicking walk the woman made look so easy.

The man he'd crowded muttered something Jack was sure he didn't want to hear anyway and made more room.

And Lauren turned her head to look directly up into his eyes.

"Hi." He smiled.

Her mouth opened but she didn't say a word.

"You left a message with my secretary."

"Yes." She seemed to throw more energy into the routine.

"You canceled our date for tomorrow."

"That's right."

"Then you wouldn't speak to me."

She turned to the right and he followed suit.

"Why wouldn't you speak to me?"

"What are you doing here?" The words jarred out as she broke into a knee-lifting trot.

Jack shuffled his feet and started trotting just in time for everyone else to shift to a different exercise. "I tracked you down."

"I'd never have guessed," she said through barely parted lips. "I thought you came here all the time and being next to you was a coincidence."

"Sarcasm doesn't suit you."

"I told you I'd decided it would be best if we didn't see each other again."

"Bounce and kick and bounce and kick!" the instructor yelled.

Jack groaned. He might not survive this. "You decided, Lauren. I didn't. I want to talk about it."

"Who told you I'd be here?"

"I never betray confidences." When he'd tried to reach her this afternoon, for the third time, her secretary had taken pity on him and told him where to find her in the evening. "Your phone was off the hook when I tried you at home after work."

"Was it?"

"How much longer does this go on?"

"Hours."

"Oh God." He'd begun to sweat. "Let's get out of here."

"I'm enjoying myself."

He groaned. "I'm not."

"Then leave. No one's keeping—" She paused, looking past him.

Jack glanced over his shoulder, into the smiling, interested eyes of the man whose place he'd usurped. He smiled back. "We're just having an intimate chat," he told the man.

Lauren, when he checked her face, had turned almost as red as her suit. He became aware, as she obviously had, that an oasis of silent, listening concentration had formed around them. The only sounds were the music, the thud of feet and the instructor's voice.

Abruptly, Lauren broke from the line and hurried to the changing rooms. Jack did the same. He pulled on his jean jacket, grabbed his gear and made a dash for the door to the street.

He made it with about a minute to spare before Lauren charged out and collided with him.

"You made a fool of me in there," she said. She wore a white sweat suit over the leotard and tights.

"I wanted to get your attention. It worked." He held her arm although she showed no sign of trying to get away. "You promised me you'd come out to the house tomorrow."

"And I changed my mind, Jack." She sounded so miserable he longed to take her in his arms and quiet her. "I've given it a lot of thought and I've decided there's no point in us spending time together."

He pulled up her chin until she had to meet his eyes. "Do you really believe that?"

"I... I think so." Her lower lip trembled and he felt a slight shift in power here.

"Let's go somewhere and talk about it."

"I need to go home for a shower."

"You can shower at my place. And then you'll be ready for that swim."

"No."

"Why? Didn't you buy a suit yet? We could go shopping and—"

"I already bought a suit." Immediately she bit her lip and averted her face.

Jack saw victory in sight. "Ah. Good. The pool will relax us. We'll talk better there."

"It's going to be dark soon."

"I'll follow you home to get your suit."

Lauren sighed deeply and he felt her giving in. "It's in my car."

"Better yet. We'll get it and leave your car where it is."

"Jack. Please don't push. I told you I've decided this is no good."

He smoothed damp hair away from her face. "But you bought a swimsuit to use at my house. Sounds to me like there's still hope for me."

"You can do much better."

"Oh, but you are so wrong," he said softly, drawing closer, feeling the pull of her sweet, full lips. "So wrong."

"All right." She stepped back. "I'll come and wade in your pool. But only if you promise to bring me back when we've done that and I'm ready to go. Promise?"

He grinned. "I promise. When you're ready to leave, I'll bring you back." But he'd make sure she wasn't ready to go for a long, long time.

Carrying her bag as well as his, he followed Lauren to her car where she retrieved a little, shiny pink box from the back seat. He eyed it curiously and she caught his look.

"The swimsuit," she said, her mouth pursed.

On the drive to his house they spoke about the fire. His idea, not hers. "The fire chief says it was definitely arson. But, like I told you on Wednesday, there's about a zero chance of catching whoever did it." By drawing her into the most painful subject in his life at the moment, he was deliberately trying for a more intimate bond.

"I've lived here a long time," she told him. "What I know about the flower business is sketchy at best, but I always thought everyone got along pretty well. Do you think this has something to do with a rival farm?"

"That seems the most obvious, doesn't it? But there hasn't been another grower who hasn't shown up in person to offer help. And every one of them is angry on my behalf, and maybe a little scared on their own."

She rested her head back. "I would be, too, if I were them. They must wonder who'll be next. But who do you think would have a reason to attack your business if it isn't someone in competition with you?"

Just being with her made him feel better—good even. She had a lucid mind in addition to all the other things that drew him to her.

"I don't have the answers, Lauren. Let's make a pact. This is Friday evening and we won't talk about my rotten business problems."

"I'll try. You might have a harder time."

He turned the truck onto the street in front of his house. "Then it's up to you to stop me if I get onto the subject again. There's nothing I can do tonight. Is that a deal?"

"A deal."

Once they'd parked, he helped her down from the cab and let them into the house.

He switched on lights and Lauren peered around. "Where's Andy?"

Not meeting her eyes, he said, "Dad wanted him for the night. The two of them are great buddies."

"I gathered."

He frowned, puzzled at the response, but didn't comment. "You must be starving. I am."

"Sort of." She followed him into the kitchen and dropped her bag.

When he looked at her, at the clean glow on her face, the way the white sweats touched every curve, his appetite fled. He smiled valiantly. "I'm glad you're only sort of hungry. We should swim before we eat."

Lauren held the pink box to her chest. It looked about the right size to contain half a dozen handkerchiefs. And Lauren looked mutinous.

"Why don't you go out to the poolhouse and change? The lights are on in the yard. There are towels and a couple of robes out there."

Balk was written all over her face. She stood her ground. "I've changed my mind. I'm very hungry. Why don't I make us something?"

"It isn't a good idea to swim on a full stomach."

"Maybe we should skip the swim and just eat."

She could be genuinely afraid of going into the water. "Look, you can stand in the shallow end where the water's only up to your middle. And I'll make sure you don't get frightened."

"I'm thirty-nine. I haven't learned to swim yet. Why bother at this stage? I know I'm not going to like it."

Inspiration hit. "You're probably right." He nodded sagely. "Absolutely right, in fact. They say it's not a good idea to force new ideas on people who don't like taking risks. You stay here and see what you can find for us to eat. I'll take a dip for half an hour or so. Then we'll eat outside. We may need jackets, but it's a nice night."

He left the kitchen via the French doors and sauntered away. Of course, he might have misjudged her personality and her pride, but he'd take that chance. The worst that could happen was that she'd make his dinner, something he usually had to do for himself and Andy on Friday and Saturday nights.

Ten minutes later, when he was already in the water, he pretended not to see Lauren walking determinedly to the poolhouse. She looked neither right nor left and her pointed chin was set at a determined angle. Jack dove, smiling to himself. He'd been right. Challenge was Lauren Taylor's middle name. She'd call his bluff at any personal cost.

When he was certain she'd gone into the little white building, he turned on his back and floated and tried to quell the jumpy excitement in his belly. He wasn't a sex fiend, he reminded himself, just an average... just a man with an active mind and body and sex drive.

The door to the poolhouse opened and a figure swathed in a large, white terry robe, slowly approached.

Jack righted himself to wave. "Hi, don't push yourself to do this. There's no shame in not being able to manage something everyone else can do. Not if you come from Laramie, Wyoming." He flipped up his toes and floated again. Nonchalance, as much as an impression of indifference, was the key here. Indifference and a few sharp digs at her clearly competitive spirit.

"Is this the shallow end?"

"Yes." Turning on his side, he stroked lazily. "Sit on the steps in the corner and get your feet wet. I had that put there for Andy to paddle. He used to wear water wings and wait for me to tow him. Hey!" With a kick, he stood on the bottom and bobbed. "I should have thought of that. Would you like water wings? I'm sure I didn't throw 'em out. Might make you feel safer."

"I don't need water wings. I'm going to get the hang of this very quickly. I would have before if I'd wanted to, but the occasion never presented itself."

"Of course." Using a slow crawl, he swam the length of the pool and rested his elbows on the wall. The outdoor lights cast a subdued glow, turning the water to transparent, iridescent turquoise.

Lauren walked to the edge and carefully bent one knee while she tested the water with a toe. Then she turned her back.

Jack started a leisurely swim back in her direction.

She undid the belt on the robe, paused, and slipped the white thing off.

His last breath might be just that—his last. Air trying to go in warred with air he'd planned to breathe out.

Lauren didn't spend time in the sun, but her skin was smooth and olive toned. What he could see of the black swimsuit, cut to a low V at the back, covered very little of that skin.

She turned. "How deep is it right here?"

Jack swallowed and managed to expand his lungs. "About three feet. Wait, I'll give you a hand."

Ignoring the hand he proffered, she sat on the edge and kicked her feet gently to and fro. He stroked close and stood up, slicking his hair back.

"Doesn't feel so warm to me."

"It will be when you get in." Looking at her, as she was now, would warm him in a freezer compartment.

The suit was something else. She was something else. Some sort of black stretchy, lacy stuff, held up over incredible breasts by a string that tied behind her neck, clung to the softly sleek and rounded curves of her body. And, where there weren't little groups of dots, the fabric was so thin her skin showed through.

"Come on." He offered her his hands. After a moment's hesitation, she slipped her fingers into his and let him help her down.

Hissing through her teeth, she looked shocked and made a grab for a more substantial hold. She found his shoulders and her fingernails dug in. Jack kept a smile on his face. He'd better also keep his eyes on *her* face. If he didn't, he was in danger of losing his mind.

"Now what?" She clung to him, the water lapping beneath her breasts.

He took a deep breath and willed the rest of him to calm down. "Do you think you could put your face in the water?"

"No." She shook her head emphatically. "I can't even do that in the shower."

In the shower. He was a cerebral man, a man more interested in minds than bodies. The hell he was, at least not right here and now.

"Floating's easy. Want to try?"

She looked dubious and moved closer. "How do you stay up?" The tips of her breasts, in the rough lacy fabric, brushed his chest.

Think, don't feel. "I'm going to turn you around. Relax and do as I tell you."

Obediently, but with every muscle rigid, she allowed him to revolve her. "Feel my hands on your back?"

"Yes." Her voice was tiny and shaky.

"Trust me. I won't let you go. Lean on my hands and let your feet come off the bottom. They'll float up and you'll be on top of the water."

"I can't do that."

"Yes you can. Try. And try to relax."

Very slowly, she put her weight into his hands. "My feet are off. Don't drop me!"

"I wouldn't drop you, Lauren." He'd like to hold her for the rest of the night, here or anywhere else. "There you go. Feel the water keeping you up?"

"Don't let go!"

"Never. Not till you tell me to."

"I'm not going to tell you to."

Gradually her body leveled. "You're doing it," he cried. "Let your muscles go floppy and get your bottom higher."

She laughed shakily. "I can't."

"You can." Sliding his hands farther beneath her, he moved smoothly until he was at her side. "Lift here." Firm pressure under the appropriate part brought her hips up.

He felt her relax. A smile softened her features. "This feels good. I never knew it would feel like this."

"You never tried before?"

"No."

"Isn't there a pool at—" He shut his mouth, furious for almost mentioning the house she'd shared with Dan.

"Dan's had one put in now. There wasn't before." She didn't appear perturbed at the reference.

"Stretch out your arms."

When she made no attempt to do as he asked, Jack took first one and then her other arm and arranged them, palms up.

He felt her beginning to trust the water. Her eyes closed. For minutes he supported her, watched the smile on her lips. With one finger, he smoothed away a strand of hair that trailed across her cheek. She opened her eyes again and looked directly up at him.

"Feel good?" he asked quietly.

"Mmm. Do I have to do more things now?"

"Not now. Floating's enough for the first time."

Her eyes fluttered shut again and he towed her a little deeper.

Very carefully, Jack eased his hand away and he watched her bob.

Suddenly Lauren flailed and grabbed. "You let go!"

He laughed and caught her around the waist. "You were doing it all by yourself until you panicked. You can do it all by yourself."

Nothing in her eyes, or in the death grip of her fingers into his sides, suggested she believed him.

"Hold me!"

"I am holding you." He was also standing on the bottom. "Put your feet down. Go on, do it."

Her face tight, she stared at him until she made contact with cement. "I thought it was too deep." She laughed, put a hand over her mouth. She looked, Jack thought, very young.

"You look lovely when you laugh," he told her.

"Thank you." She sobered.

"I like looking at you." Slowly, his hands about her waist, he circled, swinging her with him. "Shorts suit you, and tank tops, and sweatbands and leotards. Everything."

"Stetsons suit you. You look sexy in a Stetson." She hunched her shoulders and covered her mouth again. And this time she turned pink.

"I sure like it when you blush." He smoothed her cheek. "I'm going to wear a Stetson all the time. Wait right here and I'll get one."

When he made as if to leave, she laughed.

Jack glanced upward at the dark sky. "Stars. Millions of them. See?"

She followed his pointed finger. "Mmm. Millions."

"Are you warm now?"

"Very warm."

He swung her, swung her again. And she laughed softly, tilting her head.

They stopped. He didn't know whether he'd been the one to stand still, or she had, but they stood very still.

Her mouth, when he brought his lips to hers, was damp, and her face, her ear, her neck. Bending over her neck, he raised her to her toes and crushed her to him.

"You...smell...wonderful." Between each nipping kiss he heard her sigh.

She stretched up, wrapped her arms around his shoulders and kissed him fully, at first opening his mouth wide to admit her tongue, then concentrating on nibbling his lower lip.

A trembling surge burst through him, hit low in his belly, his groin.

"I don't understand," she said against his jaw.

"What don't you understand?"

"Why me? Why now?" The touch of her suit was an erotic massage. Everywhere it rubbed him he felt first the silken texture of her skin and then the rough stimulus of fabric that had to be intended for that purpose. And only that scrap of black kept him from seeing and holding all of her.

"You're not answering me."

His fingers were on the bow at the back of her neck. "The only answer I can give you is that it's right and it's what I want. Isn't that enough?" Instinctively he ground his thigh between hers. Lauren gritted her teeth and dropped back her head.

Jack recognized his own feeling as triumph. He thrust his leg harder against her and pulled the string undone.

Her eyes flew open. "Jack?"

"I think you want this, too."

"I think..." Her full lips parted and she held the tip of her tongue between her teeth.

The suit top stayed in place until he slowly peeled it down. Taking in short breaths, he supported the weight of her breasts. Wedged astride his thigh, she held his shoulders. Jack watched her flesh grow turgid beneath his touch. At the pressure of his thumbs her nipples sprang hard.

She turned her face away and muttered something.

Unable to resist, he bent to suck—and tongue. Kissing, working his way up, he asked, "What, Lauren?"

"They're too big," she said. "Too much."

He caught her chin between finger and thumb and made her look at him. "Who says so?"

She shook her head and he knew a moment's wild jealousy. He wouldn't ask the same question again.

"They're perfect. You're perfect."

"So are you." She touched him, slipped her hand inside his suit beneath the water.

His mind went wild. Struggling, he worked her suit down, took a breath and dove beneath the surface, dragged his face the length of her to pull the black wisp from beneath her feet.

Lauren's fingers in his hair, tugging him up, brought him, gasping, face-to-face with her again.

"I never wanted anyone like this," he told her, hearing the ragged pitch of his own voice. "Let me carry you?"

Her face was flushed, but she pulled away a little, frowning. "Carry?"

Grinning, he kicked onto his back, pulling her over him. "Wrap your legs around me."

She did as she was told and he was aware, as she must be, that he nudged the opening to her body. A fraction of an inch and they would be joined. But still they held back, prolonging ecstatic torment.

Grasping her waist, he urged her higher until he could take her breast into his mouth. He heard her cry out, felt the contraction of complex muscles on his belly.

"I want to take you to bed," he said, suddenly convinced that, when they'd make love, he'd want to lie with her, then make love again and finally, sleep with her in his arms.

Lauren said nothing as he towed her to the side and lifted her to sit on the wall. "I'll be back."

In moments he returned with their suits. He allowed himself an instant of desperate longing while he stared at her voluptuous body in the night's brush of white light and soft shadow.

With a single movement, he pulled himself up beside her. "Ready, Lauren?"

"Ready?"

"To come with me."

She stood up abruptly and picked up the robe she'd used. Puzzled, he watched her pull it on and belt it tightly. "I guess I'm ready."

"Are you all right?"

"Of course." She held out a hand and hauled him up.

His stomach sank. The passion, the wildness, had subtly ebbed away. Testing his will, sensing he mustn't do anything fast now, he gathered her close and rested his chin atop her head. "You never told me why you'd decided not to keep our date tomorrow." They couldn't lose what had started in the pool. *He* couldn't lose it.

"I thought maybe I would be simplifying your life."

He leaned away to see her face. "I don't understand."

"Forget it. I shouldn't have said anything. Let's go inside."

"No. Tell me."

"I . . . I wouldn't want to do anything to hurt Andy."

Her words took seconds to register. "Why would . . . How could you do that?"

"According to your father—" With a small strangled sound she wrenched away.

Jack frowned. "What's my father got to do with this?" He was afraid he might know.

"Nothing. . . . Well, he, er . . . We ran into each other and . . . he thanked me for coming out to the farm after the fire." He saw her swallow. "Oh, he loves you and Andy so much, Jack. He worries. He—he mentioned how he hoped I wouldn't be a . . . He doesn't want Andy hurt again, like he was when his mother left."

When he tried to make her face him, she moved farther away.

"My father doesn't always think far enough before interfering in my life. But he means well. He's very important to me."

"Of course he is." She gathered the sodden suit and a towel. Half turning, she raised a hand in a resigned gesture. "It's wonderful to see a family as close as you and Andy are with your dad."

"Thank you." He could *feel* it happening, the cooling between them.

"Jack. Forgive me, but I think I'd like to change and go home."

Frustrated, he searched for the right thing to say. "Don't go," was the best he could muster.

"I—I really must. It's getting late."

"But, I thought—"

"I know what you thought. So did I. Sometimes the physical gets in the way of common sense, don't you think?" She paused and faced him. "Maybe this is going to seem like an odd time to ask. But would you be comfortable telling me what happened with you and your wife?"

Closing his eyes, he bowed his head. "I don't like to go into this. It's so simple, it's crazy."

"I'd still like to know."

"All right. Mary and I met and married in college. As long as she was the center of my life we had a great marriage. Then Andy came along and she moved farther and farther away from both of us." The old tightness formed in his throat. He didn't love Mary anymore, but he loved what he'd thought she stood for. And he hated what he'd lost.

"So that was it. She changed and you decided to part?"

"I didn't decide anything. She felt she'd missed her opportunities by not pursuing her art. One day I came home and found Andy with a baby-sitter. Mary had moved out. Within two months we were divorced and she'd gone to live in Paris and paint. She's still there."

Lauren took a step closer. "She just left the two of you, to go and paint?"

"Yeah. That's why I got bent out of shape that night I met you at the aerobic studio and we went out to eat. You said you liked to paint and the dash of déjà vu sent me into a tailspin."

"I'm not Mary." She wrapped the robe more tightly around her.

"No. But I'm me and I'm only human. Warts and all."

"I'm sorry."

He didn't want pity. "Will you come into the house with me?"

"Did you send Andy away tonight hoping I'd come back with you?"

Lying wasn't his thing. "I guess it was in the back of my mind."

"How do you feel about Mary now?"

"Sad. But I don't love her." He'd taken awhile to come this far and that, at least, felt right.

"Did you know your father worries about another woman becoming important enough in your life to be able to hurt you—and Andy when the thing falls apart? And he seems convinced it would fall apart eventually."

Jack wrapped a towel around his waist. His skin had cooled. His ardor hadn't. "I know what my father thinks. He doesn't have to worry."

"Can you be so sure?"

"The only way I'd be putting Andy at risk would be by bringing in someone into our family who wasn't likely to be permanent while he's still at an impressionable age."

He reached for her, but she eluded him. "He's nine. Have you worked out some theory as to what *isn't* an impressionable age?"

Shrugging, he looked at the sky. "Who knows? Fifteen. Eighteen. I don't think about it because it isn't going to happen."

"I see," she said quietly. "Very sensible."

"I'm not a dumb kid anymore. I think things through."

"Yes." She picked up a spare towel. "I wonder what time it is."

"Why?"

"I just remembered. I promised the woman who rents rooms from me that I'd look after her daughter tonight."

He narrowed his eyes. "Don't leave now."

He heard the long sigh of her breath. "Yes, Jack, I must. Remember what you promised earlier, when I agreed to come?"

"No!" How had he allowed this to happen?

"You promised to take me back to my car when I was ready to go—"

"Lauren, in the pool—"

"Please try to forget the pool. Put it down to the stars and the water. Blame it on a frustrated divorcée, if you like."

"Lauren—"

"No." She walked toward the poolhouse. "I won't be long. I'm ready to go home."

"If it were Dan asking you to say, you would, wouldn't you?" He hated the question as soon as it was uttered.

Lauren stood still but didn't look at him. "What did you say?"

He took a deep breath. "You'd do anything for him." Why couldn't he stop himself from saying these things? "Hell, I'm sorry. I shouldn't have said that."

"I don't blame you."

"Why *do* you let him push you around?"

"I don't." She faced him. "It may look that way, but I don't. But since we're on this subject. Are you still in love with your ex-wife?"

He stiffened. "I told you I wasn't."

"Did you? It seems we don't really believe one another when it comes to the important stuff." Her black eyes were shadows he couldn't read. "Distrust is no basis for... for anything between a man and a woman."

"What are you really afraid of, Lauren?"

"Nothing, I—"

"No." He caught her hand and she didn't pull away. "Don't sidestep this. There's something going on, something you're not telling me."

"Okay." With one long finger she traced the tendons on the back of his hand. "I'm afraid of myself. I'm afraid I'm not tough enough to take a chance on getting hurt again."

"Why would you decide you're going to get hurt?" He looked away, searching for the right words. "Why can't you just let go and enjoy what we could have together?"

"Because I want it too much. And if we became lovers but never anything more, how would I feel when you eventually moved on?"

"You're getting ahead of things. Way ahead."

She laughed. The sound jarred him. "As the old saying goes, 'Once bitten...' and so on. You asked the questions and I gave you the answers."

"Could we talk some more about this... over a drink?"

Lauren brought her lips together and they trembled. "For my sake I'm going to say no. I like you, Jack. I really like you. But I want to leave now. Please stop trying to make me change my mind."

"Maybe you're right." He felt tired, beaten. "Take your time. I'll meet you in the truck."

JACK HAD NO INTENTION of risking Andy's happiness. Lauren tossed and turned in her bed. He'd ignited feelings she remembered well, but had chosen to eliminate from her life, and the reawakening of them wasn't comfortable.

Moonlight through venetian blinds drew silvery stripes across her quilt. She pushed herself to sit up and traced a pallid line.

There was no risk to Andy because Jack wouldn't get into a deep involvement as long as the boy was at a vulnerable age.

Having made his own decision, he should have asked her what decision she'd made about future relationships. Yes, she was overwhelmingly attracted to him. Lauren closed her eyes and hugged her middle, remembering the sensation of his skin on hers, his muscular limbs entrapping her willing body. But she'd made a pact for the future, too. Her independence. One marriage had taught her the perfect attitude for her to adopt with a man: never go beyond friendship.

With Jack, friendship would be impossible to maintain. The sexual attraction was too strong.

What had he been saying when he spoke of waiting until Andy was safe from hurt? That then would be the time to take a woman totally into his life, to marry her, maybe?

Lauren closed her eyes. They'd parted with no plans to meet again, but she knew they probably wouldn't be able to stay apart. When she'd told him some of her fears, Jack had responded that she was thinking too far ahead. Well, he might only be concerned with immediate gratification; Lauren already knew the price she'd eventually pay if she allowed herself that luxury.

Somewhere in the house something creaked, and creaked again like careful footsteps on the stairs.

Lauren sat very still and listened.

A door closed softly.

In one bound, Lauren was out of bed and wrenching open her door. She rushed along the hallway and stopped outside Cara's room. A line of light showed beneath the door.

Lauren tapped.

There was a rustling before Cara called out a wobbly, "Come in."

Lauren opened the door and went to the girl's bed. She sat against her pillows, her streaked, puffy face evidence of copious tears.

"What is it?" Lauren dropped to kneel beside her and reached for her hand.

Cara put small, cold fingers into hers and tried for a smile. "Hi."

"Hi. Can't you sleep?"

"Oh, yes. Um. Yes. I'm going to sleep now."

Lauren spied a suspicious bump in the bed, beside Cara's legs. "You went downstairs, didn't you?"

"Um." A huge swallow sounded painful. "Um, I was thirsty."

"Ah." Lauren eyed the lump. "What's in your bed?"

Without glasses, Cara's blue eyes were huge. "Nothing."

Lauren bit her lip. "Cara, I know it's something. And I can see you're upset. We're buddies, aren't we? Tell me what's wrong."

Cara gulped and her mouth quivered. "I didn't want you to see. I didn't want you to feel bad."

Lauren's stomach turned over.

With her gaze on Lauren's face, Cara reached into her bed and extracted the two bright green sweatshirts she'd been given.

Lauren wrinkled her brow. "What... Did something happen to them? It doesn't matter. We can get... I've got some more."

"It's...not..." Cara hiccuped. "Jimmy got in trouble and it's my fault."

"Oh, Cara, no." Lauren pulled the girl close and hugged her. "Why did Jimmy get in trouble?"

"Because I gave him the shirt. His mom got real mad and said he's not to talk about his family to anyone...about them being poor."

"I see." She didn't.

"Jimmy's mom says proud people don't like charity."

Lauren held Cara away and smiled at her. "She's right. But sometimes people mix up charity with simple kindness. Don't worry, it'll all work out."

With a little help, most things could be worked out. Lauren hunched her shoulders. She was a long way from completely giving up on Jack Irving; a very long way.

Chapter Eleven

"Why'd you come for me tonight, Dad?"

Jack sat beside Andy on his bed and stretched out his legs. "I missed you. Is that okay?"

"I guess. Grandpa didn't look too pleased."

"Grandpa understands." He'd have to. "I'm pretty good about sharing you with him."

"He misses Grandma."

Jack looked down on Andy's tousled, dark hair. "He talked to you about that?"

"Yeah. He always does."

Jack narrowed his eyes, considering. "What does he say?"

Andy leaned against him and peeked into his cupped hands where part of Strangler's two-foot length was coiled. "He says she could do anything he could do—only better."

Jack laughed. "Boy, I bet she'd have liked to hear him say that. He's right, though. She was something. Do you remember her?"

"'Course." Andy snorted. "What d'ya think? She only got real sick . . . I was six. I remember everything that ever happened. Grandpa and I talk about all that sometimes."

"*All* that?" Jack eased away to see the side of his son's face. "What kind of stuff is that?"

Andy shrugged and wound Strangler around his wrist. With a forefinger, he stroked the California King's head and stared into flat, beady eyes.

Stopping on the way back from dropping Lauren off to bring Andy home had been self-indulgent. But thinking about her was an activity to be avoided. And being alone until he could put more distance between what had to be and what had seemed possible while she was with him, was also to be avoided. Tonight he needed Andy as a tangible reminder of what was most important in life. What he also needed tonight was a way to stop dwelling on the financial disaster the figures were starting to indicate at the farm.

"What stuff do you and Grandpa talk about?" Jack prodded.

"All kinds of stuff." Strangler worked his creamy-colored body up Andy's arm.

Jack put a tentative finger on the black stripe that ran the length of the reptile's back. "I thought I told you not to bring Strangler into bed."

"Snakes are clean," Andy said thoughtfully. "We just kind of hang out for a bit before I go to sleep."

"Don't ever forget to lock him up before you do go to sleep. Not unless you want to wake up and find hamster bones on the rug. Or Jaw's whiskers."

Andy let out an exasperated puff. "Jaws is too big. And Strangler wouldn't do that kinda thing 'cause I got him when he was a baby. He's trained."

"Want to bet?" Jack eyed the sleek body. "Wait till you bring your first girlfriend home and that thing decides to do what's natural." The King was capable of vibrating its tail like a rattler. Despite the fact that the species wasn't poisonous, the effect of the rattle, particularly if accompanied by the foul-smelling fluid it could eject, might put off the hardiest of souls.

"I'm never going to have a girlfriend." Andy scowled. "Girls are dumb screamers. Anyway, Strangler gets all he needs to eat and I always put him away."

Jack hadn't missed Andy's eagerness to drop the subject of his conversation with his grandfather. "Do you and Grandpa talk about your mother?"

After a short silence, Andy slipped from bed and put his snake into the old fish aquarium where he lived on a bed of pine needles and mulch beneath a roof made of perforated metal.

"Andy?" Jack patted the bed beside him. "Do you?"

"Some," Andy said, slipping back beneath his covers.

"Your mother's a nice woman." Muscles flicked in his jaw. No kid should be brought up to believe he was the product of someone worthless, not if he was going to think he was worth something himself.

"That's not what Grandpa says," Andy muttered.

Jack rested his head against the wall. He'd been afraid of that. "Your mother calls, y'know."

"Yeah."

"She asks how you are. That's why she calls."

"She doesn't want to talk to me."

Jack locked his hands behind his neck. This conversation was overdue. "Mary... Your mother's afraid of upsetting you. Maybe, when you're older, you'll be able to get to know her."

"Nah. I don't want to. Grandpa says if she wasn't selfish she'd have stayed with us. He says she loves me, but she loves her painting thing best. He says you gotta be careful not to let people get...powerful?" Andy craned his neck to see Jack's face. "Yeah, powerful. Grandpa says a guy's gotta learn to be his own person. I think that means it's dumb to care a lot about anyone."

If Jack could put his hands on his father right now he might forget the "honor thy father" bit. He settled his features in an expressionless mold. "Do you care a lot about Grandpa?"

"'Course!"

"How about me?"

"'Course I do!"

Jack smiled down. "And I care a lot about you, so it can't always be dumb, can it?"

Andy thought about that. "No, I guess not. Grandpa says you'll never let anyone else do what Mom did to us."

"He said—" Tilting up his chin, Jack managed, with difficulty, to order his thoughts. "I know where my dad's coming from and he's right. But I don't want you worrying about these things. Did you talk about the fire?"

"Yeah. We did the other day, too. He says you'll come out of everything okay because you're so diver—diver—"

"Diversified." For now he intended keeping the lid on the truth: they were far from okay. "He's right and that's something he and my mother get all the credit for. What I inherited was the product of their foresight, and Dad's father before them."

Andy snuggled closer. "I'm gonna do what you do one day, aren't I?"

"If you want to." Pleasure swept through Jack. "College first, then come and work with me if you want to. But keep your options open, Andy. You may decide there's something else you want to do."

The boy shook his head. "No way. Len says I gotta take floriculture."

Jack laughed. "That's a helluva big word for a nine-year-old."

"Matt told me about the new poinsettia. The bud mutation stuff and everything. He says it's gonna be sold for the first time this year."

"Yup. It's going to knock the socks off every buyer who sees it." If he could figure out a way to ship the damn thing. "It's the most spectacular sport we've ever developed. I expect Matt told you sport's the word for mutant. That baby's got to help tide us over until we come back from some of the damage our pyromaniac caused." Just thinking about the new sport's debut excited him.

"Did Lauren see Lava Pearl yet?"

Jack brought his teeth together. "No. And we don't talk about it to anyone but Len and Matt and Grandpa, okay?"

"Yeah." Andy didn't sound convinced.

"I mean it, Andy. Only people really close to us can be trusted."

"Lauren can be trusted. She's kinda close, isn't she? Even Grandpa said she was nice to come around after the fire."

His father had said something positive to Andy about Lauren? There might be hope in every quarter if only she'd loosen up and give them a chance.

"Dad?" Andy elbowed him. "Lauren's our friend."

Care was still essential. "Lauren's a nice person."

"She's neat." Wriggling, Andy turned to sit, cross-legged, facing Jack. "She likes my pets and she doesn't treat me like a little kid."

Lauren, Lauren. Yet again she'd left him with the comment that she hoped they could enjoy each other as friends. Whatever had happened by the pool was probably a lesson he had to learn. She'd let him know that she was a passionate woman—God, she was passionate—but she wasn't interested in any sort of binding attachment. Clearly, sex wasn't in the cards for Lauren if the partner wasn't someone she thought she could...love? He definitely wanted sex with her. But the rest of what he felt was still hazy except that he knew he liked and respected her.

"Dad, when's Lauren coming over again?"

Jack started. "Uh, I don't know." He couldn't bring himself to say it was possible she never would.

"When the packing plant was on fire she stayed with me."

"I know. We just talked about that, remember?"

"She was nice and she was worried about you, just like I was."

"Was she?" He looked away. Andy wasn't telling him anything he didn't know, but he couldn't sort out what it all meant.

"Are we going surfing tomorrow?"

"I don't know." He felt hollow and he had a hunch there would be only one way to fill that void, which meant he would keep right on feeling hollow.

"You promised." A sleepy drawl let Jack know Andy would be asleep soon.

"Sure I did. After I spend a couple of hours at the farm, we'll go surfing. You can help me work so I can get through faster." He always found things for Andy to do that made him feel useful while they also taught him more about the business.

"Can Lauren come with us?"

Jack turned cold. "I don't think so, son. I expect she's busy."

"We could ask. Maybe we could take a picnic. Rob's folks do that. His mom makes all kinds of stuff. I've been with them."

"I know." And he knew that he was hearing how badly Andy wished he had a mom.

"I bet if I asked Lauren, she'd help us make sandwiches and things."

Jack eased his hands from behind his neck and swung his legs from the bed. "Lauren doesn't swim. I don't think she'd like it at the beach with us."

"She'd be fine." Andy looked wide-awake again. "We could teach her."

The pool by moonlight flashed before Jack's eyes and a picture of Lauren, both with and without the black swimsuit. He averted his eyes. "We'll go by ourselves this time, okay?"

"If you say so. But I bet she'd like it. Then we could come home and have dinner. She said she'd paint a picture of trees to stick on the back of Strangler's aquarium. Maybe she's done it by now."

His father had been right, damn it. Andy was ripe to attach himself to another mother figure. "Lauren told me she's busy all day tomorrow." A necessary lie.

"Oh." Andy wrinkled his nose. "So when's she coming over again?"

"I'm not sure."

"You like her, don't you? I do. And she likes you?"

Jack had the sensation that a noose was tightening around his neck. "I like Lauren very much. She's a good friend. When she's got some spare time I'll invite her over."

"Good." Scooting, Andy pushed inside his bed, turned to punch his pillow, and settled down.

Seconds later, as Jack held very still, he heard the boy's regular breathing.

Whatever was in the cards for him and Lauren, if anything, Jack had better make sure it didn't give Andy ideas about a substitute mother to bake apple pies and join the PTA. Not only was Lauren not applying for that type of position, she'd laugh at the idea.

For once Dad had been right; Andy was vulnerable, and it was his, Jack's, job to put his boy first.

Carefully he left the bed, put off the light and slipped into the hall.

Without deciding what to do next, he wandered out to the pool. He was a lucky man to have a son who wanted little more than to be loved by his dad and grandfather and possibly by a mother figure who was a distant memory now.

Jack rolled up the legs of his jeans, sat on the edge of the pool, and put his bare feet into the water.

He couldn't forget Lauren . . . not ever.

Chapter Twelve

The artist's case standing in the corner of her office served as one more irritation in an already totally irritating and confusing day. The third day of its kind in a row. If she weren't so disturbed, she'd go to the painting class tonight as planned. But she was disturbed.

Lauren got up from her desk and spared the case another glance as she went into the outer office where the accountant was packing papers away.

"Is it going to be all right now?" she asked the bespectacled man who'd been dealing with the books for Contact even before Lauren purchased the firm.

"Looks to be." Sandy-haired, pleasant looking in a nondescript way, Sam Brill was, as he always reminded her, around to keep her out of jail. As far as she knew, the comment was the only joke in his repertoire and since he was a nice man she contrived to laugh each time he used it.

"So we won't need another extension from the IRS? I really don't want to miss the June date they gave us."

"That shouldn't be necessary." Sam never made completely positive or negative remarks. "I'll probably be by for your signature in a few days."

Once he'd left, Lauren surveyed her domain and took some satisfaction from the fact that all terminal operators were hard at work . . . except Susan.

Lauren frowned at the empty chair. Probably in the ladies' room. She went there herself and found no sign of Susan.

Rather than return directly to her office, she went out to the sidewalk to breathe some of the soft warm air of a beautiful afternoon.

Sitting on the edge of a concrete planter ablaze with purple and yellow pansies, she closed her eyes to concentrate on the breeze in her hair. What a perfectly crummy weekend she'd had, followed by an equally crummy Monday.

"Lauren? What are you doing?"

At the sound of Susan's voice, Lauren's eyes snapped open. She blinked. "Hi. Taking a breather, like you. Great out here, huh?" A movement caught her eye, a man leaning to pull shut the passenger door on some sort of low, silver-gray sports car parked at the curb. Dark hair, dark glasses, a lean face. He glanced in their direction and Susan raised a hand in a brief wave.

Lauren crossed her arms and grinned. "Do I sense a lovers' tryst?"

"Hardly a tryst." But Susan sent a longing gaze after the departing car and its driver. "He had a few spare minutes so I came out to talk to him. You don't mind, do you?"

"No, I don't. As I'm always telling you, you put in your time and more. He looks interesting, by the way."

She waited, but Susan didn't volunteer any information.

"Sam Brill's finished. Looks as if the glitch in the return is finally worked out. One more nitty-gritty nuisance over with for a while."

"Good." Susan perched beside her. "Why are you unhappy?"

So it showed. Why she should imagine it might not, Lauren had no idea. She'd never been able to hide her feelings. "The usual," she said.

"Man trouble. Otherwise known as Dan Taylor."

"Dan's not the problem. I can cope with him."

Susan cocked her head. "Jack Irving, then. Did you see him on Friday?"

The innocent expression didn't fool Lauren. "Thanks to you, he found me at the studio."

"He told you I said where you were?" Susan looked outraged.

"No." Lauren smiled. "He said he never betrays a confidence. But it wasn't hard for me to figure out you were the culprit."

"I'm not confessing anything."

"You don't have to. You're a soft touch for a persuasive man, that's all."

"Well, he sounded so..." With an embarrassed laugh, Susan lifted her hair off her neck. "Caught. I'm sorry things didn't go well."

"They did," Lauren said. "At first. Let's drop the subject." Not that she'd been able to stop thinking about it for more than minutes at a time.

"What happened?"

"Nothing.... Oh, darn it, anyway. I've tried to call him half a dozen times today but his secretary keeps putting me off. Obviously he doesn't want to talk to me so I might as well forget him."

Susan turned and tilted her head to look Lauren in the eye. "Do I hear something more than casual interest here?"

"Are you more than casually interested in tall, dark and handsome with the spiffy car?" Lauren responded belligerently.

"Possibly. And I'm not unhappy. You are."

She had a point. "We got along beautifully for a while." An understatement for an interlude that would stay with her forever. "Then we got into discussing deeper stuff and everything blew up in my face."

"He turned off?"

"Yes.... No, I did."

"Ah. Why are you trying to reach him?"

Was she completely sure why? Lauren picked a pansy and shredded its stem. "I think I should tell him I was out of line reacting the way I did and that I'd like . . . I like him and I don't want it to be all over between us. Maybe I want to tell him I think we should give it another chance.''

''Then do it.'' Susan crossed her arms as if a simple dilemma had been solved.

It wasn't simple. ''We're going to start feeling the effect of the clients we've lost before long.''

Susan wound a strand of hair between her fingers. ''I know. But that's not a great way of changing the subject, Lauren.''

''This week I'm going to visit all the people who've terminated and ask some very direct questions. It makes no sense that every one of them refuses to give a reason for taking their business away.''

''I agree. And I think that's the best thing you can do. What are you going to do about Jack?''

The woman was like a bird dog after a kill. ''Forget him.''

''Will that make you happy?''

''No.'' She'd never win prizes for caution.

''Then go after him. Do it today. Tonight.''

''I already told you he won't talk to me.''

Susan got up and pulled Lauren to her feet. ''We've got work to do. Then you've got a mission.''

Lauren sighed. ''What am I supposed to do? Accost the man?''

''Exactly. And I know the perfect safe topic for the pair of you. Discuss business reversals. You've had some problems. So has he.''

''I don't see—''

''I do. Interested doesn't begin to cover that man's attitude toward you. Go tell him you need a shoulder to cry on and order him to cry on yours. There's nothing like shared trouble to bring two people together.''

WHY HAD SHE ALLOWED herself to be talked into this? The sound of the doorbell echoed through Jack's house. If his truck weren't parked in the driveway she'd have been able to hope he wasn't at home.

There was still time to hop back in her car and flee.

"Lauren!"

The door had opened and she looked down into Andy's clear brown eyes. "Hi." Hitching the package she'd brought higher under her arm, she smiled. "Is your dad in?"

"Yeah. Out back reading bank stuff."

"Well...I won't disturb him. I just thought I'd stop by." Stop by an area that was miles from her home and office where she had no reason to go if it weren't for coming to this house. She handed Andy the package and a rolled-up piece of canvas in a rubber band. "These are for you."

He held up the roll. "It's the picture for Strangler?"

"Yes. I promised, remember?"

"Yeah." He fidgeted with the rubber band. "My mom's an artist. In Paris."

Unsure how to react, Lauren caught her tongue between her teeth. "I think I knew that."

Andy rubbed a hand down his jeans. "I got a letter from her."

"That's nice."

"I haven't seen her since I was a little kid."

Lauren cleared her throat. "She must think about you a lot." Ridiculously, she felt tears prickle.

"Nah. I don't think so. But she says she's gonna come and see me." His color had heightened and Lauren saw his chest expand. He was confused, uncertain how he was supposed to feel.

Searching for inspiration, Lauren shifted from foot to foot. "Your mother wouldn't be coming all the way from Paris if she didn't really miss you." Did she also miss Jack? Did he miss her? The sinking sensation was unwelcome.

"Maybe. Dad says—"

"Who's there, Andy?" Jack's voice preceded his arrival at the door behind his son. "Oh."

"Look at this, Dad." Andy quickly unrolled the canvas on which she'd painted a miniature scene composed of rocks and greenery. "This is for Strangler. Isn't it neat?"

"Neat," Jack said, looking not at the painting but at Lauren. "That was nice of you. Andy said you'd told him you'd do it."

"It isn't great. But Strangler's probably not an expert on technique. I used canvas and oils because I thought it would hold up better than anything else. Anyway, I won't keep you."

"Hey, this is something." Andy had ripped the paper off the package. "A book on reptiles. Geez, look at the pictures. Thanks, Lauren. Are you coming for dinner? I found this new spider. My book says it's an okay one to have."

"Lauren's coming in, aren't you?" Jack said. In an open-necked, black polo shirt and dark gray pleated pants, he looked casually appealing.

She jiggled her car keys. "I guess so."

"Of course you are." He put a hand on Andy's shoulder. "Go look at your book. I'll call you when it's time to eat."

Once inside the house and alone with Jack, Lauren straightened her back and reminded herself of her plan. Andy's announcement about his mother's visit had caught her off guard, but it didn't have to change anything tonight.

Jack touched her shoulder. His arms, in the short-sleeved shirt, were tanned and muscular. "Can I offer—"

"No you can't." She interrupted tersely. "I've tried to reach you several times today and you wouldn't speak to me."

"Really. Well, now I guess you know how I felt on Friday."

"Paying me back makes you look small. I thought better of you." He could have been preoccupied at the prospect of seeing his wife after so long... his ex-wife....

"You thought better of me." Jack mimicked her tone in a way that made her squirm. "You sound like a school marm."

"Too bad. You and I have a lot in common. Besides that, we like each other, or I think we do. So we're going to get past the other night's fiasco." Her own boldness surprised her.

"Fiasco?" His face was calm, his eyes questioning. "Funny, I might have called it a lot of things. Fiasco wouldn't have been one of them. I thought it was mostly wonderful."

Her cheeks flamed. "I've come to take you to dinner. Andy, too, if he'd like to come."

"Interesting." He leaned against the wall in the entrance to the living room she found so cool and uninviting. "What is this? A guilt offering?"

Lauren took in a gulp of air. "Guilt? Why should I feel any guiltier than you? We both overreacted."

He seemed to consider what she said. "Maybe you're right. How did you feel afterward?"

"Awful."

"Me too. What do you think we can do about it, if anything?"

"Let me take you to dinner," she said, lifting her chin. "You're having some hard times and so am I. We could help each other without having to end up in bed—" Her face heated again and she glanced around. There was no sign of Andy.

Jack looked at his feet, but not before she caught his smile. "We could help each other. I agree with that much. Sure I'll have dinner with you. We're having meat loaf."

"I'd like to take you out. If we're going to try doing things as equals you should be able to allow me to do that."

"I—" He seemed to think better of whatever he'd been about to say. "Fine. There's a girl across the street who's usually available to sit with Andy at short notice. I'll call her."

"I said he should come, too," she said, suddenly panicky at the thought of being alone with Jack again.

"It's a school night. And he'd rather stick around here, anyway."

WHEN HE REALIZED they were going to Barney Middleton's place, Jack mentally cursed the coincidence but made no comment. With a little good fortune, tonight would be one of Barney's nights off. Otherwise he could imagine the gibes he'd have to endure the next time they met, or, if he was really unlucky, in front of Lauren.

"You do like Italian food?" she asked as they walked beneath the green-and-white striped awning over the door of Grazie. "I haven't been here since... The last time I was here was with Dan, but the food was very good."

He admired her evident determination to be open, regardless of how difficult that might be. "I love Italian food."

Barney was at the reception desk.

Grimacing behind Lauren's back, Jack drew a finger across his throat and prayed Barney would understand and curb the wisecracks.

"Hello," Lauren said. "Do you have a table for two?"

Barney did better than curb the wisecracks. In his best phony Italian accent—a travesty that sounded like a man from the Bronx with terminal allergies—he said, "For you, beautiful lady, the best table in the house." He glanced at Jack as if he'd never seen him before in his life and ushered Lauren ahead.

With a flourish, Barney seated her, presented a menu and whipped the napkin across her lap. "May I get the so-lovely lady something to drink?" Dropping a menu in front of Jack, he continued to ignore him.

"White wine," Lauren said, smiling warmly. "A Chardonnay. How about you, Jack?"

"He'll have Chianti," Barney said as he sailed away.

Jack waited for Lauren to comment on their reception but she'd apparently noticed nothing unusual. Across the room with its sparse Monday-night crowd, he saw Joannie Middleton and knew a moment's anxiety. Joannie made no secret of her conviction that "man was not meant to live alone." Barney went to his diminutive blond wife's side and bent to whisper something. Joannie's eyes met Jack's and she smiled. Then the smile disappeared and she turned her back.

"Not baby-sitting for the renter's child tonight?" He felt awkward, an unusual sensation.

"I did what you did for Andy—arranged for a neighbor to come in."

He looked at her over the menu. "Isn't that her mother's job?"

Her head jerked up. "I... I meant her mother arranged for a baby-sitter."

"Andy really likes you," he said without intending to.

"I really like him, too. He's very natural."

"Melon with prosciutto." The waiter Jack recognized as Colin put a large plate in the middle of the table.

While Colin spoke, Barney poured white wine for Lauren and placed the bottle on ice. He circled Jack, clicked his fingers, and took the Chianti basket Joannie bustled to put in his hand.

Lauren had finally sensed something different. She sat back, her lips slightly parted, and Barney removed the menu from her fingers.

"Did you order this?" She sounded bemused.

Jack cleared his throat. "Er, yes."

Apparently satisfied, she set to work, eating with the gusto he was coming to appreciate.

Jack ate a little melon and leaned on his elbows to watch her over the rim of his wineglass. Her hair shone like black satin. The silk dress she wore was jade green, vivid enough to wash out the complexion of a less vibrant woman. Tailored lines did nothing to detract from a curvaceous body he was having a hard time not visualizing naked.

"I had a tough time not calling you over the weekend," he said suddenly and closed his mouth firmly. This was strange. He'd never been a man to speak without thinking first.

Lauren's beautiful, shy smile wiped out the sensation of having made a fool of himself.

"I'm sorry you didn't give in." Her breasts rose and fell with her deep breath. "I kept hoping the phone would ring and it'd be you."

He speared a slice of melon, cut it mechanically into pieces, and pushed them around his plate. "I'm sorry I avoided you today." This was taking humble pie too far. Later he was bound to regret his rashness.

"I don't blame you. I was a pain on Friday night."

The air felt thinner. "You were beautiful on Friday night. Some things shouldn't be rushed and I was rushing them."

Colin's smooth approach was a relief. "Antipasto," Colin said sonorously. "We have salami and pepperoni, mixed cheeses, olives, artichoke hearts, carrots, cauliflower. The marinade is *Signor* Barney's own secret recipe." He refilled the wineglasses. "Enjoy!"

Jack hardly dared meet Lauren's eyes. He did meet Barney's fatuous grin before he swept into the kitchen.

"This looks great." Lauren rested her wrists to look over the elegant platter. "But there's so much. I don't understand how you told them what we wanted."

He made an airy gesture. At least she hadn't dressed him down for assuming she'd like what he liked. Which he hadn't. Not that she had any way of knowing...

"I don't remember them having set meals here. Is that what you do? Order by number or something? Like a Chinese restaurant?"

Jack cleared his throat and attacked the salami. Around a mouthful he made a more or less affirmative noise.

"Very unusual," Lauren said. "But a good choice."

He made a mental note to let Barney know what he thought of this effort. "You said you were having some difficulties with your business."

"Yes." She drank wine slowly, as if deep in thought. "We've lost more clients than makes any sense. Considering we give good service."

He certainly had no complaints. "Are you stepping up efforts to get new accounts?"

"Yes. That's my domain. I don't always like making sales calls, but with an operation that's still fairly small it makes sense to keep the staffing overheads down as much as possible. And I don't do such a bad job. I always seem to get an interview at least."

"I just bet you do."

"Excuse me?"

Keeping his eyes averted, he drank some of his own wine. "I said I'm sure you get interviews. You're very professional." And if she did cold calls in person, she'd only have to encounter a male to be assured of a hearing.

Joannie Middleton approached. "How is everything?" She rested a hand on Lauren's shoulder and smiled down.

"Wonderful."

"What a beautiful dress. Only someone with your marvelous coloring could wear such a strong color. I envy you."

"Thank you." Lauren smiled as Joannie walked away, then glanced at Jack with a puzzled frown. "Nice woman," she said.

"Yes." The easiest thing would be to explain his long-standing connection with the Middletons, only he'd delayed too long. "Do you have any solid theories on why you're losing business?"

"Uh-huh. I think so." Again she drank, her expression shuttered.

"I wish I had a few answers."

Lauren sat forward. "Ah, yes. More problems?"

"No, thank God. We've got enough to deal with. I've got cleanup going around the clock. That plant has to be rebuilt in record time. But I do keep expecting more trouble. I can't seem to help myself."

Colin glided toward them, holding aloft what resembled a huge, circular, yellow dish. Barney popped from behind him to clear away the existing plates.

The "dish" was a hollowed-out wheel of cheese. "The specialty of the house," Barney said with something close to a giggle. "The giant Gouda shell, filled with the finest pasta." He kissed his fingers.

Shaking his head, Jack crossed his arms. Colin retreated, to be replaced by Joannie with fresh dinner plates. She stood beside Barney as he drew himself up very straight. Hitching back a jacket cuff, he pointed and stated, "*Penne,* with a light cheese sauce, and linguine with clam sauce, naturally. And here we have the fettuccini with marinara, cannelloni stuffed with a spicy beef, *mostaccioli*...ah—" he kissed his fingers again "—with pesto, of course. And vermicelli. A feast."

"For two special people," Joannie said with quiet reverence. "Enjoy."

They withdrew together.

"Weird," Lauren said.

Jack laughed explosively, brought a fist to his mouth but gave up trying to camouflage his mirth. "I should have said something before we came in here. Barney and Joannie are old friends of mine."

"They are?" Lauren looked completely bemused. "You didn't even say hi to one another."

"Well—" he shook his head "—I'm sorry. Eat. Before all this gets cold. The Middletons would never forgive me."

Evidently Lauren decided against further questioning in favor of making a valiant attempt to attack the mountain of food.

"Wow," she said after a few minutes of silent eating. "This is really something. Is it even *on* the menu?"

"Nope. Nothing I eat here ever is. They always decide what I need and they're usually right."

"Nice," she said, wrinkling her nose. "Everyone needs to feel special and they do that for you."

He put down his fork. "You're nice. You say the damn nicest things."

Lauren shrugged, smiling at him. "So do you."

He never remembered feeling with another woman what she made him feel. He realized they were staring at each other but he made no attempt to look away.

Lauren did. "The fire was awful. But surely you won't have any more trouble now."

"Maybe. But I can't quite make myself believe it. I walk around feeling someone's watching me. It's as if there's a way for whoever's done these things to know my intentions almost before I know them myself. I've stopped writing things down at the office. I'm keeping records at home and dealing with transactions directly over the phone. But if there's any delay getting the poinsettia cuttings out, we might as well kiss this year off and look at the worst setback in our history."

Lauren laced her fingers together on the table. "I'm going to believe all the bad times are over for you," she said firmly. "And I'm going to believe you must have had the most unbelievable run of accidents. You've got to do that, too, Jack, or you'll drive yourself mad."

"Exactly what I've told him."

Jack started and turned to find Barney at his shoulder.

"Joannie and I have told Jack that all this trouble is because his stars are in the wrong place," Barney continued seriously. "Only now they've moved and everything's gonna be peachy again. Isn't that right, Jack? Isn't that what we've told you?"

Jack sighed. "Sometimes I don't think you're real, Barn. Why don't you just pull up a chair instead of hovering around, *overhearing?*"

"No, no. Wouldn't dream of it, would we, Joannie?"

"Wouldn't dream of it."

Jack swiveled in the other direction to find Joannie at his left shoulder. He faced Lauren and raised his brows in apology.

"Eat more," Joannie said. "You're too thin, Jack."

"I'm not too thin." Maybe what Barney said about his wife loving him for his body was no joke. "And I can't eat another bite."

"It was so good," Lauren said, straight-faced but with laughter in her eyes.

"Jack's like family to Joannie and me," Barney said. "We go back a long way, right, Jack?"

"Right. I've eaten a lot of pasta."

Barney punched his arm. "You and me got more between us than pasta. I get involved in these so-called civic projects and you help me figure out how to pull 'em off. *After* you tell me I shouldn't be involved."

All true.

"This is a great guy," Barney said to Lauren. "One of the best. They don't make 'em any better than Jack Irving."

Jack closed his eyes. "Are you staying or leaving, Barn?"

"We're leaving," Joannie said. "And we're glad to see two such deserving people together, aren't we, Barn?"

"Deserving?" The echo was out before Jack could stop it.

"Well." Barney made an expansive gesture. "Lauren . . . you don't mind if I call you Lauren? We met once when you were with that louse of... We met some years ago and I feel I know you."

Chewing her bottom lip, Lauren inclined her head.

"Yes," Barney said, turning red. "Anyway, as Joannie and I have said, you're not only beautiful, you're hardworking and . . . and *deserving*. Just like Jack."

"Absolutely right." Joannie nodded her blond head vigorously. "You two don't have any idea how many times Barney and I have said what a good couple you'd make. Both special, good-looking, kind and . . ." She gestured, searching for more compliments.

"Deserving?" Lauren offered.

Holding back laughter, Jack buried his nose in his wineglass and immediately realized his mistake. He began to choke.

A sharp thud in the middle of his back, delivered by Barney, left him gasping for air. "Thanks," he sputtered. "This has been some meal. I hate to suggest it, but maybe it's time I got you home, Lauren."

"You haven't had dessert," Joannie said. "Or coffee. There's ricotta cake, or maybe a little spumoni—"

"No, thank you." Lauren put her napkin on the table. "Jack's right. I do have to go."

"Of course...." Barney spread his hands. "You two young people have other things to do with a beautiful night."

Jack wanted out—now. "Could I have the bill?" He sent a little frown to Lauren who showed signs of saying she was paying.

"This special dinner is on us," Barney said. "And don't argue. We'd be offended, wouldn't we, Joannie?"

"Oh, absolutely. Offended."

"And we wouldn't want that. Good night to both of you."

Lauren got up. "Thank you very much."

Smiling with ice in his eyes, Jack sent Barney a silent warning of discussions to come, and shepherded Lauren from the restaurant.

"Could we walk for a while?" he asked when they set off along the secluded alley that housed Grazie. He felt her shaking beneath the hand he'd rested at her waist. "Are you okay? I'm really sorry about... Lauren?"

"Oh, it was great. Hilarious." Chuckling, she threaded her arm through his. "If I hadn't decided where we'd go I'd think you set me up. They genuinely think the world of you."

"You noticed?"

"I'd always heard Italian people were friendly and wanted the best for everyone, but I never experienced anything like that before."

"I hope you never will again. Incidentally, they're not even Italian."

She looked up at him, the breeze lifting her hair. "No? Well, they do think a lot of you, anyway. They think you're really... *deserving!*"

"Aargh!" He settled his hand on the back of her neck and pulled her against him. "Don't say that again, or else."

Lauren spun away, catching his hand, and broke into as rapid a jog as her high-heeled shoes allowed. "Or else what?"

"I'll think of something." He kept up easily. "To the water?"

"How did you guess?"

The alley opened onto Carlsbad Avenue at Walnut. A short distance took them across the wide road fronting the ocean. "I'm crazy about this place at night." Lauren took her hand from his and went to lean on a railing above the beach.

Standing behind her, he watched her hair blow, and the silky dress flatten to her body. "You make anything fun."

She turned her head abruptly and moonlight glistened in her eyes. Just as quickly, she looked out to sea again. Surf sighed over coarse sand and the salt air smelled fresh.

"Does it bother you that I'm saying how much I enjoy being with you?"

"I don't know how to read you, Jack."

The light that touched her hair cast a satiny streak over the water.

"I'm not very complicated." Moving close, he rested his hand on her back. Gently, he rubbed his fingers up and down her spine and felt her shudder. "I want to be with you."

"We are together."

Exerting the slightest pressure, he urged her toward him. "Someone said men and women can't be friends." Stroking her cheek, he studied her mouth.

"What does that mean? You and I are friends."

It meant he was crazy about her, body, mind, the whole package. "But it doesn't work, does it? Not that way? Is it wrong for me to want you so badly?"

She rested her face in his palm. "Why do you?"

"Why? I wish there was a simple answer. I'm human would be one way of putting it. But there's so much more." He touched his lips to her brow. "There is for you, too. I'm right, aren't I, Lauren?"

"Yes."

"What are we going to do about it? We keep edging closer and ending up with a bigger gap than ever between us. Physically, anyway. Whenever I'm not with you, I want to be. I can't seem to concentrate on much else."

She hugged him so fiercely he steadied her. "I wish I could explain what I feel. It's too soon. That means it's too soon for a lot of things."

"Try explaining." It wasn't too soon for him to feel he'd break apart if he couldn't be with her completely, and soon.

"Okay." Almost roughly, she pushed away. "Yes, I feel there could be something strong—*is* something strong between us. And, yes, not sleeping alone tonight appeals to me. But filling lonely hours, even if you're with someone you like isn't a good enough reason for having sex. Not for me."

He whistled. "You don't pull punches, lady."

"No. And in case that didn't sum it up, Andy's waiting at home for you and I'll be going back to a little girl and a baby-sitter."

Her message was clear: Lauren wasn't interested in a casual anything. "I enjoy honest people." Why couldn't he say exactly what it would take to make things good and right between them? "Lauren, I... I care about you. Will you see me again?"

"I hope so." Her hair whipped across her face and she raked it back. "Probably."

Saying he was happy would be a lie. His body wasn't letting him forget he was a man. "We'd better walk to your car. I wish I'd driven so you didn't have to go so far."

"You didn't invite me out. I invited you." She walked back the way they'd come and he followed.

"How long have the little girl and her mother rented from you?" Making conversation had become very important. The thought of letting her go again made his every step an effort.

"Over a year. It was an accident. But that's a long story. Her name's Cara. She's nine." Lauren raised an animated face. "She's lovely, Jack. Bright, and wise the way some children who haven't had enough time to just be young are wise. She always thinks of the other person first. Most adults have forgotten how to be that way...if they ever knew."

First impressions could be wrong, even second, or third impressions, and from what he was hearing he'd swear Lauren really cared about this child.

"She turned up on my doorstep—" she clasped her hands behind her back "—with Betty, her mother. They thought I had rooms to rent and... Anyway, with Joe gone, I had two empty rooms. The rest's history as they say."

He almost checked his stride. "Joe?"

At the curb, she paused until he was beside her, then turned away, toward a shack that rented surfing gear. "More dull history. Joe was my foster son for six months."

He swallowed. "You never mentioned him." He had to hold the prize for misjudgment.

"There wasn't any reason. I only had him for...for a little while. As soon as his dad could manage, he took him back. Nice kid. He'll do fine, I think, I *hope*." She gave a short laugh.

Jack looked past Lauren. In some ways she was an enigma...actually, in many ways. She seemed lost in thought.

The story went that Lauren hadn't had children with Dan Taylor because she didn't want them. The fact that Dan Taylor and his second wife immediately chose to have a child was supposed proof. Without much thought, Jack stored the gossip away. Now he'd lay bets this lady had always wanted children very badly. He thought over the comments she'd made, searching for hints. With or without anything direct, he was suddenly convinced that for some reason she'd been unable to have a baby. But if she didn't feel like sharing that with him, he certainly couldn't raise the subject.

Lauren still wasn't talking.

In the window of the surfing shack, blown up larger than she was in real life, Silky Harvey posed for posterity in a pouting, bosom-thrusting ad for a wet suit that was unzipped to the waist.

Silky was a good kid. He gazed until the smiling face and blond hair blurred. Kid was the operative. Nice in a fluffy way and with nothing more stimulating between her ears than an overdeveloped certainty that she was sexy. So different from Lauren. Beautiful Lauren who seemed oblivious to being a knockout capable of paralyzing a man's brain.

He realized she'd said something. "I'm sorry, Lauren. What did you say?"

Her face was tilted up to his. For an instant she looked toward the window, then back. "I said we should go." She stepped around him. "It's late."

"Not too late. We could walk a little more, couldn't we? I'd like to know more about Joe."

She evaded his hand. "No."

Puzzled by the sudden change in her manner, he caught her elbow. "Did I say something wrong?"

"No." Her eyes slid away from his to a point behind him.

He twisted around but saw nothing but the shack. "You make a habit of this, don't you? Switching on and switching off?" The despair he felt shook him.

"You should give up on me. I don't even seem to know my own mind."

"Try explaining it to me." His own frustration was a mirror of what he saw in Lauren's eyes.

"I can't. Do you think you could let it go? Could you be patient with me for a while? Again?"

He picked up a strand of her hair and let it slip through his fingers. "I don't seem to be able to do anything else."

Chapter Thirteen

Leaving the office for a short break in the middle of the morning had been Susan's idea. "Thank you for thinking of this," Lauren told her, appreciatively sniffing her espresso. "I didn't realize how badly I needed to get away until I was outside." They sat at one of a group of white wrought-iron tables in front of a café a few doors away from Contact.

Susan squinted into the sun and reached into her bag for sunglasses. "I'm looking for ways to leave Yolande in charge for short periods. She's still tentative about being alone in the office. Anyway, don't pin any badges on me. I've been dying to find out how things went last night."

"You're so good to listen to my woes all the time. But you don't have to today. Just sitting with a blank mind is enough for now."

"Oh, no you don't. I said I'm not up for awards. I'm curious, Lauren. Nosy, if you like. *What happened?* You said you saw him."

"His wife's coming home for a visit."

"He's divorced."

"His ex-wife."

Susan stirred her coffee slowly. "And he made a deal of telling you that?"

"No. Andy mentioned it. Jack never did. Which probably means he thought it would put me off and he'd only think that if he wants to have his cake and eat it, too. In other words, he wants someone as a safe stopgap while he's hoping for a reconciliation when his wife—ex-wife—comes home."

Susan snorted. "You've got quite an imagination. You don't know any of that for sure."

"No. But it's possible." She couldn't bring herself to tell Susan about the way Jack had stared at Silky Harvey's picture last night, like a thirsty man longing for a fresh drink. He'd made her feel every one of her thirty-nine years. She had to stop thinking about him and putting herself in line for another shot at the role of castoff when someone younger and more exciting came along.

"Lauren, don't second-guess the man."

"I'm not. It's obvious, isn't it? I'm not going to make any demands because I'm not looking for anything permanent. That makes me perfect for him." *Was* she second-guessing him?

"What does that make *him?* And are you sure you aren't interested in something permanent, as you put it?"

Lauren stared, then shook her head. "Of course not. Let's change the subject." She wasn't pining for a commitment from Jack, was she? Even the idea frightened her.

"Did you cry on each other's shoulders like I told you to?" Susan continued blithely. "I told you shared trouble is a sure way to form a bond."

"Yes. Evidently nothing else has happened. And, as he said, there's been enough trouble already. From what he said when we were driving—we went out for dinner—they've got every move they intend to make at the farm choreographed. He's dealing directly over the phone with clients and playing his cards close to his chest. And they've got watches posted, and double watches, so there should be no chance for anyone to pull anything." On the trip back to his place the choice had been between silence and safe conversation. They'd chosen the latter.

"I'd love to meet him. He sounds like a smart cookie."

Smart and with an irritating ability to crawl into her every unoccupied waking moment. "Jack's an interesting man. He thinks of every eventuality. I guess he's going to wait for the last moment to announce whatever he's doing from here on. Whatever that means. He says that'll make it impossible for certain kinds of sabotage."

"Being prepared's probably smart, but I don't think there'll be any more incidents, do you? After a major fire that got all that attention, it would be crazy."

As usual, what Susan said made sense. "You're probably right. And I hope you are, for Jack's sake." Not that she expected to be seeing much of him after the cool way they'd parted last night.

A jumping, waving figure caught Lauren's attention. "Is that Yolande now?"

Susan swiveled around. "Certainly is. I was afraid our reprieve wouldn't be very long. She's good in her way, industrious, but her initiative is zero."

"I've noticed," Lauren agreed grimly, already on her feet.

As she drew close to Yolande the woman said, "You didn't have to rush back."

Lauren heard Susan groan but put her hand on Yolande's shoulder. "What is it?"

"Someone named Betty called. She said she's going out for a while, so she'll call again later and you're not to worry."

"Thanks." As far as Lauren could remember, Betty had never called the office and she should be sleeping now.

By the time she reached her desk Susan was closing the door behind them. "I know what you're thinking and don't."

Lauren rounded on her. "You don't know what I'm thinking."

"Yes I do. And you're chewing skin off your mouth. Stop it. Just because Betty calls, it doesn't mean she's going to tell you... Well, it doesn't mean a thing."

She made up her mind. "If anything happens that I absolutely have to deal with, call. I'll either be on my way home or already there. I'll check in myself as soon as I can."

"You're overreacting."

"Maybe. Thanks for being here for me."

All the way home she alternated between feeling guilty for leaving her responsibilities in someone else's hands at a crucial time, and nerve-fraying fear of what she'd find at the town house.

The moment she opened the front door she remembered what should have been her first thought. Cara was out of school for the day.

"Hello," Lauren called. When she listened, instead of a response, she heard the sound of running water.

Relief made her weak. Taking deep breaths, she strode into the kitchen.

Cara, soapsuds swelling around the short sleeves of her blouse, stood on tiptoe at the sink. Absorbed in some task, she hadn't heard Lauren.

"Hi, sweetie," Lauren said, trying not to shock the girl.

Cara jumped and spun around, sloshing water over the floor. Billowing in the soapy water was something green.

"What are you doing?"

"Washing." She rubbed her cheek against a shoulder.

Lauren moved closer. "Aren't those the sweatshirts I gave you?"

"Yes." Cara swallowed convulsively. "I'm not doing anything wrong."

"Of course not," Lauren said gently. "But why?"

"People are proud y'know. Don't blame Jimmy's mom for being mad at him. She's had a tough time. Jimmy's told me all about it."

Lauren pulled out a chair and sat down heavily. "Should I call Mrs. Sutter and tell her it's okay for Jimmy to have the shirt?"

"No!" Cara looked horrified. "She wouldn't like it. It's better not to make her think about it. You can't fix everything."

Sometimes Cara made Lauren feel like the child. "I made things hard for you with those darn shirts."

"Nah. We love 'em. We...we put 'em on at school sometimes. It's just that you gotta do what makes things easy. Some kids say me and Jimmy are goin' together 'cause of the shirts."

"And that bothers you?" Why hadn't she left the damn things in the shop, or just bought one for Cara?

"No. Jimmy and me know we're only friends. Who wants to go with someone? That's dumb."

Dumb, except when one friend or the other wanted more than companionship, or when both of them wanted more, but one, namely Lauren, knew that the moment she gave in to her instincts she'd be on the road to being alone again.

"Don't worry about Jimmy and me." Cara had come quietly to rest a damp hand on Lauren's neck. "When we grow up we're gonna remember each other and we'll feel good about it."

Lauren hugged the thin little body, buried her face against a fragile shoulder. "You bet you will." She closed her eyes against smarting.

"Lauren! I tried to reach you at the office. I was going to call again."

She kept an arm around Cara and turned to see Betty bustling into the kitchen, more dressed up than Lauren had ever seen her.

"Cara—" Betty frowned at her daughter "—I told you to get ready."

Cara moved away from Lauren. "I was doing something. It won't take me long."

"Not now. You'll have to go as you are. It's a good job I packed your bag." Betty tutted and turned to Lauren. "I was going to let you know we'll be away overnight, if that's all right."

That Betty felt she even had to pretend to owe her an explanation pained Lauren. "Of course. Have a wonderful time."

"We will. Come on, Cara. We'll be late."

"But I've got to—"

"I'll finish up for you," Lauren said, smiling. "Run along."

Within minutes they were gone with no explanation.

Lauren felt drained. Cara was slipping away from her; she could feel it. At the sink, she finished squeezing out the sweatshirts and then took them to the dryer in the laundry room. Wise little Cara. She belonged to Betty, not to Lauren. But these trips didn't have to mean anything momentous. Why was Betty so secretive about them?

Dragging, Lauren gathered her purse and headed for the front door. She made it as far as the foot of the stairs. Just for once she'd give herself permission to be human. Let Susan cope for a few hours.

RINGING CAME TO HER dully through the quilt she must have pulled over her head. Pushing her hair out of her eyes, Lauren fumbled for the phone.

Dial tone. But the ringing was still there.

She sat up, shivering in her satin gown.

The doorbell.

Shoving at the covers, she swung her feet from the bed, grabbed the robe that matched the gown and pulled it on as she ran for the stairs.

How long had she slept? She'd decided to go to bed at around three after Susan had assured her everything was under control. The house was gloomy now.

"Coming," she called, wrapping the robe around her and tying the belt. Could Betty have changed her mind about staying away overnight?

Fumbling, she drew off the chain and threw open the door.

Jack Irving, his hands in the pockets of worn jeans, looked at her from beneath the brim of a black Stetson. Grim summed up his countenance accurately.

"May I come in?"

Before she could respond, he crossed the threshold, swinging his shoulders to pass her. "Is anyone home with you?"

"No."

"Did you check through the peephole before you opened the door?"

"N-no."

He looked her over thoroughly. "I could have been anyone. This isn't Disneyland."

She raised her head. "Really? And I thought you were Mickey Mouse."

"Don't be smart. Women alone in their homes get attacked all the time. And most of them don't come close to looking the way you do right now."

Her skin flashed hot. "You have one hell of a way of delivering a compliment. If that's what it was."

"Take it any way you want to. Do you happen to have anything to drink?"

Lauren closed the door and leaned against it. "What's the matter with you?"

He took off his hat and raked at his hair. "This has been a hell of a day. I wanted to see you," he said quietly. "I need to be with you."

Lauren felt her blood drain to her feet. Jack was in trouble. Real trouble. "Come in." She grabbed his hand and pulled him behind her into the kitchen. "Sit there," she ordered, indicating the table.

Settling his hat back on his head and tilting it low over his eyes, he spun a chair on one leg and sat astride the seat, his arms draped along the back.

She couldn't even see his eyes and, as sexy a picture as he might make, there were limits to the potency of any kind of charm. "Take your hat off."

"Huh?" He lifted his chin and squinted out at her. "Oh, sorry. Forgot." The Stetson whizzed across the table to rest in a corner.

Quelling the urge to demand that he tell her what was on his mind, all of it, immediately, Lauren surreptitiously checked to make sure the slippery robe was well in place over her skimpy gown.

"Looks great." Jack hadn't missed a move. "Something to drink would really be nice, Lauren."

Keeping one hand firmly beneath her breasts, she scuffed, pulling a step stool with her, to the cupboard over the microwave. Carefully she climbed up and opened a door. "Yuck. All this stuff must be years old."

"That usually means it's good.

She eyed the selection skeptically. "I do have some jug wine in the refrigerator."

"This isn't a jug-wine situation."

"Okay. Cherry-chocolate liqueur, separated and with what looks like pink syrup floating on top. Galliano with rust around the cap. Ah, crème de menthe. I don't suppose the little brown things floating in it mean anything."

Jack groaned. "Keep going."

"Believe me. It only gets worse." She scrabbled far back and found a cardboard cylinder she didn't remember buying, or receiving as a gift. The top came off easily and she extracted a bottle. "Full. Must be really awful. Glenfid... Glenfiddy-something."

"Glenfiddich. Thank God. Gimme."

Descending as gracefully as possible, she gave him the bottle. "What is it?"

"Single malt. First-class stuff."

"Ah." She tried to sound intelligent. Alcohol wasn't anything she knew much about. "I'll get you a glass."

"Get two. I don't like drinking alone."

"I wasn't aware you liked drinking at all."

"I don't usually." He shunned ice and half filled each of the two highball glasses she gave him. "Sit there where I can see you." He indicated the chair he pulled beside his and she sat down, so close she could see dark flecks in eyes that were the same color as his single malt.

Jack took a long swallow, coughed, wiped his mouth with the back of his hand and closed his eyes. "Medicinal purposes," he muttered. "Have some."

Lauren drank and gasped. A rasping noise came from her throat. She couldn't speak. The liquor burned all the way down, while she struggled to take a breath.

Her eyes were squeezed shut when she became dimly aware of the glass being removed from her relaxing fingers. A thud in the center of her back made her cough—and breathe again.

"You okay?"

Through teary eyes, she saw Jack's wavering face and nodded.

"Don't drink any more. You aren't up to it."

She shook her head.

"It won't be wasted." Still peering at her, he added the contents of her glass to his and sat down again. "You sure you're okay?"

"Yes," she croaked. "Fine."

Jack rested his chin on the chair back and closed his eyes. "Lauren, you ought to kick me out. I'm using you."

Her head cleared. "No you're not." She offered a hand and he grasped it. "Tell me what's happened."

He drank again. "I've been so careful. Whoever did it... Damn it. Someone found out what I thought no one knew, but the truck drivers and me. Oh, honey, I'm not sure I can pull it out anymore."

She waited patiently, stroking his fingers.

"Three Irving trucks of cut flowers arrived at the wholesalers this afternoon," he said. "Those drivers have been working for my family for years. They're absolutely clean. But when the trucks were opened there wasn't a box inside that wasn't full of mutilated blooms. Ruined, Lauren. The whole damn shipment ruined."

Appalled, Lauren got up, pushed the chair aside and knelt in front of him. She took his face in her hands, smoothed his hair. There seemed nothing to say that could come close to telling him how helpless and angry she felt.

Jack rubbed her cheek distractedly with the backs of his fingers. "Someone knew what was supposed to be completely secret—the time those trucks were due to leave. I'd swear they went from the farm in good condition. I'd also swear they left with someone in the back of each truck, working like crazy to demolish the cargo, then waiting for an opportunity to get away."

"No one saw anything?"

"Nothing. Not a damn thing. The police are on to it, but I don't expect any results."

"Oh, I hate them!" She jumped up and paced. "I wish I knew who it was."

"So do I, sweetheart," Jack said.

He sounded different. Lauren quieted, looked at him. He'd called her sweetheart. "It'll be all right," she told him, knowing she was trying to convince herself as much as Jack.

"When you say that I almost believe it. But it's bad, Lauren, really bad. I'm down to pinning everything on Irving's Lava Pearl."

She tilted her head inquiringly.

Jack laughed shortly. "A poinsettia. It's a sport—that's a mutant—out of a chance seedling called Flame Pepper. This will be the first year we offer it for sale. It's beautiful. Red-orange bracts with pearly-cream veins. Short and lush. And it's a state secret as far as I'm concerned, Lauren."

"I wouldn't say anything."

"I know you wouldn't," he said quietly. "You know, all afternoon while I was going through hell, I kept thinking about you. I promised myself I was going to come looking for you as soon as I could. I'm glad I did. So glad."

Her heart skittered, and thumped. "I'm glad, too." She wouldn't burden him with her worries about Cara—not that he was likely to understand.

"Being with you is special," he said, getting up and setting down his glass. "Come here."

Lauren went, slowly, and leaned on the edge of the table where she could see his face. "We all need someone to trust," she said. "If I can be that for you, I'm very glad, Jack."

"You can. You are. From the first time we talked, I felt—I don't know—something different, I guess. Now I think I know what it is."

She thought so, too. He felt the way she did. And she felt... Her stomach dropped and she bowed her head to hide a grimace. Was it possible that Jack could be feeling what she did at this moment? Susan had asked the question: was she sure she didn't want anything permanent with Jack? And she, Lauren, had denied it. *Wrong.* Fear of abandonment aside, she wanted Jack because she loved him, loved him more than she'd ever loved anyone.

Overwhelmed, she turned away, only to have him ease her back, and wedge her between his lean body and the hard rim of the tabletop that pressed into the backs of her thighs.

"Was it okay for me to come?"

Lauren tilted her head, rested a hand on his chest. "It was very okay, Jack. I... There's no one else I want to be with."

He raised her fingers to his lips and kissed them, keeping his eyes on hers. "No one else tonight? Or does that mean there might be other times when I'd be the preferred candidate?"

She smiled, wrinkled her nose. "I guess this is 'fess up time, huh? Well, I'll take a chance. There don't seem to be any times left when you wouldn't be the preferred candidate."

Any vestige of a smile deserted Jack's face. "Those are the sweetest words I ever heard."

Lauren couldn't speak.

"When will your little Cara and her mother be back?" Jack said, his voice husky. He rubbed his hands up and down her arms on top of the smooth satin.

She shook her head.

"Does that mean you don't know?"

"They aren't coming back tonight."

He let out a long breath. "If you want me to go, I will. But if you'd let me, I'd give my soul to stay with you all night. Just to hold you and watch you sleep. You make me believe there's still sanity in this world."

"Doesn't Andy do that?" She'd had to say it.

"Yes, sweetheart. Yes, of course." He used a thumb to tilt up her chin. "See why you're so right for me? You keep me on track. Andy's my anchor, but he's also just a little boy. You're a woman, Lauren, alive, incredibly sensitive and sexy and . . . Say you understand."

"I understand." She understood that waves of desire shivered over and into her and she was incapable of stopping what was happening.

"We can be so much for one another." His breath whispered across her mouth and he kissed her softly, took her bottom lip gently in his teeth, slipped his tongue along the sensitive skin just inside. "I've been waiting a long time for you."

Her body flamed. Jack found her desirable. He wanted to be with her when he was troubled. Surely that could be enough for as long as it lasted.

Jack spanned her waist and lifted her to sit on the table. She kept her knees tightly together, but he leaned his thigh against them, watching her eyes, smiling slightly, until she relaxed and he moved in close, smoothing away the robe and gown to run his hands up to her hips. Still smiling, he slipped his long fingers beneath the lace at the legs of her tap pants and massaged her bottom.

"Jack—"

"Ssh. You are so smooth. So soft."

She wrapped her arms convulsively around his neck and buried her face in the shoulder of his denim shirt.

"Hey," he said, nuzzling the top of her head. "Something wrong?"

"Nothing." Nothing and everything.

"Look at me."

Cautiously she raised her head but kept her eyes lowered. "It's . . ." She inclined her face and fiddled with the shirt buttons. One came undone, and another, and another, until she could pull the tails free and bare his chest.

Thick hair, dark, as she remembered from the pool, spread wide. She stroked, kissed, stroked and bent to kiss the ridges over his ribs and the flat plane of his belly and his navel.

She felt him tremble and the tightening of his fingers on her arms.

"Lauren." His voice was thick. "Is it all right?"

For a moment she didn't understand. Then she nodded. "Yes. Nothing will happen." She knew a moment's sadness that what he couldn't know meant that she was unable to get pregnant.

He worked the panties down, lifted her and slipped them away. Places deep inside her throbbed with need, but still she felt a shyness.

Jack framed her face and kissed her fully, deeply. "Relax, my love. It's right. Let go."

He must be able to feel her tension. "It's been..." Embarrassment thickened her tongue. "It's been a long time," she said in a rush. "Years, Jack."

"Do you know how good that makes me feel?" He gazed into her eyes while he slid the robe from her shoulders. The gown followed, brushed aside under hands that found and supported her breasts. Jack bent to kiss her urgent flesh, murmuring incoherent endearments and nipping, teasing, while she arched toward him in a mute plea for more and more of him.

"I'm glad there hasn't been anyone else since..." A shadow passed over his features. "I'm glad, Lauren. Forget everything, sweetheart, everything but us." Gently, he pulled her arms from the gown and it fell about her waist.

Lauren felt the last vestige of control snap. With fingers that were suddenly sure, she unsnapped and unzipped his jeans. But it was Jack who finished undressing while she touched whatever she could reach of him.

Then he was facing her, lifting her, hooking her legs around his lean hips. For an instant she tried to pull back, but he held her fast against him, used his thumbs to part the tender, engorged folds that awaited him.

Their joining was swift, a wild thrusting. Lauren cried out against the first dull ache of protest at his stretching.

Jack stopped, panting. "I'm sorry. Lauren, I'm sorry. I'm hurting you."

"No." She tried to move against him, to make him move.

He held her still. "Slower, love. It'll be okay, but it's got to be slower at first. Okay." He kissed her neck, her shoulder. "Okay, my love."

She let go, let him take her weight and do the work. And the discomfort ebbed, replaced by exquisite, mounting pain. She didn't have to tell him she was ready. As if his body read hers, he took it all and made it his own.

In the stillness of the kitchen with its commonplace trappings, Lauren found perfect passion and felt a peace that she'd never known.

Jack rested her on the table, his arms a vise around her body, the satin a pool at his feet. "You are beautiful," he said. With long, slow sweeps he stroked her back. "I'm never going to get enough of you, Lauren."

HE WATCHED HER through slitted eyes. She lay on her back, staring at the ceiling through moon-silvered darkness.

If he spoke, she might respond and say what he didn't want to hear, that she didn't feel what he'd finally figured out he felt himself. He could love this woman for the rest of his life, if she'd let him. She hadn't given any hint that she knew that's what he'd been suggesting from the minute he turned up on her doorstep, however many hours ago that had been.

Lauren turned toward him and he closed his eyes. Her touch, feather-light, settled on his neck. With the back of her finger, she skimmed the side of his face, his jaw, and brought her palm to rest against his chest.

He heard a small sound and looked at her. "You awake?" he whispered.

"Yes." She sounded... choked.

"Okay?"

"Mmm. I like having you here with me." She pressed herself to him, wrapped her arms tightly around his neck and buried her face under his chin. "I don't want to think about anything but right now."

Jack stroked her back. "I'm not going to." He didn't want to face the future, but not because he didn't want to think about the two of them. "This is corny. But I feel as if I've come home. This isn't going to be enough, Lauren. I'm going to keep on wanting to be with you." How far did he dare go? How much could he say, suggest, without some definite sign that she felt for him what he felt for her?

She pushed him to his back, rested on an elbow on each side of his head, and kissed him deeply. Her breasts were an insistent, soft pressure on his chest, and where her thighs parted over one of his, he felt her growing moist. He closed his eyes. Caution told him to let her take the lead, but she was ready for him again, and he was ready for her.

Abruptly she arched her back, supported herself on outstretched arms while she looked down at him.

Jack shifted his attention to her breasts. Gently he covered them, then raised his head to kiss first one, then the other. She cried out softly and let her hair fall over his face.

He dropped back, ready to receive her, but she rolled away and lay beside him again, staring at the ceiling. "It's . . . Jack, I'm afraid."

"Afraid of what?"

She stopped him from trying to take her into his arms. "Of myself. Lying here, feeling wonderful and wanted, I got frightened. You know why?"

"Tell me, sweetheart."

"Because there were things I didn't really admit about myself until tonight. I've come close to looking at the truth about the past, but I've always avoided it at the last minute. I—" She sighed and brought his hand to her lips. "I'm not as nice as I've told myself. I used to be able to totally convince myself that I was devastated by my divorce. And I thought it was because I was generous that I was able to keep on being there for Dan when he had problems he wanted to share with me."

He laughed. "You were. And you are. Too generous."

"No, Jack." Her eyes glittered. "I'd started falling out of love with Dan a long time before he walked out on me. Oh, I don't mean I would have ever ended my marriage, but in some ways it was a relief, and by being kind to Dan I'm paying him back for the guilt I feel because I stopped loving him." She rested the back of her hand on her mouth. "That's awful. What must have hurt me most when he finally said he was leaving was feeling I'd been…let go? Told that I was second-best?"

Jack stroked her hair, kissed her shoulder. "You're something. You think everything through so honestly."

Her small laugh was bitter. "Sure. Given enough time."

"But Dan had been drawing away from you. I heard you tell him that on the phone in your car outside the club. He'd been sleeping with Christie. A woman has to sense a thing like that. No wonder you stopped loving him."

"I'm not sure it hadn't happened even before Christie. It was almost as if we were a habit. We *were* a habit."

"With someone capable of giving you all of himself the story would be different."

"Would it? I'm not sure I believe that's possible. Dan once explained to me his theory on monogamy. He doesn't think it works for men."

Jack held himself tightly in check. She wasn't getting his message. "He's entitled to his opinions. He can't speak for everyone."

"I guess not."

He had to break the tension. "Andy keeps asking me to invite you to do things."

"Does he?" She moved her head to see him.

"Yes. He wanted to take you surfing. I told him you don't like the water much, but he said you could make the sandwiches and come and watch."

She giggled. "Already a small version of a grown male with all the role components worked out."

"He just wanted you with us. If I ever get another spare day away from the farm, will you do something with Andy and me?" She was fond of children. He was sure of that now. He'd offer her everything he had to offer and the next move was up to her.

Lauren didn't answer.

Jack frowned. "Lauren?"

"Oh, Jack. Yes. Yes, I'd love to do something with you and Andy. He's the nicest kid." Her eyes crinkled with her smile. "I'll never forget the way he set me up with Jaws."

"Neither will he." Jack laughed and touched the tip of her nose. "He still talks about you being the only girl who isn't afraid of his pets. He talks about you a lot, in fact."

Lauren grabbed his finger and held it gently between her teeth. He leaned to kiss her temple.

"Who's Andy with now?"

"My father. He often spends the night there."

The phone rang.

Jack didn't move. Lauren scooted up to sit against the headboard and turned on the light. Pulling the sheet over her breasts, she picked up the receiver. He felt as much as saw her become very still.

Silently, she handed the receiver to him. By the time he put it to his ear she'd slipped from the bed and gone into the bathroom.

"Hello."

Static and popping preceded the faint voice that said, "This is Mary."

He fell back on the pillows and checked the clock beside the bed. Nine o'clock. "Hello, Mary." He wasn't even sure what time it was in Paris. "How did you find me?"

"Denton suggested I should try this number. I had to talk to you."

He waited. Dressed in a white terry robe, Lauren came from the bathroom and sat in front of a small dressing table. She switched on a lamp and picked up a hairbrush.

"Did Andy get my letter?"

"Yes."

With slow, deliberate strokes, Lauren brushed her hair. In the mirror, her eyes held his.

"Is he excited?"

"Excited?"

"About my coming to see him? I wondered... I'm not sure I should."

He rested the back of his wrist over his eyes. "I'm sure you should."

"Why?"

"Because you said you would, that's why. You don't make contact after so long and get people's hopes up, only to turn around and say you've changed your mind." He felt murderous. The violence of his reaction stunned him.

"I wrote because I was a bit low. Things weren't going so well and suddenly it seemed appealing to come there for a while."

Nothing had changed with her. She was still first, second and always in her own mind. Use the people who love you if it suits you, then shove them away when you don't need them. "Doesn't it still sound appealing to come?" He couldn't bear to have Andy undermined again.

"Well...I'm going to have a show, Jack. Finally, it's happening and I'm so excited. Maurice... Jack, tell Andy something came up, will you?"

"No." Not this time. He was out of excuses. "Look, this isn't the best time to talk. I'll call you later—tomorrow. Bye."

He shoved the receiver into its cradle and threw back the covers. In two strides he was behind Lauren, pushing his hands beneath the robe to knead her shoulders.

She wouldn't meet his gaze.

"That was Mary...my ex-wife."

"I gathered. You asked her how she knew you were here."

"My father gave her your number as a possibility." And later he'd have more to say about that.

"I see." She set down the brush and sat immobile.

"Come back to bed." He bent to kiss her neck.

"I don't think so."

The robe fell open under his hands. Watching her in the mirror, he pulled her back against him, covering her breasts, moving his hips slightly at her back. "Come with me, Lauren."

"You were telling her you wanted her to come."

He turned cold. "Only for Andy's sake."

Lauren stood, ignored the robe that slid to the floor, and faced him. Tears were in her eyes.

"Please don't look like that. Mary has nothing to do with us." His desire for her was something neither of them could miss. "We're what matters. Doesn't that mean something to you?"

She sighed. "It means more than I can explain."

"Same here. But you don't trust me, do you?"

Pink washed her cheeks. "Men haven't given me a whole lot to trust."

"Men?" He raised a brow. "You already admitted the one man in your life who let you down had probably fallen from favor before he dropped the bomb. Does one man who didn't know what he had, or what he was losing, mean the rest of us are no good?"

"No," she said, shaking her head. "But I saw the look on your face when you were talking to her. You were persuading her to come."

He raised his hands to hold her, thought better of it and turned away. "For *Andy*. I can't force you to believe me, but that's the only reason, Lauren."

She rubbed her shoulders.

His attempt at a laugh failed. "Can you believe us? Two people who just made wonderful love, but who don't trust each other?"

"I don't want to feel this way."

"Then don't." He faced her again. "I could say that I wonder if you're the type of woman who'll grow bored with any man after a while. After all, you got bored with Dan."

"It wasn't the way you make it sound."

"Maybe. But I've only got your word for it." If he had to shock her to make her see reason, he would.

"It's true."

He picked up the robe and held it while she slipped it on. "Do you really think I want my ex-wife to visit?" While he spoke, he picked up his jeans and pulled them on.

"I don't want to, but I know what I heard."

"Yeah. Okay. Well, I guess you're going to have to decide what you believe, all by yourself." He was too wound up to think straight.

Lauren laced her fingers together. "It wasn't my ex-spouse who called while we were in bed. It was yours."

"I've spent more than my share of time listening to you and your ex-husband. You're still joined at the hip."

"That's not fair!"

"No," he said quietly and put on his shirt. "None of this is. It's damned stupid. But you don't get it about me, do you? You don't get any of what I've been trying to say to you for hours, or why I'm upset right now."

"Jack—"

"It's okay. It's fine. Just the way it should be. Two people helping one another through some lonely hours. You don't have to be able to really know me, or read my mind. But there's unfinished business between us. Remember that."

She made no attempt to argue, or to stop him from leaving.

Chapter Fourteen

Lauren slammed her car door with enough force to jar her arm to the shoulder. The whole world was so damn high-handed, so ready to be drawn into mean little intrigues.

She needed a few more minutes to calm down before going into the office. Leaning on the hood of the Honda, she took deep breaths. Damn Christie Taylor, anyway. Jealous, treacherous, but without the smarts to carry off her tricks and not get caught.

Another car rolled into sight, sun scintillating off its silver hood. It stopped a few yards from Contact's premises. Within seconds, Susan appeared and ran to the driver's side of the sports car. The tinted window rolled smoothly down and the man Lauren remembered from before smiled up at Susan, who bent to kiss him.

Lauren smiled, folded her arms and looked at her feet. She didn't want to spy.

There was no way to get to the office without being seen. She went to the back of her car and opened the trunk. Within seconds the sleek silver beast slipped past.

"Lauren?"

She winced and shut the trunk, grateful to have found a pile of folders to fill her hands. "Oh, hi, Susan." Looking both ways, she trotted across the street. "Wait till you hear what I just did."

They went into the building together and were soon closeted in Lauren's domain. "You're in a better mood today," Susan said.

Throughout yesterday, Lauren had found it impossible to think of anything but Jack and the previous night when they'd been together. "I'm busy today. And I've got what I want."

Susan settled into a chair. "What would that be? A way to work things out with Jack?"

Lauren already regretted having confided in Susan the day before, but she'd needed someone and Susan had been her only choice. "I just came from seeing Mrs. Arthur Wakefield and I was right."

"Right?" Susan looked blank.

"Mrs. Wakefield had been told by a little bird that Contact wasn't to be trusted, that we tend to be careless with privileged information."

Susan shot to her feet. "What the hell does she mean?"

"Calm down, calm down. It's all right. All I had to do was figure out the common denominator between our defectors and I was home free."

"I'm not following you."

"Catering services, beauty supply firms, a beauty salon, a tanning salon, one of the best children's clothing shops in town and on and on. Ring any bells?"

Susan thought. "No."

"Christie Taylor!" Lauren swung around to stare through the window. "It was the clothing store that gave me the idea. Then I took a chance. I managed to confirm that Christie uses We Serve U. And that Mrs. Wakefield socializes with Christie. Then I followed up and it was easy to find out Christie's connections with the other businesses."

"What did you do then?" Susan sounded incredulous.

"I went to Mrs. Arthur Wakefield and told her I know Christie had suggested she no longer use us."

"Good grief. What if you'd been wrong?"

"She'd already quit us. How much more egg could I have on my face? Dan wouldn't have allowed Christie to take things any farther. But Mrs. Wakefield folded like a house of cards. Christie told her we run around chatting about our clients' business to anyone who'll listen."

"But what difference is it going to make?" Susan still didn't sound enthusiastic.

Lauren spun to face her. "I reminded Mrs. Wakefield that her husband has his sights set on public office in this town and that it wouldn't do for his wife to be linked to malicious gossip. She couldn't agree with me more. The lady is very sorry and is going to make sure everything possible is done to put right the terrible wrong that's been done us. She's going to speak to the other clients personally," Lauren finished triumphantly.

Susan shook her head. "Sick," she muttered. "I'll never figure out why Dan married the little toad."

The door opened and Lauren jumped. Dan marched into the room, glaring at Susan who planted her hands on her hips and showed no sign of leaving.

"I want to talk to you," he told Lauren. "Alone."

"I'll stay," Susan said belligerently.

Lauren looked at the ceiling. "I don't want to talk to you, Dan. And if you say one thing out of line, you're gone. I can handle things, Susan. Thanks for the support."

"I don't think I should leave—"

"Go ahead," Lauren said quickly, raising a brow significantly. "I expect you'll be getting some interesting calls."

A smile spread slowly over Susan's face. "Yes." She eyed Dan. "I'm looking forward to them."

As soon as the door closed behind Susan, Dan advanced on Lauren. "You're not going to like what I intend to say."

She smiled tightly, oddly sorry for him. Evidently, news traveled even faster than she'd thought in this town. Someone must already have told him about Christie's vendetta.

"Why don't we sit down, Dan? Would you like some coffee?"

He frowned. "No. You know I don't drink coffee."

Lauren sighed and went to the coffee maker to pour herself a much-needed cup. "I seem to have forgotten a lot of things about you. There isn't any need for me to remember, is there?"

"There's no need to be nasty. I'm not staying. I just want to warn you about Jack Irving."

She turned, almost spilling from her mug. "What do you mean?" Jack was a subject burned permanently into her brain, she thought of little else, but Dan was the last person she intended to discuss him with.

"You two have been getting pretty tight."

Lauren realized her mouth was open and she closed it firmly.

"He's not right for you," Dan said. "I'm only telling you this because I care—"

"What happens to me?" Lauren finished for him. "How dare you? Get out!"

"Now, Lauren. Calm down. If there's one thing I can't stand, it's a hysterical woman." His chin came up and he looked down at her with those familiar, striking blue eyes—eyes that showed he considered himself superior in intellect and that the possibility of being wrong never occurred to him.

A deep breath, intended to calm her, only served to stop her from shouting. "I wonder how many women, at this very moment, are being told they're hysterical by insecure men who want to control them. Off you go, Dan. The end. Finish."

"Don't be ridiculous. When I asked if you were seeing Irving you didn't deny it."

"I would have if I'd known you were going to make the subject your business."

"You told me how bad business has been for him."

Lauren leaned on her desk. "No, I didn't. You told me you'd heard a lot of rumors about Jack having difficulties. I didn't disagree." And in the future she wasn't going to be having any personal conversations with Dan. "I've got work to do."

"It is true that he lost a whole shipment, isn't it?"

"This discussion's over."

"You said so. I know it's true. And I know he needs money. Has he talked about money with you?"

"Talking about other people's business runs in your family, doesn't it?" Lauren said, crossing her arms. The statute of limitations on being nice had run out.

Dan, immaculate in a light gray suit, appeared to turn over her comment. "Answer my question about Irving and I'll let that pass."

"But I won't." In a few succinct sentences, she told him about Christie's meddling. "For old times' sake I don't intend to take any legal action," she concluded.

For the first time in her memory, Dan appeared at a loss for words. He pulled a pack of cigarettes from his inside pocket and sat down in front of her desk.

"I prefer people not to smoke in here."

"I'm not just people." But he put the pack away.

The prick of pity Lauren felt quickly died. "It's time you were, to me—long past time. Goodbye, Dan."

"Lauren—"

"No. There's not going to be any changing my mind this time."

He gripped the arms of the chair, searching her face for any sign of weakening. "You really mean it." Pushing himself upright, he straightened his jacket. "So be it. But don't say I didn't warn you about Irving."

Disgusted, Lauren went to sit behind her desk. Shading her eyes with a hand, she bent over her papers and, after an interval, heard the door open. From the outer office came the muted patter of keyboards and the sound of her operators' voices. Dan hadn't even said he felt badly about what his wife had tried to do.

The door closed.

Letting out a sigh, Lauren fell back in the chair and threw her pencil down—and looked up at Jack Irving.

"Been having another cozy chat with ex-hubby?"

She couldn't think of a thing to say. Dressed in worn jeans and a light denim shirt open at the neck and with the sleeves rolled up past his elbows, he looked as if he'd come from helping clear charred debris at the packing plant.

"Commiserating with him, were you? He must have broken his neck getting here after I kicked him off my land."

"I don't know what you're talking about."

"Sure. You didn't tell Dan baby I'm in so much trouble I don't know where next week's grocery money's coming from. You didn't tell him how badly devastated we've been by the fire."

"Hey, wait a minute." She got up and walked around to stand in front of him. "Just a minute. I don't know what brought this on, but there isn't any one in town, or a lot of other places, who doesn't know about the fire."

He came a step closer. "And the flower shipments? Does everyone in town know about something I told you yesterday? You didn't mention that to Dan?"

Her blush was instant.

Jack's laugh was unpleasant. "What did you do? Wait just long enough for me to be out of your bedroom and call the guy? Did you tell him I was ripe to make a cheap sale on a bundle of land that's been in my family for generations?"

"I admit I mentioned the shipments when he called this morning about—about nothing in particular. And I'm sorry. I should have been more careful, but it never struck me..." Maybe she deserved criticism for being too trusting, but not for maliciousness. "Do you mean Dan came and tried to buy property from you?"

Jack scowled and averted his face. "As if you didn't know. That wasn't the guy's ghost I just passed. Don't tell me he wasn't giving you a progress report. He *told* me, Lauren." He shoved his hands in his pockets and stared at her. "He told me he knew from you how bad things were and so, as a gesture to a friend of yours, he was offering to take some property off my hands."

"Jack—"

"*Let* me finish. Of course, what he could offer wouldn't be top dollar because he'd be making a long-term investment 'at best,' taking a flyer for a *friend* and hoping he could come up with a way to turn a *small* profit in the future. But at least I'd get some of the operating capital I obviously need right now. I almost puked."

"I knew absolutely nothing about this." And she didn't know what she felt more strongly—amazement at Dan's underhanded tactics, or fury with Jack for believing she was involved.

"You can't let him go, can you?"

Lauren flinched, stepped back, and came up against the desk. "That's not fair. I told you . . . I was honest with you about Dan."

"And I trusted you with things I haven't told another soul." He regarded her steadily. "Do you still love him?"

Lauren made fists at her sides. She felt the sting of tears. "How can you ask that?"

"I *am* asking. You shared things with him that I thought were between the two of us."

"They were.... They are. I... Jack, I..." Why couldn't she tell him she loved him?

"When it comes right down to it, you don't have any defense, do you?" Jack made a disgusted sound. "I'm out of here."

He strode from the room, closing the door firmly behind him.

"Jack!" But it was too late. Just as it had been too late last night when she'd finally run downstairs only to find he was already driving away.

MIRRORS DIDN'T LIE? Lauren twisted from the mirror on her dressing table. She wasn't young anymore. But neither was she old. There were lines where once the skin had been smooth, but her face would be described as good, even interesting. And although she didn't like everything about her body, it, too, was good, fit.

But Jack Irving was younger, eligible, possibly still in love with his ex-wife and, if not, would undoubtedly find it easy to find someone younger and more exciting than Lauren Taylor.

The house was silent. She'd come home to a note from Betty saying she had the night off and had taken Cara out for a few hours.

Dressed in sweats, Lauren left her bedroom and started downstairs, in time to meet Betty and Cara coming in. Betty carried a brown paper sack, Cara, a huge bouquet of flowers.

Lauren frowned. "What's going on?"

"These are for you." Cara dumped the cellophane-covered blooms in Lauren's arms. "And Mom's got champagne."

Lauren looked questioningly at Betty, who ducked her head and hurried into the kitchen. Cara's hand, slipped into hers, made Lauren jump.

The girl smiled up at her, a whimsical smile with her lips pulled in. "Come on."

Lauren allowed herself to be led into the kitchen. Betty had set two wineglasses on the table and was struggling with the champagne cork. "We're going to drink a toast." For a woman with something she thought should be celebrated, Betty sounded miserable.

"Come on," Cara whispered, urging Lauren to a chair. She took the flowers back, half filled the sink and dumped them, cellophane and all, into the water. "We gotta find a vase."

The cork finally popped, shooting across the room. Cara hunched her shoulders, never taking her gaze from Lauren's face.

Very carefully, Betty filled the two wineglasses and then poured a small amount of champagne into a juice glass. This she gave to Cara.

Lauren's heart beat so hard she felt sick. "What are we celebrating?"

Betty stood up very straight, her face flushed. "The flowers are because you've done so much for Cara and me. And the champagne's because I wanted you to be glad for me and for Cara. I'm getting married again."

AT THE TAP on her door, Lauren rolled away, toward the window. There was nothing else to be said, nothing she could say without crying and, so far, she'd managed not to do that in front of Betty and Cara.

The tap came again, and, at the same time, the door slid open, then closed again.

She felt the covers at her back lift, and a small, bony person slipped in behind her. "I listened outside," Cara said. "I've been crying, too."

Lauren squeezed her eyes tightly shut. Evidently Betty's romance with a policeman she'd met through her job had been blossoming for months. Now he'd accepted a job as a sheriff in a small Wisconsin town and wanted nothing more than to live a quieter life there with Betty and Cara as his family.

Cara shook her shoulder. "Jimmy and me are gonna write. You and me can write, too."

"Sure." And she should be too glad for the child to be sorry for herself. "It's wonderful, Cara. You and your mom, and Bill, you're going to be a family and that's what you need most."

"He's nice," Cara said. "He took us to see Gram. His mom lives in San Diego and we went there. She likes me."

"Of course she likes you."

"Mom helped me clean my room this afternoon."

Lauren couldn't speak.

"She knows you're gonna feel sad so everything's gonna be gone before you come home tomorrow." Cara gulped. "Is it all right if I leave Sam?"

Lauren reached to turn on the bedside light and sat up. It no longer mattered that Cara would see the tears.

Cara sat up, too, and leaned against Lauren. In her arms was the most decrepit, the most loved of her stuffed animals—a bear worn shiny and hairless by years of cuddling.

"Oh, you can't leave Sam behind." Lauren laid a finger on one of the bear's mismatched blue-button eyes. "Before you knew it, you'd be missing him so much I'd have to send him to you."

Cara raised her pointed face. "No. Things get lost in the mail. You look after him and then I'll have to come back and visit him one day."

Chapter Fifteen

"It's true, then?" Matt Carson asked.

Jack glanced at Len Gogh and back at Matt. The younger man had never been someone who'd shown signs of wanting to know people. Jack certainly didn't know him—and Len, in his noncommunitive way, had made similar comments about his second-in-command's social skills.

"Matt—" Jack struggled to keep calm. "Look, the fact is our backs are against the wall and we're going to have to come out of this any way we can. Irving's isn't going to be written off as history."

Matt, tall, slim, dark-haired and with an angularly good-looking face, shoved round, wire-rimmed glasses up his nose and settled expressionless hazel eyes on Jack. The baggy jeans and loose brown shirt he wore blended into the background with the greenhouse from which he'd just emerged.

Silently Len handed over several photographs of poinsettia.

"Son of a bitch," Matt said. He peered closely, then thrust the photos at Jack. "These are shots of Lava Pearl."

"Wrong," Len said tightly. "That's what we're telling you. They're shots of what look like Lava Pearl. Flame Talon is what Edgerton's are calling this one."

Matt let out a long, tuneless whistle. "And they've beaten us to it. Right? They've got it on the market first?"

"Yeah." Jack shuffled the photos. "I can't believe it. Damn, it's going to be hard to come back from this one."

"That's it." Matt threw up his hands. "Count me out. I'm gone."

"Just like that?" Jack shook his head. "You're needed here."

Matt pulled a floppy canvas hat from his back pocket, rammed it on his head and pulled the brim down around his ears and eyes. "Three years' work down the tubes is all the prodding I need. I'm sorry for you, Jack, but I can't help. I'll be clearing out of Carlsbad now."

"And going where?" Len asked. His neutral voice didn't fool Jack. Len thought Matt was escaping a difficult situation and Len wasn't a man who'd be likely to approve of quitters.

"Home for a start," Matt said, walking away. "Back to Montana as fast as I can make it. I've already been approached for a professorship in floriculture. I guess I'll take it."

Standing with Len, Jack watched Matt walk away. "I never understood the guy," he muttered. "But he's good at what he does."

"Yeah." Len pulled a stick of gum from his pocket, unwrapped it and stuffed the wad into his mouth. "Look on the bright side. We're going to need every penny we can save and he was expensive."

Jack only half heard what Len said. A familiar red Honda wound its way up the track. He should feel frustrated at the sight of that car, furious at the prospect of having to deal with the biggest dilemma in his life—even bigger than the disaster that had smashed down around his ears this morning—but what he felt was a lifting of the blackness simply at the thought of seeing Lauren.

"My wife and I live very simply."

"Hmm?" Jack realized Len was talking to him.

"Cecelia sells every piece she makes. Somehow or other her pottery's become some sort of status symbol in the art world."

"I'm glad," Jack said politely. Lauren got out of her car and, amazingly, Andy appeared from the passenger side and pointed in Jack's and Len's direction.

"Anyway," Len continued, "with no kids and no expenses to speak of, I can afford to work without pay for as long as it takes."

Jack turned to him, momentarily speechless. "That's not necessary."

Len sniffed and hitched at his overalls. "It may be. We'll pitch in, Jack. We'll pull it off."

If he hadn't been unsure how the other man would react, Jack would have embraced him. "Let's take it a day at a time. Thanks, Len."

"Gotta go." Evidently Len wasn't as concerned as Jack about the effect of his actions on others. He thumped Jack on the back and ambled away.

Lauren and Andy had moved from sight behind the open trunk of her car. Andy was supposed to be at his grandfather's house where he often spent Saturday mornings. Jack started walking, but moved out of the way as Matt Carson drove by in his ramshackle green truck with sagging wooden railing rigged atop the bed.

The truck drew to a stop in front of the Honda. Lauren appeared, waved apologetically, and moved her car to the side of the track to allow Matt to pass.

Jack reached the Honda as Lauren got out again. She glanced over her shoulder. "Who was that?"

"Matt Carson. He's my...until this morning he was our poinsettia guru. Why?"

"No reason." She faced him and the uncertainty in her eyes made him want to grab her and just hold on. "I just wondered."

"He was rude," Andy said, carrying what appeared to be a picnic basket. "He told Lauren to move her... He said to move her car fast," he finished, coloring slightly.

"Figures," Jack said. "He's in a hurry to get back to Montana—today by the sound of it."

"Andy," Lauren said, "would you take the basket into your dad's office?"

"Well... Yeah, sure." He caught his father's eye. "I was walking over here from Grandpa's and Lauren saw me. She gave me a ride."

"I hope that was all right," Lauren said, resting a hand on the back of Andy's neck. "I told him I didn't think I qualified as a stranger."

"You don't," Jack said, unable to stop staring at her. "We'll be right in, Andy."

Once the boy was gone, Lauren stood in front of Jack. She pushed back hair that was blowing in her eyes. "What I'm doing is out of character," she said simply. "I decided maybe it's time I tried something a little daring."

In tennis shoes, red walking shorts and a baggy white cotton shirt, with her legs bare, she looked young and vulnerable.

"Daring how?"

"Forcing a confrontation. I've never been good at that."

Jack screwed up his eyes against a sudden squall that whipped fine rain into his face. "Your timing couldn't be worse." Even if he did wish he could take her into his arms and pretend the world was a wonderful, safe place.

"I'm sorry." Lauren pulled in the corners of her mouth. "I called your place and your housekeeper said she was there to drop off dry-cleaning or something."

That sounded like Bernice, always ready to spill her own and his business to anyone.

"She told me you were working today. So-o, I decided to bring a picnic lunch. Bernice said you don't eat properly out here."

"Bernice says too much." But maybe he should thank his housekeeper, grab the woman in front of him, and kiss her until he forgot he might be on the verge of bankruptcy.

"I could just go away again," Lauren said. "But you do have to eat. And now, since Andy's here, he does, too. And then, if you're interested, I think the least we owe each other is a chance to say our piece. We've got unfinished business, Jack. I don't like that."

"Neither do I." And he admired her guts. The effort this was costing showed clearly in every tense line of her body. "Let's get inside out of the rain."

They ate in his office and he found he took second place to Lauren in Andy's attention. Lauren didn't appear to notice that all Andy's remarks were aimed at her. The two talked about Andy's menagerie, and soccer, and Mr. Baggs, Andy's hated math teacher.

"Do you know Cara Flood?" Lauren asked suddenly.

Jack noticed the tone of her voice changed, lowered, and she distractedly wrapped the remainder of her sandwich in her napkin.

Andy's brow puckered, then cleared. "Yeah. She's a whiz. Even Baggsy leaves her alone."

Lauren nodded. "Cara's going to do well." She fell quiet.

"Jimmy Sutter's her friend. He's okay, too."

"Cara's moved away," Lauren said and Jack saw the corners of her mouth twitch.

"Yeah?" Andy's mouth was full of cake.

Jack frowned. "Why don't you take a piece of that out to Len? He's probably in Sixteen." Much as he'd like to just sit and observe these two, he was going to have to figure out what direction to take in the months to come.

Within seconds, Andy had left with a sandwich and a huge piece of cake for Len.

Lauren began repacking the basket. "I've obviously chosen a bad time for this," she said. "But maybe there wouldn't be a good one."

He hated the flat, empty feeling the thought of her leaving brought. "Thank you for coming," he said. "We'll talk. We do owe each other that much. But—" He covered his mouth. There was no reason not to tell her what had happened, but he didn't want to hear the saga aloud again.

Lauren looked at him sharply. She straightened slowly, a crease forming between her brows. "Something else has happened," she said, gripping the arms of her chair. "You said my timing was bad. Why?"

"Because, metaphorically speaking, I got kicked in the teeth this morning. It's going to take years for me to climb out again, if I ever manage to do it at all."

"What—"

"Don't ask." He opened the top drawer of his desk, took out two sheets of paper and pushed them toward her. "These tell the story. They came in overnight. Then these arrived by courier this morning." He fished the crumpled photos from his pocket and threw them down.

Lauren began to read. "Flame Talon?" She glanced up at him and back at the first sheet. "Edgerton's in Florida producing sport. Flame Talon," she read aloud. "Photos to follow. We've already advertised product. Name change won't be problem. Can't risk unreliable delivery. Cancel Lava Pearl. Will advise on other orders."

Jack waited for her to raise her face again. "Final straw," he said. "That's the first of a rash of cancellations we're probably going to get. I'm going to be building from scratch, or trying to."

"I don't get it." Lauren stood up. "Why should this Flame Talon affect you?"

He snorted and pushed a photo into her hand. "That's Flame Talon. Describe it to me."

She stared down. "Orangy red," she said very softly. "With cream veins. Oh, Jack, how can this be? This is the same as Lava Pearl, isn't it?"

"Sure looks that way. And I can't tell you how it happened, except that it seems like I've gathered a lifetime's bad luck in a couple of months. Unfortunately, customers have been alerted to the sport. When I warned them we could be a bit patchy with delivery, they were naturally disappointed, but we could have been up to full production by next year. Only along comes this Florida outfit with something that looks like a duplicate and they're ready to step right into our shoes. Uncanny. And I can't do a thing but retreat and regroup."

"It won't affect the other varieties you produce, will it?"

She was bound to see all the possible ramifications. "You see what that customer says? Will advise on other orders. We're in limbo. Edgerton's could push their advantage. They must think they've died and gone to heaven."

"Or gotten very lucky," Lauren murmured. She looked at the second piece of paper. "They came in under your price, too? It's so close. How could that happen?"

"Damned if I know." He felt cold, and tired. But having Lauren here was more comfort than he'd hoped for. "The response came in on the service. It was waiting for me this morning. I guess that means Edgerton's got their prices out yesterday and they just happened to be barely lower than ours. Add that to the other factors and we don't look good at all—even with customers we've had for more years than I've been alive."

Lauren dropped the memos and the photo back on his desk and sat back, staring into space. "Service? You mean my service?"

"Uh-huh. Of course. With the time differences across the country I often get messages overnight. The customer likes that option."

"Of course." She chewed a knuckle.

Jack sat forward. "What are you thinking?" As he waited, she appeared to become paler. "Lauren, what is it?"

"I've got to go."

He stopped her before she reached the door. "What the hell is wrong with you? Tell me."

"Please." She breathed rapidly through her mouth. "You tell me one thing, then just let me go."

"Lauren—"

"I'll be back. I promise." She clutched his arms now. "It wouldn't be possible to... How would you deliberately copy someone else's special poinsettia? Are they hybrids or whatever you call them? Do you keep records about them?"

"They aren't hybrids." His stomach knotted. "It's what they call bud mutation. And it's complicated, Lauren. Sure there are records, but I guess the only way you'd get an exact copy would be by getting hold... That's not possible. No one could have taken cuttings without Matt noticing. He watched over everything as if they were his kids. No, this is just one of those crazy things that can happen."

"And the fact that it happened after you had so many other things go wrong has made it perfect for these other people, because you don't have the resources to fight back right now?"

He nodded.

"And Edgerton's timing their pricing quotes and probably other things just right, tied the whole package up for them?"

Suddenly incredibly weary, Jack nodded slowly. "It sure did. Are you making some other point?"

Lauren opened the door. "I hope to God I'm not. I'll get back to you."

PEOPLE COULD BE PULLED into situations over which they had no control. Then it could become difficult, or impossible to get out. That had to be the explanation. Or she could be completely wrong and her whole theory was a myth.

She'd only been to Susan's apartment in Oceanside once. When Lauren left Vista Freeway, she drove slowly north, feeling her way. In the misty rain, the landscape appeared sodden brown.

Via Clara. "Darn it." The street sign caught her eye as she drove by and she found a place to turn around.

What if she was wrong? She took long, slow, calming breaths. Discovering she was wrong was exactly what she should hope for.

Susan lived on the upper floor of a house owned by an elderly woman. A separate entrance had been made via an outside stairway.

Lauren parked beside Susan's decrepit brown Dodge and turned off the Honda's engine. Jack's face was what she had to keep before her, the way he'd looked when she left him: dully angry, disappointed, resigned. If she could change that, she would, even if it signaled the falling of the curtain on any hopes she still had for the two of them.

If she *was* right, no more time could be wasted.

Susan opened her door before Lauren could ring the bell. "Lauren?" She looked surprised and pleased. "Hey, what a surprise. Come on in."

The apartment was small and threadbare, but very clean. Lauren stood in the middle of the sitting room where a Paganini violin concerto played softly from a tape deck. The choice of music surprised her. But then, there was very little she really knew about Susan Bailey.

"Coffee?" Susan asked. "Or a drink? I have wine or—"

"Nothing, thanks."

Susan bit her lip. "I'm sorry about Cara, Lauren."

"You already told me that. So am I."

"You're lonely, aren't you?"

"Yes." She was wrong. She had to be. "I'm trying to keep too busy to think about it."

Susan smiled and straightened the cushion on a green velvet chair. "Sit down. What were you doing? Just driving around? I'm glad you came here."

Lauren turned away. Yes, she missed Cara—so much it hurt—but what was happening here could eclipse even that. "How's Matt Carson?"

"He's..."

In the silence that followed, Lauren pressed a fist to her mouth. She could scarcely breathe. The man in the green truck had seemed so familiar; the way he'd stuck his head out the window. Sitting in Jack's office, she'd mentally replaced the round-framed wire glasses with dark lenses, removed his floppy hat, and then she'd been almost sure. Now there was no doubt.

Susan walked around her, a puzzled smile on her lovely mouth. "I don't remember telling you his name."

"You didn't. Oh, Susan, how could you do it? How could you take privileged information and give it away? That's what you did, isn't it? You copied messages meant for Jack and gave them to Matt Carson."

"I—" Susan backed away. "—No. Matt's good. He's done all the work out there and he deserves to get more for that than a pat on the back while Irving's takes all the credit."

"Oh my God." Lauren sat down abruptly. "You encouraged me to keep on seeing Jack. Then you asked questions and I answered them. I thought you were my friend."

Susan spread her hands. "I didn't know you'd meet him. That was chance. And I already knew most of what you told—" Her hand went to her mouth.

"You knew about the awful things that happened before I did," Lauren said quietly. "But I was the one who warned you that Jack would be sending messages himself at night."

"He always did that!" The panting noise Lauren heard turned to jerky little sobs. "Matt says Jack's going to be okay again in a year or so. This is Matt's one chance, that's all."

"And where do you come into this? How is Matt's one chance going to affect you?"

"We're getting married." She began to cry. "Does Jack Irving know?"

"Not yet. He will."

"Don't," Susan begged. "I'll tell Matt he's got to stop now. He left for Los Angeles last night. When I talk to him, I'll make him stop and we'll go away. He'll be back in a few days."

"What exactly is he supposed to stop?"

Susan sank to the edge of the couch. "All he wants is to start his own farm outside L.A. He's already got the land. He used the facilities at Irving's to do some research for what he's going to raise. He won't be in competition with Jack . . . not really."

Lauren gritted her teeth, trying to sort through what she was hearing and how it might connect to what she'd seen earlier. "Matt left last night?"

"Yes. I gave him . . ."

"You gave him copies of some messages that came through Contact."

"Yes." Susan's voice was barely audible.

"Do you know what they meant?"

"No. But Matt said it was time for him to leave for a while."

"And what about you?"

"When he comes back, he'll settle things here and we'll go away together."

Lauren struggled to stay calm. "Do you have his address in L.A.?"

"No." Susan laced her fingers tightly together on her knees. "Matt said it was best that I didn't."

"Susan, how could you want to be with a man who would set fire to part of another man's livelihood? What if someone had been killed in that plant?"

"Matt didn't have anything to do with that!" Susan jumped up. "He was as upset as anyone. He told me."

Lauren stared, incredulous. "And he didn't have anything to do with any of the other bad things that happened to Jack?"

"No! All he did was raise some sort of plants. Starters, he called them." She paced. "He was upset about all those things."

"Because they weakened Jack's business?"

"Yes. Exactly. Matt said Jack wouldn't have much to fight with for a year or so. But all I did was give Matt copies of messages so he could time some of the things he was going to need to do to get going himself."

"And you didn't think that was wrong?" Lauren was aware of how urgent it was for her to get to a phone, but not without all the facts. She had to ask one more question. "How often did you give messages that referred to prices?"

"I don't know. Sometimes."

"Like last night?"

Susan rocked rapidly. "Yes. There was something like that last night."

"And then Matt left for L.A.?"

"Yes."

She rushed to the door and outside.

"Lauren!" Susan was on her heels, running down the steps. "What are you going to do?"

Lauren opened her car door and paused. "I'm going to find a phone. What you do is your business... for now. Matt Carson didn't leave town last night, Susan. I saw him less than two hours ago. He'd just told Jack he'd be leaving today. For Montana."

Chapter Sixteen

Lauren put a mug of coffee in front of Susan and returned to the swivel chair that had been Cara's favorite.

"Thanks," Susan said. She picked up the mug and scrunched into a corner of the couch. "I wanted to see you, but I didn't know if you'd even talk to me."

"Staying angry was never something I was good at," Lauren said. "If I had been it wouldn't have taken me three years to tell my ex-husband to stay out of my life." Even now, while she despised what Susan had helped cause, she couldn't help feeling sorry for the woman. But she hadn't expected Susan to turn up on her doorstep at seven in the evening, without a coat, and damp from the drizzle that had seemed perpetual for three days.

"The police came to see me a couple of hours after you left. I thought they'd arrest me or something, but they just asked lots of questions and said I shouldn't try to leave the area. Then they came back again yesterday and asked more questions about Matt."

Lauren used a foot to rock herself back and forth. "Did they tell you anything that's happened?"

"No. I hoped you would, though. What does Jack think they're going to do about Matt?"

"I don't know." She lowered her eyes. Since her telephone conversation with Jack on Saturday afternoon, two days ago now, she'd heard nothing from him. "The police talked to me, too. They came to the office this morning."

"Did they say anything about Matt?" Desperation loaded Susan's voice. "Have they talked to him?"

"I don't know about that, either. Have you talked to him?"

"No."

"I didn't think so." And she couldn't condemn someone else for loving too much for their own good. Her own future felt like a mine field to be crossed, but she knew that whatever happened she'd keep right on loving Jack.

"You don't think Matt's going to come back for me, do you?" Susan whispered.

"From Los Angeles? Or from Montana?" Lauren asked and felt ashamed of herself. "I'm sorry. No, I don't think Matt's going to come back because I think he did a lot of illegal things here and knew it was time to get out. He never expected anyone to find out about him, of course. After all, when he didn't show up again the way he promised you he would, what could you do? Where would you start looking? You certainly wouldn't tell anyone what he'd been doing at Irving's because you had a part in that."

Susan seemed oddly smaller. Lauren knew it was an optical illusion, but the other woman appeared to diminish in her corner, becoming like an aged child with too much hair that was too red and luminous green eyes too big for her face.

"You'll be all right," Lauren said, with absolutely no conviction. "You'll come through this. There'll be someone else for you one day." How could she be saying those words? Did she hope, at some level, that the empty message she spread, like a Band-Aid, over Susan, would somehow become true for herself?

"Do you think Matt did all those awful things to Jack? The fire, the damage to the flowers, the seeds mismarked?"

"I'm sure he did. Those things and more."

"He couldn't have been in three trucks at one time."

"No. Obviously he had help. But that doesn't make him less guilty."

Susan put down her mug with a clatter. "I think he did them, too," she said in a low voice. "I don't want to, but I do. He should have called me by now. Why did he lie to me? Why didn't he want me to go and be with him?"

"He couldn't ask you to go to his farm, Susan, because he doesn't have one. Or that's what I think. I think he sent cuttings to another farm somewhere else so they could pretend they raised a special plant themselves and made a lot of money that should have been Jack's."

"Why did he hate Jack?"

Lauren closed her eyes. "That's what's so awful. He didn't hate Jack. He didn't care one way or the other about Jack. Matt was just doing a job for money and the job entailed hurting Jack. That's all of it." And her own supposedly innocent little business had helped Carson time everything beautifully.

"I'd have gone with him, anyway."

Lauren started and opened her eyes. "What?"

"I love him. You think I'm bad for that, don't you?"

She settled her hands on the chair arms. Tears welled and she blinked. "I think you're a good woman who did something bad. And I think Matt Carson is crazy that he didn't see what he had in you and that he couldn't forget whatever money he was going to make by ruining another man."

Susan got up. "I'd better go. At least you and Jack have each other now."

Lauren saw Susan out, knowing she'd try to help her if she could.

The phone rang and she hurried into the sitting room.

No. The calls that came in every hour or so were only from Contact. Susan had been the one who fielded after-hours queries. Until Lauren could find a replacement lead, she'd have to deal with the questions herself. This one could wait. She had to get out of this house and run, run so hard she wouldn't be able to think.

Already dressed in sweats, she pinned on her door key. The phone stopped ringing, then started again.

Slamming the front door behind her, Lauren set off for the beach without bothering to stretch. *At least she and Jack had each other now?* Did they? She intended to keep on praying that they would one day.

No more feeling sorry for herself. She'd get on with her life, even if it eventually had to be somewhere other than in Carlsbad.

"LAUREN!"

Wind off the ocean, laden with moisture, muffled his voice and threw the name back at him.

That wind was good, clean. He felt as if he'd been holed up in smoky offices for weeks instead of only since Saturday afternoon.

Where the hell was she? He leaned over the railing above the beach and tried to make out the shape of anything that might be moving.

Nothing.

The night was black and filled with noises. Her car was parked in its usual spot and there were lights on at her place, but there'd been no response to his telephone calls earlier, or to his ring at her door minutes ago.

She could be inside and just not answering. He should have tried to reach her before tonight, but things had proceeded so quickly and the police had either been with him, or coming or going.

And, if he were honest, he'd admit he'd needed a little time to think about what he was going to do about Lauren Taylor.

Lauren liked the wind and rain. When they'd run together on the beach he'd been the one to want to quit.

A light farther down the promenade sent an illuminated stripe across the sand. A shadow slipped across that stripe.

Jack vaulted the railing to a ramp and broke into a run. His jeans, damp now, and his jacket hampered him. He ran on, grateful he wore sneakers rather than boots.

"Lauren! Wait!" He still couldn't see her, but he could feel her now. Wet sand gave beneath his feet and he pushed harder with each stride.

He reached the pale line of light on the beach and paused. The wind quieted momentarily and he glanced around. She couldn't have gone too far.

A sound came to him and he turned to his left. "Lauren? Are you there?"

"Yes. By the wall." He heard her clearly this time.

His eyes had grown accustomed to the darkness. Something pale waved. He smiled and broke into a jog, stopping when he stood over her. "Hiding?"

"Not really. Sheltering. This is where we came before, remember?"

Jack dropped to his haunches beside her. "I remember everything I want to remember." He touched the back of her hand with his forefinger. "I want to remember everything about you."

"Am I needed for something?"

Her face was indistinct and he leaned nearer. "Oh, yes."

She sighed. "The police again? Do I have to go to them this time?"

"I'm the one who needs you." Carefully, he moved to sit beside her on the triangle of more or less dry sand in the lee of the wall. Just looking at her, feeling her near him, made his throat ache with longing.

"You know I'll help you if I can," Lauren said. "I'm sorry, Jack. I guess I'm not much of a judge of character in the employee department."

"Because of Susan Bailey?"

"Who else?"

"I employed her boyfriend."

She was silent for a moment. "That was different."

"Really? One day when we've got nothing better to do, you'll have to explain the theory behind that."

"I don't blame you for wanting to stay away from me."

"If I wanted to stay away from you, why am I here now?" He was going to have to make sure they shared the work needed for whatever relationship they were to have. The reward would be worth anything it took to get it.

"Jack—" Her voice broke.

He scooted close and pulled her against him. "What? I'm sorry it took so long for me to be with you. It's been mad. Lauren, you're not going to believe what I've got to tell you."

A cold hand found his neck and slipped inside his collar. He drew in a breath and held it.

"Tell me," she said.

"Matt Carson didn't go to L.A."

"We knew that."

"We didn't know anything, sweetheart. He didn't go to Montana, or anywhere else."

Lauren craned around, her face close to his. "He's still here? Why? Did they catch him before he left?"

"Nope. On all counts. It was Martin Edgerton they caught, at the Palomar Airport where he was about to take off in his own plane for Florida."

"Edgerton? The name of the people in Florida with the poinsettia," she whispered. "Do you mean . . . ?"

"Exactly. There never was a Matt Carson. The guy who supposedly worked for me is heir apparent to the Edgerton operation. He does have a degree in floriculture. He really knows his stuff or he couldn't have pulled off what he did in the three years he was here, but the credentials he showed me, everything he presented to me was phony."

"Why did... I don't understand how they chose you, or knew what you were doing here."

"We were successful. They were successful, but less so. Evidently they decided to send Matt—or whatever his name is—up here to see if he could figure out a way to get what we had. And he eventually did it."

"With help from me."

He shook her gently. "Sometimes I can really tell why the male is the superior sex."

"What!" Lauren grabbed the lapels of his jacket.

Jack chuckled. "You females don't always think too clearly. You lead with the heart or something equally unreliable. If it hadn't been for you, my dear, the guy would have gotten away with the whole thing. Thanks to you, the police got to the house he rented in the middle of nowhere near the airport in time to see him leaving in the Alpha Romeo you described.

"They followed him to the airport where they let him board his plane, the plane they were told Martin Edgerton flew back and forth to Florida regularly."

Lauren tugged on his coat. "It doesn't sound real."

"Fact is invariably stranger than fiction. Isn't that what they say? Anyway, our strong, silent saboteur didn't do so well under interrogation. He spilled the lot and cried for Dad to come and bail him out, which he tried to do. Daddy also folded and filled in a few other details. Sonny boy flew my rooted cuttings down to Florida in his little plane—tidy as you like. Lauren—" he raised her chin to look into her eyes "—I'm serious. If you hadn't come along, they'd have gotten away with it."

"Then I'm glad I did," she told him softly.

He heard his own nervous laugh. "So am I. But this isn't all about flowers, is it, sweetheart?"

"Isn't it?"

"No. Two people who irritate one another as much as we do have to have a hell of a lot going for them."

She didn't laugh.

"It's cold out here, Lauren. And damp."

Without a word, she nestled her face against his shoulder.

"Hey," he said, stroking her damp hair. "Aren't you going to talk to me? Do you want me to leave you to think, or something?" She smelled of fresh air and salt. If he kissed her, she'd taste of salt.

"No!" Her head shot up. "I just don't know where you're coming from. Or where I want you to be coming from, for that matter. Or where I'm coming from. Or—"

She caressed the side of his face. "Or maybe I know what I want and I'm scared to death you don't want it, too."

"Shh." He rested a finger on her mouth. "I don't think it's very complicated. Can we go some place warm to talk?"

"I don't want to go home."

Her vehemence tightened his jaw. Maybe things were slightly more complicated than he wanted to admit. "Would that be because the little girl isn't there anymore?"

She nodded. "Partly. Jack, I really miss her. I can't pretend about that."

"I thought so. I was going to suggest my place anyway."

"You must be tired. If you need to go home I'll understand, Jack. We'll talk tomorrow, or whenever."

"Uh-uh." He stood up and pulled her to her feet. "Nothing doing. You just said you didn't want to go to your place."

She gave a shaky laugh. "I'm glad you said that. I lied when I said I'd understand if you left me. I need you. And I really don't want to go home."

"Even if you did, you couldn't. I've got to take you to my place."

"You've *got* to?"

He held her arm and started to walk. Lauren didn't move fast enough and did a rapid sidestep to keep her balance.

"Hold it!"

Jack kept going. Bulldozer technique was required.

"Jack! You're pulling me off my feet!"

"I'd rather you said *sweeping,* but I'll take what I can get. Come on. We're late."

"Late for what?"

"My father's waiting for us."

Now she dug a heel in the sand and tried to wrench away. Jack swept her easily into his arms and gritted his teeth at the effort it took to make headway on the sand with the added weight.

"Why is your father waiting for us? He doesn't like me."

If he bent his face a few inches, he could kiss her. Jack looked straight ahead. Self-control could be learned in small increments. "You only *think* my father doesn't like you. Andy's waiting, too."

"Why?" She shrieked the question.

"Because they sent me to find you."

KIDNAPPING IMPLIED being taken away against one's will. Leaning against the window in Jack's pickup, Lauren admitted to herself that kidnapping didn't apply in this situation.

He drove too fast.

"What's going to happen about the poinsettia?" she asked timidly.

"Edgerton's is closed down at this point. The rest—what happens with our supply this year—remains to be seen. Things aren't going to be miraculously cured because the truth's been exposed, but at least I think we're going to get a fighting chance."

Too soon, he swept into the driveway at his house, leaped from the cab and came around to open her door. He half lifted her, sliding her down his length until they stood, toe-to-toe. Lauren took a jerky little breath, and another. Jack bent slowly over her until she felt the warmth of his mouth a whisper away from hers.

Lauren closed her eyes.

"Hey, Dad! Lauren!"

Jack groaned and rested his forehead on hers.

"We've been waiting for you!"

By the time Andy reached them, Jack stood beside Lauren, his hands in his pockets, his weight resting on one leg. "Hi, sport. Sorry we took a while."

"Yeah, well. Grandpa's getting . . . well, you know how he gets."

"I know." Jack sounded grim. He rested one hand on Andy's neck, the other at Lauren's waist and walked into the house.

Denton Irving sat in an ivory satin chair in the living room, looking out of place in his red plaid shirt and baggy navy blue corduroy pants.

He stood up and cleared his throat. "All sorted out, is it?"

Lauren glanced at Jack whose face showed no expression.

"Not quite, Dad," he said.

She longed to ask what it was that was supposed to have been dealt with, and by whom.

Denton made a disapproving, snuffling noise, jutted his chin and thrust a hand in Lauren's direction.

She only hesitated an instant before accepting a bone-crushing shake.

"Thank you for what you did," he said, sounding ferocious. "Good head on your shoulders. Always admired that in a woman. Jack's mother was that way. You ask him."

"I will," Lauren said, taken aback.

"Get your coat," Denton ordered Andy. To Jack he said, "I put what we talked about beside your bed."

Lauren looked at Jack just in time to see him turn an interesting shade of red.

"Going to be all right, is it?" Denton almost shouted.

Jack finally moved. "We hope so, Dad. These things take time."

Denton snorted and aimed a dark stare in Lauren's direction. "Young people never think their elders know anything. You think an old man doesn't remember. You ready, Andy?"

The boy zipped his windbreaker. "Yes, Grandpa."

"That's all right then." He ambled from the room, shooing Andy before him. "Never mind what I think," Lauren heard him say, "go ahead. Throw it all away. But don't come to me with a long face afterward."

"What was all that about?" Lauren asked when she and Jack were alone. "And where on earth is he taking Andy at this time of night?"

Jack shuffled his feet. "I don't know what it was about. Dad often takes Andy. You know that."

"I think nine-year-old boys belong in bed at almost ten on a school night."

"Nag," Jack said, not quite under his breath.

"I'm not a nag," Lauren said, incensed. "I believe in responsible parenting is all."

He seemed about to speak, then changed his mind.

"What? Say what you're thinking, Jack."

"When I first started to get to know you, I thought you didn't care much for kids."

Her sweats were damp. She concentrated on how uncomfortable she felt.

"Lauren? You do like them, don't you?"

She sighed deeply. "Yes, Jack. I love them. Do I get to go home now that I've seen Denton and Andy?"

"No," he said simply. "You don't have a car."

"You do."

"You said you didn't want to go home."

"I don't like fencing matches. I'm not much of a game player."

"Hah!" He shrugged out of his jacket and tossed it on one of the pale chairs. "You could have fooled me. You knock the socks off me every time we play any kind of game."

She tried not to appear smug. "Your coat's wet. It'll ruin the chair."

"Good. I hate that chair. It's time we redecorated the place."

She forebore mentioning that the time to redecorate wasn't while you were trying to dig yourself out of potential financial ruin.

"You're wet," he told her.

"I'm all right."

"No you're not." Taking her hand, he led her into the hall. "We'll find you something dry to wear."

She thought, and immediately discarded the notion of his coming up with something belonging to his ex-wife. Her next thought was that he was undoubtedly leading her to his bedroom.

Heat sped into every part of her.

He did take her into his bedroom. Big, untidy—and with a platform bed that showed signs of having been hastily made. The black-and-white striped quilt hung slightly askew and matching pillows were piled carelessly on top. Books, heaped higgledy-piggledy on a lacquered table, pushed two black-and-gold Chinese vases perilously close to one side.

Lauren looked around curiously. Here she felt Jack. There was strength and style and a masculinity that was more comfortable than overwhelming. She turned to find him looking at her.

He smiled, his gaze lingering on her, before he went to pull shut the wooden louvers at a recessed floor-to-ceiling window.

"Now," he said, all business. "Take everything off and I'll see what I can find."

She sucked her bottom lip between her teeth to stop a laugh. But she didn't move.

"You can put on my robe if I can find it." He strode into the bathroom and checked behind the door, then, grumbling, disappeared into a closet to emerge with a dark green terry robe. "You should be warm enough in this." He tossed it to her.

"Thanks." Suddenly tired, she eyed the bed longingly, but bypassed it to go into the bathroom. "Jack, are you going to put my things in the dryer, or what?"

"Probably not," he called.

Trying not to look at herself in the mirrored walls of his black-and-white bathroom, she stripped to her bra and panties and donned the robe. He was probably in some sort of shock after all that had happened and didn't even know his behavior was bizarre.

Lauren did look at herself then: damp hair hanging around her face, almost no lipstick, and dark smudges from the remnants of mascara. The latter did a great job of making sure no one would miss the little lines at the corners of her eyes. Quickly she washed her face and scrubbed it dry with one of Jack's black towels. Clean and shiny was preferable to sallow and grubby. Since all she had with her was her door key, there was nothing more to be done.

She emerged to find Jack wearing only very skimpy red briefs. "Red!" She grinned, then made the mistake of laughing.

There was no hope of evading his flying tackle. They landed together in the middle of his comfortable bed and Lauren made no attempt to move beneath his weight.

The gentling in his eyes, the softening around his mouth knocked out any humor the moment had held. He stroked back her hair and tilted his head sideways to study her. "We promised each other that we'd have a chance to say our piece. Isn't that what we said on Saturday before the balloon went up?"

"Yes, Jack."

"I was an idiot about Dan and the real estate thing. You didn't know anything about it."

"No, I didn't. I tried to tell you, but—"

"I know. But the man's an ass. I can't imagine what you ever saw in him. And I hate the way you let him stroll in and out of your life like—"

"I don't anymore. When you came roaring in, I'd just told him a few truths he won't forget in a hurry—or forgive."

He rested a thumb on her bottom lip. "You know what all my bluster was about, don't you?"

"Tell me."

"I'm jealous of him."

"You don't have to be. Not anymore."

Jack propped his head. "No. You may have to remind me of that, though, I warn you. I love you, Lauren. That's kind of blunt. Not too flowery. But I do love you so very much."

"I—" She closed her eyes and felt a tear squeeze free and course down her temple. "Great. Now I'm crying."

"Women are strange. I've always thought so."

"I love you. I love you. I love you." Lauren sniffed and laughed. "More than I can tell you."

"Oh, sweetheart." His lips brushed hers lightly. "We're going to have good times together. Lots of good times."

She took a deep breath, rubbed the tears from her eyes and looked at him. "My turn to be blunt. I've never talked about my not being able to have babies."

"You don't have to now. I guessed as much a long time ago."

He always seemed to make things easier for her. "Jack, I would have said something, but it seemed weird to talk about an issue that didn't matter if we had no future together."

"It still doesn't matter, darling." Carefully he lifted her head and cradled it against his neck.

She became very still, very quiet inside. "I'm thirty-nine. That's past a sensible age for having babies, anyway."

"Yes it is. All that matters to me is you." He rocked her slowly.

"I could never get pregnant." Her skin felt icy. "The reasons can be parroted off, but they don't mean much, even to me except that I'm infertile."

Jack rested her back on the pillow and sank his teeth into his bottom lip.

There was nothing he could say, she knew that—nothing she wanted him to say. But she didn't want him to view her as less than she was: a complete woman.

"I mean it when I said I already figured this out, you know," he said finally. "It still troubles you, doesn't it? That's why you tend to draw back when children start to get close to you. It's why you've only gone so far with Andy."

She laughed before she could stop herself. "Half right, half wrong. Not such a bad attempt at analysis. No, not being able to conceive doesn't bother me anymore. I think I adjusted well to that. But I am afraid of coming to love children only to lose them again. It's happened twice—with Joe and Cara. And I'm afraid of loving Andy, then having to move away from him." Only it was already too late; she'd begun to care for the boy.

"How about his father?"

She wriggled to see him more clearly. "Am I afraid of loving you? I already do. I told you." And he'd told her. His words still rang in her brain.

"I'm cold." Scooping her to sit on one side of the bed, Jack threw back the quilt and blankets. Settling himself against the pillows, he extended an arm. "Lie with me."

Lauren swallowed almost painfully. Never removing her eyes from his, she took off the robe, tossed it aside and joined him beneath the covers. "What did you mean just now?"

As if he hadn't heard her, Jack bent his head and kissed Lauren, a gentle but infinitely demanding kiss. Gentle now, was the message she received, but that it was only the beginning.

He raised his head again and looked at the lips he'd left parted and waiting. A lamp, behind Jack on a bedside table, cast deflected light over his powerful shoulder and threw graded shadows over his strongly muscled chest.

"I wondered," he murmured, "if you might be afraid of your love... of loving Andy's father for some reason."

Her breathing became shallower. "I was. But I don't think we always have a choice about these things."

"You thought I still cared for Mary. I don't, you know. I only felt that it might be bad for Andy if his mother didn't come to see him when she'd said she would. He knows he's less important to her than her painting."

"I understand."

"It doesn't matter. She's not coming anyway. But I guess I tend to worry too much about Andy sometimes because he doesn't seem to care." This time he kissed her throat. "He seems a whole lot more interested in making sure you keep coming around."

"Does he?"

"Mmm." His attention centered on her shoulder while he carefully moved aside her bra strap. "Smart. Like his dad. Same taste exactly, evidently. You said you don't think we have much choice in these things. In who we love, you mean?''

''I've got to say it again, Jack. I love you so much.'' And her eyes chose this moment to fill with tears again. And her throat felt so closed, it ached. ''I can't help it,'' she managed to whisper.

For what felt like forever, he looked at her. ''Do you know,'' he said, ''I actually worried about losing you because you might decide something else was more important than I could ever be to you? I invented every reason not to let myself love you.''

''But it didn't work.''

He smiled then, tipped back his head and grinned down at her. ''No, it didn't work. Wow, am I glad it didn't work.''

She wanted to laugh and leap about but more than that, she wanted to make wild love with him. ''We take the prize for insecurity. Who do you see when you look in the mirror?''

Jack shrugged, and frowned. ''A man. An ordinary man, I guess.''

She did laugh at that. ''Ordinary? You're spectacular.''

''Okay.'' He framed her face. ''Who do you see in the mirror?''

''A slightly overblown woman approaching middle age.''

He flopped onto his back and shouted, ''That's hysterical. My toes curl just at the sight of you. And that's the mild part. Come here, you.''

The phone rang.

''Oh, go away.'' Jack moaned and pulled her into his arms. ''We're not answering that.''

''It might be an emergency.''

''I don't care.'' He tried to kiss her.

''Maybe something's wrong with Andy.''

Jack drew back his head, reached across her and snatched up the receiver. ''Yes.''

Lauren watched his face. He sank to the pillows and closed his eyes. "Yes," he repeated. "Just a minute. Hold the line."

Promptly, Jack thrust the phone under the pillow and crawled from the bed to kneel on the floor. He took her hand and laced their fingers together. "I want to spend the rest of my life with you."

"What is it?" Lauren whispered hoarsely. "What's wrong?"

"Forget everything but what I'm saying to you." Propping himself on his elbows, he kissed her lingeringly. Slipping his hands around her neck, he pulled her into his arms. "How did I get so lucky?"

"Thank you." She smiled and shook her head. "Everything I try to tell you comes out wrong."

Reaching behind him, Jack scuffled among the books on the table until he produced a tiny brown leather bag. "Will you marry me?"

"I beg your pardon?"

"I'd like you to be my wife . . . please. And—" he wrestled the bag open and pulled out an old fashioned ring set with a square-cut emerald and diamonds in a starburst "—this was my mother's. It would mean a great deal to my father if you would agree to marry me and accept this ring, to seal the pact? Good grief. That sounded asinine. Please, my darling, *will* you marry me?"

"Yes." Lauren eyed the phone cord leading to the pillow. "Is this being recorded or something?"

Jack ignored the question, took her finger and put on the ring before retrieving the phone. He hesitated. "Thank you, Lauren. You've made me very happy."

"Me, too."

Into the phone he said, "Sorry to keep you waiting. Yes, Lauren loves the ring, Dad." He closed his eyes once more. "Yes, you can tell Andy it's okay. We'll see him tomorrow. Good night."

Lauren took the receiver from him and hung up. "You came looking for me tonight knowing you intended to ask me to marry you and expecting me to agree?"

"Knowing you'd agree," Jack said. "Occasionally your logic is almost flawless."

He switched off the light.

Harlequin Intrigue®

QUID PRO QUO

Racketeer King Crawley is a man who lives by one rule: An Eye For An Eye. Put behind bars for his sins against humanity, Crawley is driven by an insatiable need to get even with the judge who betrayed him. And the only way to have his revenge is for the judge's children to suffer for their father's sins....

Harlequin Intrigue introduces Patricia Rosemoor's QUID PRO QUO series: #161 PUSHED TO THE LIMIT (May 1991), #163 SQUARING ACCOUNTS (June 1991) and #165 NO HOLDS BARRED (July 1991).

Meet:

***Sydney Raferty:** She is the first to feel the wrath of King Crawley's vengeance. Pushed to the brink of insanity, she must fight her way back to reality—with the help of Benno DeMartino in #161 PUSHED TO THE LIMIT.

***Dakota Raferty:** The judge's only son, he is a man whose honest nature falls prey to the racketeer's madness. With Honor Bright, he becomes an unsuspecting pawn in a game of deadly revenge in #163 SQUARING ACCOUNTS.

***Asia Raferty:** The youngest of the siblings, she is stalked by Crawley and must find a way to end the vendetta. Only one man can help—Dominic Crawley. But will the son join forces with his father's enemy in #165 NO HOLDS BARRED?

Don't miss a single title of Patricia Rosemoor's QUID PRO QUO trilogy coming to you from Harlequin Intrigue.

QPQ-1